HAULIN'

———————— *HAULIN'*

A Novel by PHILLIP FINCH

Doubleday & Company, Inc., Garden City, New York
1975

Library of Congress Cataloging in Publication Data

Finch, Phillip.
    Haulin'.

    I. Title.
PZ4.F4925Hau [PS3556.I456]   813'.5'4
ISBN 0-385-01313-2
Library of Congress Catalog Card Number 74–22838

HAULIN'

"... Well, boys, get this. Durin' that last record, I got a call from a fella haulin' a hot load of dry chemicals from Mobile to Casper. Says his name's Moondog, from Commerce, Texas. Said all you guys out there with Citizens Band sets would know 'im. When I talked to old Moondog, he was flyin' along at seventy toward Salina, talkin' on his CB that was patched through on Big John McCallum's home phone in Lawrence. Way to go, Big John, thanks a bunch. Anyway, Moondog wanted all you truckers haulin' along the Kansas Turnpike to know that the Smokies are playin' with their little black box about seven miles west of the Bonner Springs interchange on the eastbound side. That's what he said. 'Course, I don't know what he meant by that. And Moondog said he wanted to hear a song, too, so here she goes. This one's goin' out for you, Moondog, you and all the other over-the-road truckers bombin' along somewhere out there. We know you're out there, boys. You bet! We know who brings our vegetables to the store and the steel to the construction job. Yessir! You're doin' a great job, boys. Just keep 'em rollin', you mother-truckers . . ."

1

Chapter 1

Logbook, check. Electrical tape, two rolls of silver duct tape. Check. Road flares, check. Reflectors, check. Road atlas, check. Spare bulbs, spare fuses. Check. Windshield scraper, check. Lenny Lewis flicks over the page of his notebook and continues down his list. From under his seat he pulls a green plastic fishing-tackle box. Inside: ballpoint, mechanical pencil with a well-worn eraser, bottle of aspirin, large bottle of Di-Gel, credit cards and traveler's checks tucked into a vinyl wallet, one roll of quarters, one of dimes for automobile toll gates, one dozen individually wrapped Naturalamb condoms, one tube of burn ointment, one roll of gauze, another of adhesive tape, and one capped glass jar bearing the label of a vitamin supplement and containing pills in an astonishing variety of colors, names, and shapes—Black Beauties, Big Reds, Greenies, alabaster Hummers, and the gleaming white capsules that Pickett calls "Turnaround Specials." Lenny shakes the bottle. They are running low, down to the last three dozen, but no problem. Pickett can get them by the gross the next time they go through El Paso or San Diego. Lenny snaps shut the cover of the tackle box, their survival kit, and slides it under his seat, beside the pistol in its holster.

The gun is Pickett's toy. It is a gleaming Ruger .44 Magnum Blackhawk revolver, single-action, powerful enough to stop a bear, firing a blunt-nosed lead slug as long and as thick as the first joint of a man's thumb. Some nights, after he has finished a long stretch of driving and turned the wheel over to Lenny, Pickett will reach under the seat for the pistol and the handsome tooled-leather holster. He is still too jazzed to settle into the sleeping bunk, so he pulls the box of cartridges from the glove compartment, drops the bullets one by one into the six chambers, flips the cylinder back into place, and then unrolls the window on his side to bring the air bucking into the cab. He cocks the hammer, steadies the gun with both hands, and squints through the sights until a highway sign pops into the range of the Mack's high-beams. Aiming through the strut of the outside mirror, he squeezes the trigger into a cataclysmic explosion that jerks the revolver back into his face, shaking the cab with a roar that drowns, for a moment, the whine of the tires, the bellowing of the wind, and the growl of the Cummins diesel engine chuffing away somewhere beneath their asses in the cab-over tractor. And Pickett laughs like hell. All this while Lenny guides them down some dark, forsaken stretch of road in Nebraska, maybe, or Utah or Iowa, blasting along at sixty-five, seventy miles an hour, his right foot pegged to the accelerator, one hand on the wheel and the other maybe fiddling with the volume on the stereo tape deck.

Lenny has learned to live with this noisy pastime and even laughs along with Pickett now. It is, he has decided, fairly normal behavior for a man who has finished fourteen hours of popping pills and herding a thirty-ton beast down the road.

Lenny flicks over the notebook again to the last page on his checklist. Flashlight . . . bright enough, he decides, but he remembers that the big electric torch in the tool locker is beginning to dim. He will remind Pickett to buy new dry cells when he stops for fuel sometime during the night. A change of clothes, socks, and underwear are stuffed in a small gym bag behind the seat. And a Thermos bottle of hot coffee. Jesus, yes, the Thermos. On his second run with Pickett, Lenny filled the bottle at a truck-stop diner near Coeur d'Alene and left it in the booth where he and Pickett ate. Lenny nearly got his ass kicked out into the Montana countryside when Pickett asked for coffee two hours later. Now, after almost three years, they laugh about it. But Lenny still checks carefully for the Thermos. As always, he lays it between the seats, beside the Interstate Commerce Commission logbook, a clip board holding copies of the weight tickets and manifest sheets for this trip, and a plasticbound looseleaf notebook that holds trucking permits for the forty-eight continental states, the Mack's papers, medical certificates for Pickett and Lenny, and a photostated copy of Pickett's contract with Mercury International Movers. With the checklist complete, with paperwork in order, with spare parts, tools, and tire chains packed away, Lenny and Pickett feel ready to sally forth onto the highways of America.

They are long-haul, over-the-road truckers who spend more than three hundred days a year either filling and emptying a van with household goods or hustling across the countryside with those goods in the Mack diesel that is owned by Pickett and leased to MIM. Lenny Lewis is technically Pickett's relief driver, but he functions mostly as squire and swamper, as apprentice, accomplice, and audience. And they are friends.

They have spent the last two days loading the van with furniture from three different homes around San Francisco, all bound for Massachusetts.

In San Bruno, they loaded ersatz Early American furniture and miscellaneous effects belonging to a young executive for a paper products firm and his pregnant wife. He had been promoted from the West Coast sales branch to a management position with the home office in Newton. The promotion arrived before the baby, their first. Pickett and Lenny showed at 8 A.M., having already weighed the truck with full tanks and empty van to find their tare weight, which was recorded on a weight ticket and signed by the weighmaster. They loaded sofa, freezer, bedroom chests, and china cabinet into the trailer, wrapping the wooden furniture in quilted blankets, and listing each item on their manifest. The legs came off the dining room table and the table-top went against the wall of the trailer. Mirrors and framed pictures were wrapped in cardboard and secured with straps to the side of the van. Pickett and Lenny hefted out boxes of china, crates of dishes, and an open cardboard box crammed with the detritus of daily life, fragments of family existence: family albums, three small potted cacti, a fondue pot, the contents of the woman's cosmetic drawer, a brass crucifix. This, the wife said, is the last of it, the things that never got catalogued or collected until the very end. Pickett and Lenny worked quickly, almost without a word. As moving jobs go, this one was soft and quick. The house was a single-level cottage. The doors were wide enough and it was a mere eighteen paces—Lenny counted them—from the front door to the ramp of the van. When the heaviest pieces were secured, Pickett and Lenny piled boxes and crates flush to the ceiling of the van. By noon, they were finished. The load was bound into the recesses of the van, held in check by thick belts and by its own inertia. They were cinching the last strap when the woman walked to the sidewalk. Inside, the trailer still looked roomy enough to accommodate a game of two-on-two basketball. She seemed dismayed at what a small pile their possessions made. The husband rode with them to

6

the weigh station, where they found the new gross and computed the net weight of the shipment: 4,330 pounds.

They lunched quickly to arrive by one P.M. at the Pacific Heights flat of a San Francisco State University professor. He is, he told Lenny, accepting a big raise to teach English literature at Wellesley. He talked in a nasal, piping voice about the way he had acquired his furniture, haunting auctions and estate sales. They would, of course, be especially careful. Pickett and Lenny only nodded as they went about checking the clearance of his front door and marking boxes in black crayon. It was the top flat of a two-story building, which was not good. But the flat was old, built when space was not at a premium, so the doors were wide and the ceilings were set far above their heads. Pickett looked at the furniture. Rummage-sale stuff, he decided. He could not imagine why people go to the time and trouble, let alone the expense, of hauling such junk across country. Pickett saw one problem: a long leatherette sofa that occupied nearly one wall of the living room. Yes, yes, the professor assured them, the local company that moved him here three years ago got the sofa up the staircase without much problem. They took out dressers, boxes of books, coffee tables, and stereo equipment. Finally, they could avoid the sofa no longer. They angled the thing down the hallway, then through the door. They eased it by inches until the back of the sofa rubbed against the door frame and another corner of the piece butted against the far wall of the staircase.

"Try again," Pickett said. "This time with the backside down."

This time they were nearly out the door when one stubby leg of the sofa caught on the edge of the door itself, just as Pickett, on the downstairs end, ran out of room again.

Lenny lifted his end higher, working for another half inch of clearance.

"Pickett," he said, "you got any room?"

"The thing is flush against the wall already, Lenny. Don't shove it any more or you'll scrape the plaster."

"Pickett, if we had just another half inch. The damn leg keeps catching on the door. And I can see that the leg isn't supposed to come off."

So they laid down the sofa, knocked the pins from the door hinges and lifted the big oaken door out of the way. Then the sofa slid through the frame with a pencil-width clearance on both sides. The rest was quick and easy. Pickett and Lenny were finished before dark. They found a weigh station ten minutes before closing, and the weighmaster put his signature to a net of 4,825 pounds.

Now, most of this second day has been spent in loading 10,220 pounds from the hillside home of an aerospace engineer in Los Gatos who is taking a new job and is moving himself, his wife, their four children, and an incredible volume of Danish furniture to live in Worcester. That job has filled the trailer almost to capacity, certainly without room for another decent load. Their total cargo weighs 19,375 pounds. Already, they have worked two days. The load will keep them on the road more than fifty-five hours if they drive without rest, and they will spend two more days unloading. Pickett will receive 50 per cent of the moving fee, about $2,200, in a check from Mercury on the first of next month. He will pay every penny of his own expenses. He figures that with tires costing almost $800 a set and lasting 70,000 miles, with a 6,000-mile lube job costing $35, with diesel fuel up near fifty cents a gallon and disappearing at the rate of a gallon every five miles, with state governments co-operating in taxing every mile he drives around the country, with all that, Pickett calculates

8

that he pays out about thirty-five cents for every mile he puts on the odometer. Add to that his $250 every week for Lenny, plus $600 a year in license fees, plus insurance premiums of $1,500 a year, plus depreciation on his Mack and with six months of truck payments at better than 300 bucks each still left in his coupon book, Pickett figures he is working for less than $4.00 an hour. He tries not to think about that too often.

Pickett's home is far removed in spirit and in substance from the elegantly shingled townhouses, the casual and classy hillside homes or the thickly carpeted prestige apartments where he and Lenny sweat, strain, and curse.

It is a subdivision split-level, among the first tract of homes built in the city of Antioch, California, about sixty miles from San Francisco. Pickett's home has not aged well. The neighborhood is not shabby, but neither is it the first choice of the young couples who come to the city to work in the town's paper mill or chemical plant. Antioch is not one of those places that generally adorns picture postcards. It is broad and flat, immoderately wet in the winter months, as dry and as hot as the plains of western Kansas during the summer. There used to be a certain grassy, rural charm to the place, when farmers' pastures, green in the spring, dry and golden in the summer, pushed into the city limits. Now the most apparent features of the city are high-tension power lines on massive steel struts, smokestacks, and the utilitarian lines of industrial architecture. On the road, Pickett likes to tell other drivers that he lives "near San Francisco," and they are likely to shake their heads in envy. But he and Lenny both know that Antioch could just as well be "near Dayton" or "near Charlotte" or "near Allentown." Pickett's neighbors are mill hands, linemen for the power company, construction workers. They are not the sort of people who would ever pay someone else two thousand

9

dollars to haul their furniture across the continent. And neither, for that matter, is Pickett.

And where the hell is Pickett? Already, it is dark. They have eaten dinner in Pickett's home and Pickett has sent Lenny to the truck to run over his list one more time, promising that he would be out soon. That was a half hour ago. Lenny has been through the list twice, has traced a route to Boston they both know by rote. Still, Pickett has not appeared. This is not like him, Lenny thinks, because Pickett is not one to waste the hours of darkness that make for fast, uncluttered driving. Pickett has spent a week at home since the last trip, longer than usual for him, and Lenny wonders whether Pickett is becoming weary of the business. Lengthy good-bys are a bad sign for a long-haul trucker. Lenny flips through the road atlas, drums his fingers on the padded dash and is ready to step down from the cab and knock on the front door when Pickett steps out into the gloaming. Head down, hands shoved into his pockets, he hurries down the walk. He opens the door and, with practiced grace, he lifts himself up toward the cab, one foot on a grooved metal step, his right hand wrapped around a chromed brace. He swings into the cab and settles into the seat. He looks straight ahead, staring down the street as he speaks:

"Must've been on the phone with that damn dispatcher for an hour," he says. "Anyway, the sonuvabitch says if we hustle our asses out to Boston, they might be able to put together a full load for us from there to Dallas–Fort Worth."

Pickett pumps the accelerator, turns the ignition key, and taps the pedal tentatively as the diesel burps and then catches. The rumble is hesitant for a moment, then eager and powerful. It is a familiar sound, and the cab seems full and alive again. Pickett reaches for the shift lever, finds a low gear, sets the truck in motion without the suggestion of a hitch or jerk. Lenny sees Pickett's son waving from the living-room window. But not his wife. Pickett's wife has never watched them leave.

When they reach State Highway 4, outside the city limits, Pickett works up through the gears and the truck gains speed, heading for Stockton. There, they catch Interstate 5, for a short hop to Sacramento, where they turn down a cloverleaf for Interstate 80 East. Ahead of them lie the Sierra mountains, the wide and arid stretches of the Nevada desert, and a long night of driving.

Chapter 2

His given name is John William, but nobody has called him that since his mother died in 1952. To certain pump jockeys, truck stop waitresses, load brokers, bartenders, and truck drivers around the United States who have known him since he hit the road in his first White twenty-nine years ago, to his wife and to Lenny, he is Pickett, invariably Pickett. To everyone else, he is J.W., and they say it with respect.

The independent truckers' trademark is anonymity, a facelessness that is almost inevitable when a man spends most of his life on the road. The characters in the trucking world's cast are divided by a simple distinction; there are those who move and there are those who stay put. One who stays—say, a mechanic at a big truck stop and service center in the middle of Kansas—sees a parade of faces pass before him, pause for a few minutes, maybe an hour, then disappear. Faces and the names that go with them are not remembered because the effort pays no dividends.

But there are exceptions, men who by sheer persistence, longevity, and magnetism are hailed by name in Tuscaloosa, Duluth, Wheeling, Salinas, Bozeman, Texarkana, and Grand Junction. Such a man is Pickett, partly because he has been on the road so *damn* long and partly because he is the sort of person who tends to leave lasting impressions, one way or the other.

Physically, he is memorable: six feet, four inches and weighing not much more than the 210 pounds he tipped in 1946, when he was twenty-one. His face is red and beefy, his hair once so dark and straight that he found it easy to believe his father's claim of some Shawnee ancestry. Now it is still straight, but heavily mottled by streaks, splotches of white. His shoulders are broad, his back still straight, and he is strong enough to squat down, wrap his arms around a packed wardrobe box, straighten his legs, and carry that box out of a bedroom, through a hall, down two flights of stairs and up the ramp into his van.

So Pickett is imposing, even before he opens his mouth. There are no surprises when he does. Pickett tends to leave the impression of loudness, but that is not really so. His voice is deep, throaty, rumbling, resonant, with a distinctive edge. It is a quality that talks of too much bad booze, too much good booze, too many cigarettes, and a fist that slammed into his larynx during a fight in a barbecue joint near Tyson's Corner, Maryland, in 1948. He was speechless for three weeks after that.

And with the voice he says outrageous, improbable things. He is cocky, confident, challenging. He is the purveyor of some of the more outlandish stories ever told across a table in a roadside diner. He is likely to lean out the window of his Mack and inform a surly pump attendant that he is speaking to J. W. Pickett, a trucker just as mean and tough as any gear-jammer who ever hustled a rig down a highway, so it's *Mister* Pickett to you, and be sure to watch your tongue next time.

Then there is the matter of his clothes. No obscurely titled fop who ever strolled into an Ascot tea party was ever considered more stylish and tasteful than Pickett is in his own milieu. That is not to imply that his tastes run in the Savile Row vein. When Pickett has loaded his van and sets out on the road, he strips off his cotton overalls to reveal straight-leg gabardine dress slacks which he buys for twenty-six dollars at a Kansas City haberdashery, pressed to a delicate edge, the neat cuffs breaking slightly over the top of his polished Acme boots with stacked heels. Silver plated buttons inlaid with mother-of-pearl gleam on his shirt. Cinched loosely around his neck is a string tie, secured by an ornament in the shape of a longhorn's head. From Bismarck to Brownsville, that is style of the first order.

One September evening in 1951, Pickett tried a left turn from a right-hand lane along Clear Lake Avenue in Springfield, Illinois. A local patrolman spotted him, stopped him, cited him for the moving violation and then charged him with disorderly conduct when Pickett protested too loudly. The incident cost Pickett $135, plus a night in jail, and a rap sheet that listed his two distinguishing marks: a salmon-pink scar on his left cheek, along the jawline, and a tattoo on his right forearm. The scar was his souvenir of a fire one morning as he hauled a shipment of women's coats and dresses from New York to Cincinnati. He was making good time toward Mansfield, about daybreak, when he glanced into a mirror and saw smoke trailing from a right-side wheel on the trailer. The tire had been overinflated. It had heated and begun to burn. Rubber fires are dirty, smelly, and frustrating; tire compounds glower and smolder

13

until they are exhausted, and the heat from one burning tire will very likely ignite another close by. Pickett was out of the cab with his extinguisher when the tire blew with a mortar-shell pop, shredding the thick walls and blowing a half-liquid scrap of hot rubber onto Pickett's cheek. Pickett brushed it off, shook the extinguisher to life, and saved the cargo, but the burn left a ragged scar about two inches across, the approximate shape of Greenland on a Mercator projection.

The tattoo is a real work of art, acquired one night in Manila, when Pickett was on leave during the war. An inspired needle artist noticed how the muscles along the underside of Pickett's right forearm bulged when he clenched his hand. Deftly, outlining in blue dye and shading with the most delicate red tones, the artist reproduced Betty Grable in her famous backside pin-up pose, looking coyly over one shoulder. Only, he left off the bathing suit. Otherwise, the reproduction was perfect. So finely was it traced and so strategically was it placed, that for the rest of his life, every time Pickett was to make a fist with his right hand, Betty would do a classic bump-and-grind shimmy as the muscles rippled. It became, and remains, one of the true delights of Pickett's existence.

With all of that, Pickett stands out in stark relief from his trucking fellows, the way a squawking, florid macaw might stick out in a cage full of peeping parakeets. He is remembered.

Lenny learned early that no place is too unlikely to run across someone who knows Pickett. It might be the dumpy, gray-haired waitress in Green Bay who has been serving Pickett ham and eggs (four, over easy) at erratic intervals for the last twenty-seven years. It could be the parts manager of a Mack service department in Little Rock who sold Pickett a box of fuses two years ago. Or it might be a produce hauler who once swapped stories with him across a pot of coffee in the early hours of a forgotten morning, who spots him and calls his name from across the room when Pickett and Lenny walk past the TRUCKERS ONLY sign of a restaurant at the interchange of an Interstate highway near Newark. That, in fact, is how Lenny saw it happen the first time, the first week he was with Pickett. They were hungry, headed for a table, when a trucker stood up in a booth to hail him.

"Hey, it's J. W. Pickett. I'll be damned. Hey, J.W., come over here."

Lenny saw Pickett grin. They walked over to the booth, sat down, joining three other men.

"J. W. Pickett. I'll be damned, J. W. Pickett. Last time I saw you was at that Skelly stop in West Memphis, Arkansas, the one that serves those great omelets all night."

"Right," Pickett said. "This is my relief driver, Lenny Lewis. Lenny, this is, umm, let's see . . ."

"Jack Jenkins," said the man, "produce hauler out of San Berdoo, remember? This is Bill Robinson. He's got that real nice Diamond Reo conventional outside, leased out to Standard Oil of New Jersey, and this is Julio Marquez. He's haulin' a load of dry goods from Bridgeport to St. Pete."

"Boys, J.W. here has got some stories to tell. Been on the road about thirty years. Damn, that's a long time. Remember that story you told in West Memphis? The one about the time you jackknifed your rig with a load of steel girders. You remember?"

"Sure," Pickett said. "Back in the winter of '54, I think. But, hell, it's a long story. I'd better order first. Waitress! Hey, honey, how about swishin' that pretty little tail of yours over here, okay? Fine. Real fine. Now, we'll take a pot of coffee, and it better be fresh and hot. My buddy here wants a plate of scrambled eggs, American fries on the side, big

15

glass of milk. I want four eggs, four *big* eggs, over easy. A slab of ham. I mean real ham, none of that Spam, and don't skimp on it. And I want a big pastry or two honey-dipped doughnuts, if you can find any that aren't stale. Don't forget the bottle of catsup, neither.

"Anyway, boys, I'm a furniture hauler now, but I spent near twenty-five years picking up loads from brokers, haulin' anything I could get my hands on, didn't matter what. I run the wheels off two White tractors and one Kenworth before I bought the Mack I got now, and it ain't in such great shape any more. So I'm in Gary, dropped off a load of dry goods, been on the road three and a half weeks and I figure I'll try and find a load goin' back to the West Coast, so's I can go home. Stop by this broker. Oh, he's got stuff headed for Portland, Seattle, and he's always got lots of loads for L.A., San Diego, but not a damn thing headed for Frisco this particular day. I'm ready to walk out when the guy says, Hey, wait a minute, Pickett, what kind of shape is your tractor in? I tell the fucker it'll haul anything he can hook it up to. So he says, Pickett, they're building this new warehouse up near Burney, north of Frisco, and they need sixty thousand pounds of steel. That's a real pisser. You don't want to break it into two loads but it's overweight if you haul it as a single. I said, buddy, just point me to it. I'll worry about the weigh stations. So I take off on a beeline, and the beeline takes me right into the Feather River Canyon. Oh, I could-uh taken the long way around, but I was itchin' to get home and I figure I can handle it. And did I mention that this is the first week of January? Shee-yit. Snow on the ground, gray clouds all over the place, it's gettin' on toward evenin' and I'm headed down the canyon. Road is dry, all right, but icy in spots. Any of you guys ever driven that fuckin' road? Too much, too much. There ain't another highway like it

16

in the states. Jest mile after mile, down through the trees, switchbacks every few hundred yards, inchin' on down.

"And I'm in a hurry. Too big of a hurry. Plus, it's been a tough year and maybe my tires are not in too good a shape. So I come down off this switchback in low, my brakes startin' to smell, and instead of playin' it smart I jump about three gears, put my foot into it and really start to move because I see the road straighten out for about a half-mile ahead of me. Well, I'd been drivin' about three straight days and my brain was not working as quick as it should-uh been. Because all of a sudden, I'm bombin' down the road at maybe forty-five, fifty, I eat up that straight stretch of road that way a hungry dog gobbles up a scrap of beef suet, and here is this road sign that says, slow, fifteen miles per, with a big crooked arrow swoopin' all over the place. Well, you can laugh at them signs anyplace else but they mean business on the Feather River Canyon road. You bet. So I get on the brakes and nothin' happens. I could-uh been draggin' my foot, all the good it did me. So I'm right on top of the curve, still blastin' right along, and I try to pull it out of fourth, jam it real quick-like into low, and hope I could slow down and not blow the engine into little bitty pieces.

"Can you believe it? I missed the shift. I was so excited I forgot to kick the revs up. I just grind the gears. I try it again, finally I catch the thing but it's too late. I figure I'm goin' over the side. I give one big heave at the wheel, try to stay on the road, and somehow I do it. To this day, I don't know how that big fucker got around the curve, but it did. The motor is screamin', the tractor is buckin' all over the place and then I see that my worries ain't over yet. 'Cause I look in my mirror and here is my trailer, just slidin' its rear end out sure as hell. And here I am, comin' up on another curve, still headin' downhill. I twitch the wheel, nothin' happens. It's too late. That trailer has got a mind of its own, and it's pushin' me right down the road, thirty-five tons. Well, if you've ever jackknifed your rig, you you know that feelin'. You just sit there and wait for somethin' to happen. The trailer slides right up beside me, so close I can look over and read the tiny yellow letterin' they've got stenciled on the girders. Man, I'll never forget it. I thought maybe I should jump out the cab, leave by the passenger side. Then I didn't have any more time to think, because here comes the next curve. You know what? The tractor hits a patch of ice, the trailer catches traction on the pavement, and the rig just sort-uh whipsaws right through the curve and plows right into a big snowbank. And there it stops.

"Sweet Jesus, I could *not* believe it. I was so scared that I jump down from the cab, fall flat into the snow and then scramble across the road. I didn't want to be *near* that truck. I just stand there across the road, maybe five, ten minutes. It's chilly as hell, but I'm standin' in my shirt sleeves, sweatin' like a pig. I remember, it's quiet as hell, 'cause I killed the engine somewheres on the way down. There's no traffic whatsoever, just me and the snow and the exhaust cracklin' on the truck as it cools down. I calm down a little bit. I start thinkin' how close I came to buyin' a plot. I take a few deep breaths and the air really feels good, you know, like a mouthful of clear water when you've been hot and thirsty all day. Funny how a little thing like breathin' can feel so good. So I look over at the truck. Looks okay. I'm startin' to get a little cold. I walk across the road, want to take a closer look at the other side. Looks okay. Check all my fittin's, my brake lines. Everything looks okay. I'm startin' to get a little colder, positively chilly now that my sweat is startin' to dry. Then I remember how anxious I am to get home. So I climb back into the cab.

"You know, it's funny as hell. I think if that truck had jackknifed on some main artery, I would have caught a ride home and I never would have gone near that cab again. But there wasn't any traffic. I didn't have any other way of gettin' home. I had to drive back myself. And I think that's what kept me in the truckin' business. Otherwise, I'd prob'ly be sellin' Fuller brushes or somethin'. So I get back in the cab, settle back in the seat, and sit there a minute, takin' my time. But I'm cold, and the heater doesn't work till the engine is running. So I find neutral, start 'er up, let it idle. Then I drop it into low, ease it out of the snow, and head down the road again.

"Well, you can bet that I never took it out of low till I dropped my load and headed for home. But that was all right. Just so long as I was back at the wheel, just so long as I proved to myself that I had the *cojones* to get back into that cab, everythin' was okay. Hell, I've jackknifed my truck five different times since then, and I never got shaken up as bad as I did that day back in '54. No sir."

So it is, time and again, in places where they have no right to be anything but strangers. Pickett they see and Pickett they hail. Pickett with his gray eyes flashing a dare while he piles one preposterous yarn upon another, taunting the men across the table to call him a liar, yes, pin him down, show him where he has screwed up a time or a place or somehow slipped on some small, telling detail. Pickett fumbling for a name he never tried to remember, Pickett backslapping and glad-handing, Pickett bending grammar and dredging up an Oklahoma twang just for the occasion the way some people dip into the cellar for a vintage to go with a special dinner, Pickett finally swaggering off to his Mack with a last burst of bravado about the road ahead, leaving his listeners numb with awe like a farm kid from Kansas who has left the state, who now sees the Rockies for the first time, speechless because what the hell do you say, anyway, about a spectacle that exceeds by any measure anything you've ever imagined before?

In three years, Lenny has only once seen a trucker offer more than casual, diffident objection to a Pickett anecdote. Most often, Pickett ignores the faintly disbelieving smiles or the questioning furrows on the forehead because Pickett in the middle of a story is a runaway, no easier to arrest than a forty-ton semi steaming down a steep grade. But once, it happened. Pickett, rolling halfway through his story, slurring his participles in fine fashion and arching his eyebrows, lowering his voice at just the right moments, had screwed, for perhaps the four-hundredth time over hot coffee and glazed doughnuts, the two daughters of a Mormon shopkeeper on his way through Logan, Utah. Pickett had just finished with the first on a one hundred-pound sack of flour and was preparing to put away the second—all this while father pumps gas, unsuspecting, outside—when a young punk of a trucker, a line hauler on a regular L.A.–Chicago run, decided he could take it no longer.

"Oh man, what a load of horseshit," he said loud enough to be heard. Pickett stopped talking. Everyone else at the table stopped breathing. The young trucker drew back, looked at Pickett, ran his fingers through an especially oily version of a flattop haircut that used to be called a "Chicago Boxcar."

Pickett stared at him.

"I mean, Chrise sake," the line hauler said. "I mean, that kind of stuff doesn't happen. I really can't see why the hell we waste our time listening to this bullshit, when we've all got a job to go out and do."

Lenny had been with Pickett six months by this time, long enough to imagine what kind of mayhem this could provoke. He waited, watched Pickett draw deliberately on a cigarette, lean on his elbows across the table, stare into the line hauler's eyes.

"You know all about it, right?" he said. "You been on the road, what? Three years? Four years? You drive from Chicago to L.A. prob'ly twice a week, you got a pay check comin' in from some goddamn freightline, just like clockwork, you eat at the same crummy fuckin' turnpike restaurants, drive the same crummy fuckin' highways so often you could prob'ly do it asleep. Am I wrong? C'mon, tell me I'm wrong. No? That's what I figured. You drive a goddamn six-lane Interstate from L.A. to Chicago, twice a week, and you think that's truck drivin'."

Pickett stopped here to pull on the cigarette again and jab his finger in the air as the smoke billowed from his nostrils.

"Well, buuullll-shit, buddy. For my money, you might as well be a bricklayer or an accountant. That ain't your rig. You ain't payin' a hundred-thirty dollars a month to insure that truck and your cargo. You ain't takin' the first risk when you pull that truck out on the highway, 'cept maybe pickin' up a dose in some cathouse along the way. You're trying to tell me about truck drivin'?

"Well, tell me about it, asshole. Tell me about the trucks thirty years ago, the ones with suspensions so bad that you peed red after eight hours' drivin'. You think I got these shoulders twirlin' power-steering wheels with my pinkie? Fuck me, I did. I wrestled those bastards every inch of the way. There wasn't any other way. Oh, and while you're at it, dick-head, tell me about the roads. You know, the roads we had to take before some genius in the Defense Department thought up the Interstates. You remember that, don't you? Drivin' from Miami to New York on two-lane asphalt all the way, goin' through every goddamn little town on the map, gettin' hassled by every shit-kickin' cop in every one of those little towns, and I mean *all* the way from Miami to New

York. You ever drive Route One from Miami to New York? Man, I can see it now. Lookin' into your mirrors, waitin' to get pulled over by every redneck sheriff from Waycross to Fredericksburg. Then right through the middle of downtown D.C., Hyattsville, College Park, Baltimore . . . Fuckin' Hyattsville used to be so bad they gave fuckin' President Harding a ticket for speedin'. Delaware, Philadelphia, right through the middle of the fuckin' city, I mean right through the middle. Nowadays, it's toll roads, turnpikes, Interstates the whole way.

"Same with the mountains. When I close my eyes, I can see every fuckin' foot of every mountain pass in the country. Know why? 'Cause I've driven 'em all, in every kind of weather, every month of the year. If they was open, I drove 'em. Shit. I'll bet you don't even bother gettin' a weather report, most times.

"Wild times, strange places, puttin' your ass on the line every time you kicked over the motor. That's all gone, just about. You got to go lookin' for trouble now. And I'll bet you don't, either. You drive your L.A.–Chicago run twice a week, just like punchin' a time clock, and you don't want to hear about anythin' else.

"But you're gonna tell me about truck drivin'."

That was the only time he knew that anyone ever challenged Pickett. Most of them, Lenny has decided, want to believe the stories, want to believe that the man mixing this verbal concoction with his heaping dollops of absurdity actually has done these things, has balled these women and crashed these trucks and laid out these cheating brokers with a single right cross just as he says, has done these things and still survives and prospers. Pickett's stories are the trucker image chiseled to a sublime edge and buffed to a high gleam, perfect in the finest detail.

His listeners are not bothered that the stories might be

apocryphal, for it is an unspoken axiom of trucking stories, even the most unlikely of Pickett's tales, that anything which can be conceived probably has happened to some trucker somewhere. The capricious reality of trucking life is surely equal to even the most outlandish imagination.

And while the action in Pickett's stories may stretch credulity, their backgrounds and settings are rich in gritty detail, reeking of an authenticity that comes from having driven four million miles, spending more time behind the wheel than most people do in bed, driving two White tractors, one Kenworth, and finally his Mack so long and so hard that they were of only nominal value on the trade-in lot. Pickett talks of times past, such times as the younger truckers have never seen, never will see. Technical advances have made the trucks far more dependable and powerful, with a comfort that borders on luxury. Sleeper compartments now can be ordered the size of a double bed. Inflatable seats mean that the trucker can literally ride on a cushion of air. Power steering, stiffer and heavier suspensions, stronger brakes with back-up systems all make driving easier and safer. Multilane Interstate highways, designed to accommodate military convoys and even rolling ballistic missiles during a war emorgency, make the driving so uneventful and uniform as to be almost boring.

The changes have not been without their disadvantages. No longer, for example, can the best food on the road be found where truckers park their rigs. That, Pickett assures Lenny every time they eat a sawdust hamburger, really used to be the case. The two-lane roads that cut through small towns in the countryside were once full of man-and-wife operations serving good, quick, honest food. But the big turnpikes brought truckers off the back roads and the task of feeding thousands of truckers plus tourists and traveling salesmen fell to the chains with their neon signs and, sometimes, exclusive franchises. Now the food is only quick. Wholesome truck-stop food still can be found—Pickett has his places: among them a red frame house in Lovelock, Nevada, specializing in broasted chicken and a diner in Vaughn, New Mexico, that dispenses thick gravy and flaky biscuits twenty-four hours daily—but those places are scarce. The drivers who know of them are few and those who care are even fewer. If the food is hot and served without delay, if it stays in the stomach and doesn't talk back too sharply, then it satisfies the requirements of most truckers. Pickett may wince when he dips a fork into a mound of instant whipped potatoes, but he also wipes the plate clean. He knows, after all, that he has very little choice.

Things were far different when Pickett wheeled his White out of Tulsa with a full load of propane, bound for Chattanooga, on an especially muggy summer day in 1946. The truck was new, Pickett was young and too brash to permit any doubts about his new career. It was his first run as a trucker, and he saw himself being carried away from a grubbing existence, roughnecking on somebody else's oil derricks.

Trucking was a way out that he hadn't seen until the year before. His older brother had moved to Oregon in '41, and spent the war hauling logs from the cutting forests of the Pacific Northwest to the lumber mills. He was at the airport in Tulsa when Pickett came home from the South Pacific. He was visiting from Oregon and he drove Pickett and their widowed mother home to Bartlesville in a 1941 Lincoln.

"I've got m'money saved," he told Pickett on the way home. "I'm buyin' me a new Caddy when they start makin' new cars again. Business is goin' real good."

Later that night, they talked alone, sipping coffee and hacking away at a cherry pie as they sat across the kitchen table, a single bulb burning above them in an otherwise dark house.

"Well, John, I'm glad I took off to come see you. You look good. It's my first vacation in five years. We been pullin' them logs out of the forests faster'n you could imagine, what with the war and all. God, but it's pretty up there. You wouldn't believe it. They take ton after ton of logs out of there every day and it's still just as green and pretty . . . You know, you ought to think about comin' up and joinin' me. I'll be able to afford a new truck, maybe this time next year. You could do it, John. Have you thought about what you want to do?"

Pickett shifted in his chair.

"Hard to say. I worked weekends with Paul Johnson and his rigging company before the war. I'm strong. He'd hire me back, I guess. I figure I could roughneck for just about anybody. Work's hard, but the money's good."

"Okay, John, but think about it. We'd be a good team. If business stays good, I'll pay you more than you'll make bustin' your ass in an oil field."

Logging truckers are almost universally regarded within the industry as the kamikaze branch of the business. It is frantic, insane work that involves short stretches of driving, usually over poor back roads, often unpaved. Because there are no Highway Department weighing stations sequestered in the forested wilderness, truckers are limited only by the practical consideration of how much weight their tractor can haul at a reasonable speed. And what is reasonable for logging truckers would seem suicidal to almost anyone else. So they grind out of their driveways and into the forests at daybreak, ready for the first load of the day. They stand by anxiously as log upon ponderous log is eased onto their trailer. And then they are off, speedometer needle tapping fifty, fifty-five on single-lane dirt roads, leaving a pall of dust

25

trailing a half-mile behind them. They ask all concession on the road and they give none. Slowing 100,000 pounds of projectile from fifty miles an hour to zero within a reasonable distance is a task beyond the capabilities of the brakes of any tractor-trailer. So the logging truckers don't even bother to try. They barrel down to the mills, fretting as the load is weighed and lifted off, and then they are off to make the trip again.

The risks are great and the rewards for the hustling trucker are not inconsiderable, although maintenance and mechanical attrition cut deep into the profits. Still, it is good money. Pickett's brother lived well until the spring day in '46, when a load broke loose as he stood beside his trailer, nervously snapping a piece of chewing gum, anxious to get in another run before nightfall. Pickett and his mother were the two beneficiaries on his life insurance policy. With his share of the money, Pickett put a down payment on his first White, and he walked away from the oil fields forever. He was twenty-one years old.

For ten years, he was a quintessential gypsy trucker, working six, eight, ten weeks at a time on the road, picking up loads from brokers in whatever city he found himself, never pausing anywhere for more than a night, dodging weigh stations, scurrying from city to city, tucking his money away at the end of a job in the afternoon and probably spending most of it that night before hitting the road again the next morning, driving hard and living harder. He loved it. He had his own name painted in script on the door of his cab and he was careful to keep it clean, wiping the road grime from the flowing yellow letters. When his clothes were filthy and he found road-weariness settling into his mind, Pickett would shop around for a load back to Tulsa or Bartlesville. He would stumble into bed in the old room, sleep around the

26

clock, spend a day sorting through his mail, maybe waiting for an overhaul on his White. Then he would be off again, eager to run thousands of miles of pavement under his wheels, anxious to feel the wheel in his hands again and to let the rumble of the engine, the whining tires, the vibrations, the moving scenery, wash over his mind and his body.

In '54, he married, moved to California, and the trips became shorter. He stayed at home four, five days at a time. He spent his money less freely, sometimes stuck a wad of cash into an envelope and sent it to his wife when he had been paid for a job. In '52 he traded in the tired old White after having rolled up almost 1,200,000 miles. His new White held him until 1959, when he used it as part down payment on a new Kenworth. Just under 900,000 miles showed on the odometer. In 1968, he was leafing through a trucking magazine, knowing that after 900,000 miles on the Kenworth, he should be looking for a new tractor. He saw an ad placed by a major interstate moving company.

"Security and independence!" the headline said.

"Truckers," the ad continued, "you can keep your independence and still have the security of working for one of America's largest and most prestigious moving firms. Excellent benefits under our working agreement include family health insurance. Steady work with a company that cares. If you own your own rig in good condition and have a good driving record, call collect or write . . ."

Pickett thought about that. Furniture movers are not highly regarded in the trucking hierarchy. In the fraternity, they are known as "flea haulers," and Pickett himself had made snide jokes about that branch of the profession. The reason for the contempt is that furniture movers are called on to do regular physical labor in loading and unloading their vans, and most truckers feel that this offends an unwritten code of dignity for their profession. It is tough work. But the job has its advantages. Instead of dickering with brokers from city to city, the furniture hauler deals daily with a single national dispatcher. Unlike those of perishable commodities, furniture deadlines are flexible. Time still is of economic essence for the owner-operator, but a two-day delay because of a breakdown does not turn the furniture hauler's cargo into twenty tons of garbage.

Finally, furniture haulers are untroubled by a concern that is utmost for many truckers, and that is complying with the varying weight limits posted by individual states. A van crammed full of sofas, dressers, and clothing will never come close to exceeding even the most stringent weight limit in any state. Corollary to this is the fact that furniture haulers do not overtax their machinery and do not need the most powerful tractors to climb steep grades at a legal highway pace. So, the driving itself is generally easier than usual for furniture movers, these bug-haulers, than for most other truckers.

As trucking goes, it is a steady job, certainly an honest job, not the sort of work that will make a man rich but, yes, more secure than some, and still with a certain degree of independence, which for the owner-operator usually means taking his own risks. The truck is Pickett's own. He pays all operating expenses, including his co-driver. He works when economic necessity tugs at his sleeve and he rests when he can afford it.

Pickett read the magazine ad three times, then sent a postcard to the address listed in the last line of the text. Six weeks later, he signed a working agreement with Mercury Interstate, and a week afterward he took possession of a new Mack, partly because of his enduring childhood conviction that every trucker ought to own a Mack at least once.

Chapter 3

Billy-Frank Freeman is hustling, eating up the pavement of North Shore Road just as quickly as he dares, but checking his mirrors, because if there is one hassle that he does not need right now, it is the flashing lights and the unsmiling face of a Massachusetts state policeman. Still, he knows he had better get his ass to the airport to meet Rivera's flight from Miami, because Rivera is not a man to be kept waiting.

Billy-Frank whips out of his lane to blow by a station wagon, downshifts the XK-E to third when a VW looms in his path, flicks the wheel, stabs the accelerator, and feels the Jag nearly leap past the slower car. It is that way for almost seven miles through midday traffic, Billy-Frank terrorizing the North Shore Road, blasting past Revere Beach and the dog track, straight down McClellan to Logan International. No time to mess with legal parking; Billy-Frank flies up the approach road, four-wheel drifts in front of a honking airport limo to screech into the only open space in front of the Northeast Airlines concourse. Then he is out and gone in a flash of flowing hair, high-heeled seven-league boots and embroidered brocade. He is at the gate, panting and sweating, when Rivera steps off the plane.

"Mr. Rivera," he says, and then he remembers to wipe off his damp palm before he offers it.

"Hello, babycakes," says Rivera, unsmiling. He steps out of

the gate, never breaks stride, swinging a briefcase beside him. "Talk to me. Parilla called me in Miami. Said you had business to talk. I hope to hell it's good. I took a trip special up here and my flight to the Coast leaves in twenty-three minutes."

Billy-Frank falls in beside him and they step down the hall at a smart pace, heels clicking on the tiled floor. In a less cosmopolitan city and setting, they might have drawn stares: one, in his twenties, with hair cascading to the squared-off shoulders of his brocade jacket, this an embroidered version of a Union Army general's dress coat, complete with epaulets; the other perhaps twice his age but holding off the years well, his face still tight, his hair black and brush-cut, tanned like a man who makes a point of spending time in the sun, wearing his sharkskin suit and alligator shoes as though he truly belonged in them.

"Right," says Billy-Frank. "Well, it's bargain time. I've got myself in a fix and I've got to get rid of some merchandise. It's good stuff, the best. Absolutely Grade-A, primo stuff."

"Sure. I'm looking for that lobster shop, the one where they sell 'em to you live. Down this way, I think. So, what's the problem?"

"My courier, my main man, meets his contact on a freighter from Bogotá, just like usual, about two weeks ago," says Billy-Frank. "No problem there. Then he's crossing the border, up near Derby Line, and the U. S. Customs agents haul him out of the car, take his luggage away, strip-search him, and keep him sitting on his ass for about two hours. He figures the game is up. But after all this crap, they give him his clothes, give him the luggage, give him a thank-you-sir, and send him on his way."

Billy-Frank watches Rivera's face while he is saying this. Nothing is getting through, he thinks, nothing at all.

30

"Sure," says Rivera. "Hey, here's the place. Buddy, you the clerk? I want a couple of lobsters. I want that one, the one with the humpback. And over there"—jabbing a finger toward a corner of the murky tank—"the fat one scrunched over at the side. What an idea, huh, lobsters at the airport? Right, that's the one. The big sucker over there, the one with the big claws. My wife would kill me if I stopped off in Boston without bringing her home a couple of Maine lobsters. So go ahead, babycakes, I'm listening."

"Yeah," says Billy-Frank, and he talks while Rivera watches the clerk dip a sieve into the cloudy recesses of the tank, dump the lobsters into a plastic bag, and walk to a scale. "Anyway, my courier is no dummy. The stuff is still in his bags and he figures there is no way they could have missed it. And he also figures they aren't letting him go without keeping pretty close tabs on him. So do I. Right now, I've got my courier cooling off one place and the merchandise is stashed somewhere else. But I can't go near it. And I don't know how long I can keep sitting on it."

"Uh-huh. And what do you want from me?" Rivera says, as he flips a twenty-dollar greenback on the counter.

"It's bargain time. I'm giving it to you half price just to get back my overhead so I can stay in business. See, I think the Feds got greedy. They wanted to see where my man went and who he talked to. There was an awful lot of stuff in those suitcases, more than I've ever handled before. Like, twenty pounds."

Rivera does not whistle or slap his knee. He is not given to vulgar display. Instead, he registers his surprise by blinking his eyes while Billy-Frank talks and the clerk counts change into his palm.

"Now I've got to get rid of the stuff," Billy-Frank says, "get it out of the area, until they figure they've blown the play and I can get back to business. So I'm giving it to you, twenty pounds for the price of ten, and this is top-grade stuff."

They walk away from the counter and stand beside a row of foam-and-chrome chairs in the airport lobby.

"Ordinarily," says Rivera, "I would say I don't need your troubles. But I'll take my chances because I could use a few pounds of the stuff. Back on the coast, we're stepping on that crap four times with xylocaine, and the freaks are lapping it up. But I want the transfer to be neat, neat and professional. I want it handled right, because I don't need your heat. Understand, babycakes? So you hire good professional help to get it out to the Coast. Pay the man good. Give him five at your end, and you tell him it's worth another five when he gets it to California. Ten thousand is a lot of money, but it's worth it for good help. Find him yourself, because I don't want my people mixed up in it, okay? If the stuff is as good as you say it is, you'll get the money just like usual, from my man in Providence."

"Okay," says Billy-Frank. "I'll get to work. I'll find somebody. It won't be easy. If it's the Federals, I figure they've got a line on every carrier from New England to Frisco. But I'll find somebody."

"You better," Rivera says, turning his left wrist to check a gold wristwatch. "And it better be good. I'm taking chances, just talking to you. I'm laying out good money for twenty pounds of cocaine, and I don't want it to be so hot that I've got to drop it."

Then he is gone, stepping on his left heel and hurrying off for his afternoon flight.

Billy-Frank Freeman's lips are pursed and his hands are kneading air, working nervously, as he walks to the concourse, in time to see a cop slide a parking tag under the windshield wiper of his Jag.

"Thanks a lot," Billy-Frank says.

"My pleasure," the cop says.

Just don't call me babycakes, Billy-Frank thinks, and he slips the ticket into a pocket of his skin-tight velveteen pants.

Chapter 4

After twenty-one years of marriage to a truck driver, Doris Pickett has learned something about saying good-by to the man you love. She figures: You treat him good when he's home, but when he's ready to leave, no fuss, no scene. You take your arms off his neck, you step back and you let him walk out the door. And when he has, you get on with whatever has to be done, so things will be right when he returns. Doris Pickett has never believed that a weeping woman could stop a man who had made up his mind to leave.

But now that he is gone, now that the dishes have been cleared from the table and now that John William has been sent to bed, now that the darkness and the silence leave a vacuum for her sorrows to fill, she weeps. She lies alone in their bed, and tears well up in her eyes, then fall to dampen her pillow. It is a cruel, heartless joke that her body has played on them, she thinks. A baby. A baby after twenty-one years. It is crazy enough to be carrying a child at age forty-one, but for that child to be conceived after so many years of fruitless trying is brutal and insane.

Doris Pickett, even without knowing it, is a true stoic. Her husband may bring her expensive trinkets when he returns after six weeks on the road, but he has never pampered her.

33

Things could have been easier, but Doris Pickett has never questioned her life because she has never seen that she could change things. But now, in the darkness of her room, Doris Pickett is confronted by the plain unfairness of it all. The baby that she once prayed for is now a burden and a misery; ten years make that much difference. If the first forty-one years of her life were less than ideal—and Pickett had warned her that marriage to a trucker would not be easy—then the next twenty could be insufferable. She cannot see bringing up a baby without a husband at home again. She cannot see Pickett staying at home, either, not if he is to live like a man and support his family. But there is no way of avoiding the baby now. The doctor said so a week ago. Oh, she could have gone earlier to the doctor, and she had heard that women were supposed to know about these things. But not her. After so long barren, she had no idea until it was too late that a baby was growing within her.

Pickett never mentioned anything like this the day he brought her into his life. She was slinging hash and filling coffee cups in a truck stop near Mobile one day in '54, when Pickett came bounding in and sat at the counter. He was loud but he was handsome and he looked at her with cocky, approving eyes, a cloth cap with its narrow black visor tilted back on his head, a package of Luckies rolled up in the left arm of his short-sleeved shirt. He joked with her, he kidded her about the coffee, and when he finished his meal, he threw four bits on the counter, started to walk away, then turned back to her and said in an offhand way, listen, honey, don't go fallin' in love with any other truck-drivin' man, y'hear? Because I'm comin' back this way soon, and when I do, I'm takin' you away with me to be my wife.

"Hey, fella," she said to him before he reached the door, "ain't you at least going to tell me your name?"

"Honey, I'm J. W. Pickett. Everybody knows that."

She laughed. But he was back a week later, and then she did something she had thought about for seven nights but had never dreamed she would be able to do. She untied her apron. She phoned her stepfather to say that she wouldn't be coming home, she walked away and never looked back. From that time on, she was Pickett's woman, no argument about that. She sat beside him that day in the cramped cab of his second White, and she could not keep from crying as they bounced down the highway, away from Mobile.

"Damn, honey, what's that for? What are you leavin' behind, anyways?"

"Oh, I don't know," she said. "Bad stepfather, couple of sisters, my job . . . my ma died a couple of years ago . . . but it's home, you know?"

She wiped away those tears and looked at him through blurred eyes, and she smiled.

"After all," she said, "what am I getting myself into now? A trucking man who's going to go off and leave me alone half the time. Lord, I must be out of my head, running off to get married to you. Hey, you are going to marry me, ain't you? Because if you ain't, you can just let me off right here."

"Oh, I'm goin' t'marry you, all right," he said. "We'll move to California, raise us three or four kids, and I bet you won't never want to come back to Mobile. I'll be on the road quite a bit, but don't worry none about that. You don't want some crummy guy with a half-ass job, home at five-thirty every day and bringin' his troubles home with 'im. Hell, a trucker is a better man part time than most anybody else is when he's home seven days a week."

A week later, they were married in Carson City. Then they drove straight to Antioch. Actually, they were driving to San Francisco for their honeymoon, married four hours, when Pickett noticed the neat tract of homes set into the side of a slightly rolling hill, a small island of brick and wood in a sea

35

of swaying golden grass. There were just a dozen homes in the development then. Pickett walked up to the real estate agent in the model home, pulled a thick wad of money from a breast pocket of his shirt and counted out a two-thousand-dollar down payment. He picked out a house at the end of the street, told the agent he would return the next day to sign the papers, and that has been their home ever since. For ten years, they talked about children and families. Then they stopped talking and adopted John William.

If she could have changed things, Doris Pickett would have had her husband home more often, but that would have been all, because those were good days in their way. They had money and they spent it well. They were kids and they were unshaken in an implicit belief that nothing could ever go too far wrong in the life of a trucking man and his family.

Now the new life in her body mocks those joys and dreams. Something is very wrong now. The ironic conjunction of seed and egg in her womb and the heartless arithmetic of the years have put a pressure on her and Pickett unlike any other.

It was during Pickett's last trip that she visited the doctor. Pickett, she remembers, never even blinked when he came home and heard the news.

"A baby. Our baby? Hell. Oh, hell, Doris." And that was it. He spent the rest of that week looking and acting like a man who had been skulled by a sledge hammer but who hadn't yet realized that he was supposed to fall on his face. She knew that he could count the years. She saw him pull the bankbook from a dresser drawer and tote up the figures. No solace there.

He brooded all week and she never mentioned it again until after this last dinner, after Pickett had sent Lenny to wait in the truck. They sat together, silent, holding hands at the table while John William watched television in another room. When she saw that he was ready to leave, she squeezed his hand and said, Pickett, what are we going to do?

When he looked at her and shook his head, she bit her lip for having said it.

For it was the first time she had ever seen him look helpless.

Chapter 5

Pickett and Lenny are out of Sacramento, over Donner Pass and booming down toward Reno before either of them speaks. This is not unusual. They are adjusting, settling back into their environment, because the knowledge that he is going to spend the next three days strapped into a missile traveling across a continent inevitably alters and revises the way a man talks and thinks.

To begin, no vignette in life can be considered very thoroughly or seriously when it is viewed through a thick plexiglass window at seventy miles per hour. So, what is seen is taken at total face value, as best the eye can perceive it as it approaches and then vanishes within a few seconds.

The result is that while the trucker's body and his machine hurtle down the road, his mind is decelerating. When the stimuli of the outside world are so fleeting as to be negligible, then the trucker's consciousness shrinks into a narrow range bounded by the road immediately ahead, his gauges, and the compartment of living space he shares with his partner.

And with wearying expanses of time and distance ahead

of them, there is rarely a rush to conversation between truckers. Pickett and Lenny may go silent for several hours at a time, their minds in blank suspension and each understanding why. When conversation comes, it may last for an hour or more. The topics may range from the economic bind of the independent trucker to the suspected hygienic shortcomings of the girls at Jack's Blue Heron near Elko, Nevada. Their talk may lapse for a half hour or more until one of them picks it up again as if they had paused for only a deep breath.

Pickett and Lenny are comfortable with silence and with the estrangement imposed by the tractor cab. Others are not so lucky. There are truck drivers who feel compelled to bridge the gap with heaps of palaver, filling the hours with mindless chatter and absurd anecdotes. There are three options for such a driver. He drives alone, or he goes through a succession of partners the way marathon runners use up sweat socks. Or he finds another like himself and they bore each other into a perpetual silence.

More seriously afflicted are the truckers who cannot abide a lengthy separation from the world outside their cabs. Far too often than is economically feasible, they pull off the highways and into truck stops for a cup of coffee and a taste of humanity. They are likely to drive in freezing weather with their windows half open, feeling in the wind a chilly comfort that there is, indeed, real life outside their compartment of metal and glass. If they are smart, or lucky, they sell their rigs and go to work as insurance salesmen.

Pickett and Lenny, then, silently go through the ritual, disconnecting themselves from the existence they left behind when the truck grunted away from Pickett's house a couple of hours ago.

Finally, as they crest Donner Pass and Pickett gears down for the downhill stretch to the state line:

"God damnit but it's getting cold out there, Pickett. Let's have a little more heat. And what is it, the end of October? I'll bet you a steak that we've got to get out the chains before the end of this trip."

From Pickett, a soft, low laugh.

"Lenny, I ain't lettin' you take my money all that easy. They had snow in Colorado this week, I heard on TV. We'll be lucky if we make it out of Laramie tomorrow without puttin' on them chains."

Pickett glances over to see how Lenny is taking this. Hmmm. He is taking this fine.

"But you don't mind, do you?" Pickett says.

"What?"

"I say, you don't mind that we're goin' to be spendin' the next five months kneelin' in the snow to put on them chains, freezin' our asses off. Not to mention slippin' and slidin' down the road on ice and snow half the time."

"Come on, Pickett, I don't look forward to that any more than you do."

"Okay, college kid, whatever you say. But I saw you lappin' it up, just thinkin' about it. Yessir, you can hardly wait."

"Pickett, you get crazier by the minute. I sure the fuck hope you stay together long enough to get us to Boston, is all."

It is gentle joshing, but when it is over, Pickett thinks: He likes it, the kid really likes it. He likes the driving and the greasy spoons and all the rest of the bullshit.

And he thinks: I'm going to have a talk with that boy.

They are an hour out of Reno when Lenny begins to feel the day's hard work. He yawns, sees only the yellow dividing stripes flying by on their left, hears only the booming of the diesel and the urgent, high-pitched hum of the tires.

39

"Pickett," he says, "one of us might as well get some sleep. I'll take the wheel for a few hours."

"Forget it, kid. I'm feelin' good. I'll get wired, drive 'till daybreak. We'll make Salt Lake about that time. I'll wake you up. Pull the box out, though, and leave it on the seat."

Lenny climbs into the sleeper, unfolds a woolen blanket, is ready to draw the curtains. First, there is something he must get straight.

"Pickett, you okay? You've been strange. Different. You got something on your mind? It's nothing I've done, is it?"

Something on his mind? Oh no. Not much, Pickett thinks. Nothing that about fifteen years and fifty thousand dollars wouldn't fix. But he says, no big thing, kid. It's got nothin' to do with you.

From his first run with Pickett, Lenny has never had trouble sleeping in the truck. Diesel's growl recedes into the fringes of his awareness until it is no more obvious or obtrusive than breathing. It is hypnotic, a lulling thrum as Lenny pulls the blanket over his body, feeling safe and untouchable, lost to the world and flying free somewhere in the Nevada desert. He cannot be touched. It is a good feeling. He is quickly asleep.

Pickett has the truck free-wheeling at seventy, the speedometer needle unvarying, his foot steady on the accelerator. Before he can feel drowsy, Pickett leans across the seats, opens the fishing-tackle box, lays his hand on the glass jar, and holds it between his knees as he unscrews the cap with his free hand. He dips into the jar twice with his beefy forefinger, then holds the handful of pills up to the shaft of moonlight that beams through the passenger window. Two Reds, three Greenies, one Hummer and one Turnaround Special. He drops the Hummer, two Greenies and a Red into the jar, gulps the rest without water. He screws back the lid, replaces the jar and lays the fishing-tackle box on the floor beneath his seat. He works a pair of headphones around his ears, slips the jack into the tape deck and picks a stereo cartridge off the top of his instrument console. Hank Snow. That will do very well. Yes, indeed. And he whistles to the beat laid down by The Singing Ranger as the truck blasts through the night.

He is feeling much better already. He is putting miles between himself and his predicament. And thus, the problem seems not half so imposing as it did before. In the morning, he will be able to talk about it.

Chapter 6

Lenny, Lenny. Lenny with the stringy, sun-bleached hair. Lenny the Freeway Legend, from Ventura to La Jolla. Surfboard Lenny, Loverboy Lenny, Freak-out Lenny, the last of the Kalifornia Krazy Kids.

Lenny, they have been asking about you.

Where they hit the surf at Malibu, in all the old sandy-floored hangouts, they still think about you, Lenny. Big Willie and his street-racing bunch over in Pasadena miss you, too, you and your crazy, fishtailing, rubber-smearing, ninety-mile-an-hour excursions down Washington Boulevard. Down at Ascot, they are still wondering whatever happened to that fast Novice flat-tracker who rode his Bultaco right into the Turn Four boards one memorable night, that crazy dude in the purple and white leathers who smacked off the wall, did a complete three-sixty somersault through the air in front of the grandstands, bounced down the track, slid on

41

his ass about a hundred feet more and came to a stop still right-side up, yes, still holding onto the handlebars, nothing else. Oh, Lenny, they loved you for that. The wide-open freaks in Venice and the closet freaks in Tarzana and the girls, the girls from Oxnard to Altadena to Oceanside, they all ask about you now and then. And when they hear that you are haulin' around the country with a pill-popping Okie truck driver, they say: Lenny? Lenny Lewis? Oh, man, you must be talking about somebody else. Then they think about it for a minute and they say: You know, that kind of figures.

If they only knew. Because Lenny has changed, mellowed. New York to L.A. in fifty-five hours is a fast and rugged trip, but even at that speed, the trip should be boring. Not even the strongest sense of urgency can sustain itself over fifty-five hours. So Lenny has accommodated himself to the realities of the trucking life. He thinks more, talks less, takes life and the miles as they come. Age and the trucking life have done that to him. Lenny likes himself this way. He would have to agree that it was the best of fortunes that brought him to Idaho Route 26 between Arco and Blackfoot the day late one June when he became J. W. Pickett's third, best, and probably last relief driver.

Pickett drove alone for more than twenty years. Signing with Mercury, though, meant that he had to face up to hiring a co-driver to help in loading and unloading the truck. He didn't like it, but he had little choice. Theoretically, he could have driven alone and hired casual help in different cities, recruiting muscle for a day or two, either off the streets or at a Mercury terminal. But such help tends to lose enthusiasm for the work at hand when the job includes easing a four-hundred-pound armoire down a steep and narrow staircase. Such help, Pickett suspected, might be prone to quit on the job at critical times. Besides, having two drivers in the cab would end his career-long battle of keeping the daily logbook within the bounds of credulity and federal regulations. For the first time in his trucking career, he might not have to spend hours erasing, laboring over his doctored entries, trying to explain how he had managed to cover fourteen hundred miles from one midnight to the next without violating an astonishing number of traffic laws and trucking regulations. A co-driver simplified all that. With two men in the cab, they could legally be on the road twenty hours a day, driving ten hours each, provided each got eight hours off duty in the sleeper. Well, there was no way of telling that Pickett actually had driven sixteen of those twenty hours or that neither man had spent more than two hours in the sleeper compartment, no way at all. And if Pickett wanted to haul non-stop for a day or two, he could squeeze in the last four hours a day with a little creative reporting in the logbook.

So Pickett hired on a man who had been suggested by the Mercury representative. He was a twenty-nine-year-old trucker from Manteca who had gone broke trying to earn a living for himself, his wife and three pre-school children as owner and operator of a twelve-year-old International. His name was Eldon Tucker, and he was a disaster. Taking on a co-driver is no mean step for a man after twenty years of genuine independence. The psychological process of surrendering territory to another human is imposing enough. Eldon was no hitchhiker, no guest in the cab. He had proprietary rights to a share of the two or three cubic feet of living area that the cab comprised. Eldon belonged there. It was not his cab, but he was working with Pickett, entitled to stake out part of it as his own.

The cab of a diesel tractor is a trucker's home and his office, his world on the road. Contact is close. Pickett tried, he truly did, but this mating was doomed from the start.

43

Hours, days, and weeks spent together in a cab will strip away the insulation of human feelings so that the slightest irritant gnaws at the mind and dominates the consciousness like a pebble in a hiker's shoe, and Eldon had his share of eccentricities. Mostly, Pickett could not abide the man's insistence that Pickett was doing everything bass-ackwards, from the method he used to coax a settee out of a doorway to the fashion in which he tapped the accelerator before kicking down to a lower gear. After eleven months, Pickett and his bank account were approaching the breaking point. His trips were becoming shorter and he found excuses to stay at home simply because he dreaded being in the cab with Eldon.

One day, as they passed through Bend, Oregon, Pickett could take it no longer. Silently, he reached into his wallet and produced bus fare home to Manteca for Eldon.

"Go," Pickett said softly. "Go now, Eldon, before it's too late."

On his next trip, Pickett took along the brother-in-law of a neighbor down the street, a man who had been fired from his job at a local body shop because of a disagreement with the foreman. The disagreement had been over the man's ability to take the creases out of the dented right rear quarterpanel of a 1971 Torino after he had consumed a pint of Canadian whiskey during a half-hour lunch break.

His name was Jack Sanders, and he had never driven a truck. That was of little consequence to Pickett, who was happy enough to have the driving chores to himself again. He wanted Sanders' muscle. Sanders would have been invaluable in loading furniture if he had applied half the energy to this task that he gave to finding and consuming a bottle of booze wherever Pickett might park the truck. Pickett had to give him credit; the man had a positive nose for the hard stuff. One night they pulled into Burlington,

Vermont, at 2 A.M. to rest before beginning to unload in the morning. Pickett curled up in the sleeper box, and Sanders strode off into the darkness, toward a moonlit and lifeless downtown. He returned less than an hour later, a quart of off-brand gin and two styrofoam cups tucked under his arm in a paper bag. He shook Pickett awake because Sanders did not like to drink alone.

"I'm not a gin lover," he told Pickett as he filled the cups, "but sometimes a man has to make some concessions."

Pickett liked Sanders. He was quiet. Being an absolute novice in the profession, he never tried to advise Pickett on running the trucking business. But there were some uneasy moments when Pickett had to explain away his obviously inebriated "co-driver" at inspection stations. Besides, Pickett had to believe that Sanders, sober, would carry a little bit more and carry it a little bit longer than he did with a couple of stiff belts boiling through his system. Still, it was with genuine regret that Pickett, that morning late in June, sent Sanders on his way back to California. It was after eight o'clock when Sanders appeared, barely coherent and even less co-ordinated, to help Pickett empty a large home in Seattle for a trip to Tucson. Pickett hired two teen-aged boys in the neighborhood, gave them thirty-five dollars each for seven hours' work, and set off alone that evening for Arizona.

Silent desperation prodded Pickett and Lenny toward that meeting on Idaho Route 26. Pickett was truly up against it, for the weeks from early June through Labor Day are frantic times in the interstate moving business. There is non-stop work for those who can handle the pace, and Pickett knew he could handle it, if only he could find help. Lenny's problems were far less specific. He felt them as a vague uneasiness, an amorphous alienation with his life's directions. That feeling had been with him for some time.

He grew up in Beverly Hills, the only son of a minor motion picture producer and a onetime starlet who had pitched her career for marriage. Lenny knew that she had given up the movies for her husband. Lenny knew it and everybody else in Beverly Hills knew it; she never ceased telling about it. Their house was not a Beverly Hills masterpiece, but it was nice, very nice. Lenny went to high school with the sons and daughters of movie stars and millionaires. What Lenny lacked in inherited fame and wealth, he made up for with his insane derring-do. Crazy Lenny Lewis would do anything, go anywhere, just for the hell of it. Lenny was smoking grass in the high school lavatories when slipping vodka into the punch bowl at school dances was considered daring. He surfed, he raced motorcycles at Ascot Speedway, and he astounded everybody by enrolling at UCLA to study psychology. It seemed like the thing to do, he said. But Lenny was not finished astonishing people. He breezed through UCLA *cum laude* and still made it to the surf and to the backstreet dragstrips without fail on weekends. He earned two letters on the wrestling team, he sweated his way to the finals of the Pacific-Eight Conference 159-pound championships in his senior year, and when it was over, when he had strolled onstage at Pauley Pavilion to receive his diploma, when he had shaken hands with well-wishers at a party at his home, when he realized that his days and his weeks were his own because he had nothing, just nothing to do, he stuffed jeans and a workshirt into a backpack and told his parents that he was going to hit the road.

He promised to keep in touch, and he was gone the next day. He was traveling light, and that meant without a car. He hitched up the coast for three days in Big Sur. Friends in San Francisco. Six days in Yosemite, feeling the moodiness of the high country. Then a ride to Yellowstone and the Tetons, but too cramped there. Arizona, maybe. Canyon de Chelly. From Jackson, Wyoming, he caught a ride with a man returning from vacation to his work as a technician at an atomic energy research station several miles off Route 26.

"It's classified stuff, pretty high security," the technician told him. "I'll drop you off here at the highway. You'll get a ride sooner or later."

It was seven in the morning and Lenny found himself sitting beside a highway cutting through the most desolate stretch of land he had ever seen. He pulled an apple from his pack and dug his teeth deep into it. He tore at the fruit with huge bites, then gnawed until he reached the core. He tossed the core alongside the road. Fifteen minutes, and he had not seen a car. The silence was awesome.

Route 26 is not one of America's more heavily traveled highways. Interstates 80 North and 15 bear the burden of Idaho's tourist traffic. Sheep, sagebrush, and unfenced range land are 26's chief scenic attractions. So quiet and so lonely is the road that jet fighter pilots passing overhead delight in swooping down on an occasional speck of automobile below, hurtling down from the sky, past Mach One, so that they seem totally silent as they slide down and level off maybe a hundred feet high. They flash by the car and they are followed, milliseconds later, by the unbelievable boom of a sonic shock wave. The driver is lucky if he keeps his car on the road.

Pickett himself had been victimized that way, but he has his diversions, too. One of these is terrorizing long-haired hitchhikers. This, then, was the scene on Idaho Route 26, between Arco and Blackfoot, on this particular June morning. Pickett tooling down the road, clipping along at sev-

47

enty, wondering what the hell he is going to do for help when he gets to Tucson. Lenny beside the road, wondering what the kids are doing on Malibu and cursing himself for not leaving the technician at Idaho Falls, when he had a chance. Then he heard the drone of the diesel in the distance. Up on his feet. Stand straight and smile, he thought. Stick the thumb resolutely down the road.

Pickett saw him. Pickett also saw the rumpled workshirt and, most distressing of all, the long California hair. So Pickett bore down the road and then, ever so gently, set the right front wheel of his tractor off the asphalt and onto the shoulder of the road where Lenny was standing. Pickett grinned.

"Scramble, hippie," he said.

But Lenny did not scramble. He did not even blink. He squared his shoulders. He caught Pickett's eyes and he stared straight at him as the truck bore down, churning dust. Holy shit. Pickett saw that the longhair was not about to retreat. No time for braking. He cranked the wheel hard left, saw the truck flash past Lenny, who was still standing there, as if transfixed. He wrestled the truck back on the pavement, glanced into his outside mirror on the passenger side, saw nothing but billowing dust. He clamped hard on the brakes, downshifted, slowly brought twenty-five tons to a standstill. When he stopped, a wind was blowing the veil of dust away and he saw the longhair picking himself out of the dust. He slipped into reverse, and the differential whined as he eased backward to where Lenny brushed the gray dust from his pants.

Pickett leaned over to look at him.

"Redneck cocksucker," Lenny said.

"Get in," Pickett said, and he stretched across the seat to open the door. Lenny stood there, hands on hips, running his tongue speculatively over his lips.

48

"Christ sake, kid," Pickett said, "if I wanted to kill you, you wouldn't be standing now. You'd be scattered all over the place."

Lenny lifted his pack to the floor of the cab and then climbed clumsily to the seat. He shut the door. Pickett set the truck rolling again, worked through the gears, and talked.

"Last I seen of you, you was standin' on the shoulder like a cigar-store Indian," Pickett said. "How'd you end up in the dirt? You lose your nerve and bail out?"

"No way," Lenny said. "Your trailer got a little sideways. It hit me a glancing blow, just brushed me, but it was enough to knock me down."

"You're lucky," Pickett said.

"You're a laugh."

"I mean it. Somebody pulls a stunt like that, he deserves to get hurt. What're you tryin' to prove?"

"Me? Hey, mister, I didn't jump out into the road, you know. I didn't wear some sign that says 'Hit me if you can.' I didn't ask for these problems. Just because I've got long hair doesn't mean I'm fair game for every redneck truck jockey on the road."

"Hey. Fuck you, kid. I'm givin' you a ride, ain't I? Look, I'm no hardass. I just get bored now and then, is all. I seen you standin' along the road, I figure no harm done if I scare you a little bit. How the hell was I supposed to know you weren't goin' to move? What you tryin' to prove, anyway?"

"I'm not trying to prove anything. I've got just as much right there on the shoulder of that road as you have."

"Oh hell, I can see I'm up against a real mental giant in this discussion," Pickett said. "Kid, ain't you ever heard that might makes right? You ever heard of the right-of-way? Well, I had the right-of-weight. Anybody too dumb

49

to see that deserves to be put out of his misery. Man, they'd shoot a mule for bein' that dumb."

But Pickett's tone by now was not abusive. He was amused, intrigued.

"Tell me," he said, "are you brave or just plain fuckin' dumb?"

"What's the difference?" Lenny said, smiling.

They blew down through Idaho, into Utah, Pickett using deserted back roads, making time. And they talked. For both of them, it was an education.

"How come you ain't workin', kid?" Pickett asked at one point.

"I just got out of school. Don't know, I can't think of anything I really want to do. I studied psychology, but that's kind of a dead end for me. Not much you can do with a bachelor's in psychology, except go to graduate school or become a social worker. I can't see either one of those. So, I thought I'd spend the summer just bumming around."

"You mean just doin' nothin'? Just travelin' from place to place without a job? What do you get out of that?"

"I'm seeing the country, meeting people. I never would have met you if I hadn't been sticking out my thumb back there on the road, would I?"

"Don't it bother you, though, bein' without a job all summer?"

"Bother me? No, I can't say so. I've never had a job for long, not for more than a few months at a time when I needed some extra bread."

"I'm not puttin' you down, but I can't imagine that. I really can't. Man, when I got out of the Army, the first thing I did was to run out and get a job. I've been workin' my butt off in this truck since forty-nine. I wouldn't

50

know a vacation if it ran across the highway in front of my high-beams."

"Come on, this job is one long vacation. Just driving back and forth around the country. This is the life."

"Shit, buddy-boy, that shows how much you know. I've seen every stretch of road in this country so often that it's like walkin' across the street. I ain't drivin' around 'cause I enjoy it. It's a job. It's the way I make my money. How'd you like to spend six weeks livin' out of this cab, drivin' your tail off all day? It's no vacation, let me tell you."

"Six weeks? You spend six weeks at a time on the road?"

"Sometimes. Sometimes more. I go where the work takes me, and as long as the work is good, I stay on the road."

"That doesn't seem so bad. I think I might like that. I really do. Don't laugh at me, mister, but I think I could dig that. I think I could get behind that."

"You do, huh? You think you could *dig* that? I don't think you could. This is heavy work. You got to be tough, because there's more to this job than just drivin'. You think I've got a crew of helpers waitin' for me to unload this truck when I get to Tucson? Like hell I do. That's all part of the job."

"Just the same, I think I could do it."

"I wonder. You look kind of light for this sort of work."

"You offering me a job?"

"I didn't say that. Only, I do need some help when I get to Tucson. I had to get rid of my co-driver this morning and it's goin' to be just about dark when we get to Tucson. It'll be pretty late to hustle up some help. So, what I'm sayin' is, if you'd like to pick up a few extra bucks, say forty for about eight hours' work, maybe less, then I could use you."

"I don't know. I was thinking about getting off around Flagstaff, heading east for Canyon de Chelly, maybe."

"Suit yourself. I said I was givin' you a ride, and I will. But if sightseein's all you're worried about, there's plenty farther south, around Tucson. They got the Picture Rocks there, and the Saguaro National Monument. I hear they're real nice."

"Yeah? You been there?"

"Well, never to stop, actually, but I've heard talk. Supposed to be nice. And the desert is real fine down there, too. If you like desert, that is."

"Okay," Lenny said, "you got yourself a deal. Only, I don't want any money. You're already doing me a favor, just giving me a ride like this."

"Bull*shit*. Man, you are dumb, turnin' down cold cash when it's offered. You work, you'll take the money. That's all. And since we're goin' to be workin' together, you might as well know my name. I'm J. W. Pickett, world's finest over-the-road hauler."

"I'll bet you are, J.W. And I'm Lenny. Lenny Lewis."

"Okay, Lenny, glad to have you aboard. How's it feel to be an honest workin' man again?"

"I feel like a real American," Lenny said. "If I had an American flag decal, I'd stick it on my backpack right now."

With that deceptively elaborate tango was kindled one of the more improbable friendships on the road. All things considered, it was not a difficult détente. Pickett, for one, liked Lenny's independence and his grit. And Lenny figured that any man who had spent more than twenty years in a business such as this could not be all bad. After an hour in the cab, Lenny knew he liked trucking.

Strange, the sensation. He was on the move, really stepping out, not without direction but with a specific goal—Tucson before dark—dangling tantalizingly before him. He felt Pickett's unspoken sense of purpose and he took it to himself. Bouncing, growling down the highway, he felt Tucson drawing nearer. He watched the mile markers tick by the cab and he grinned inside. He liked Pickett, too. The

52

man had his rough edges, but there was no bullshit about him, not if you could read through his redneck smokescreen. Pickett was a real man and trucking was a real job and he truly regretted seeing it all end in Tucson when they finally carried the last crate in from the van after midnight.

"Well, did I do okay?"

"Kid, you did good, real good. You were a big help, no kiddin'."

"Thanks."

They were standing outside the home, near the truck, Pickett having checked the manifest, collected the fee and completed the job with the homeowner's signature.

"Where are you headed now?" Pickett asked.

"I don't know, I was going to ask you the same thing. You going home?"

"Not me, kid, I called the dispatcher inside, and he says I've got fifteen thousand pounds sittin' in a warehouse in Phoenix. I'm pickin' that up first thing in the mornin', headin' for Chicago."

"Chicago. No kidding. You really do see the country."

"I guess so. Well, listen, kid, here's your forty. You earned it. I'm gettin' back on the road. I'm drivin' to Phoenix now. I'll sleep in the warehouse lot until mornin'."

"Okay. Uh, what are you doing for help? You going to hire another co-driver?"

"Don't ask me. I'll hire help for the mornin' at the warehouse, then I don't know. I've got to find somebody."

"J.W., I'll come right out and say it. I'd like to ride with you. I'll work hard, just as hard as I did tonight. I've never driven a truck, but I'm pretty good with mechanical things. I'll learn quick."

"I'm sure you would, kid, but the thing is . . . well, I'm lookin' for somebody full time. Somebody who'll stick around for a few months. No offense, but I think you'd prob'ly get tired of this after a while. Then I'd have to go through all the bullshit of hirin' somebody again. You understand."

"If that's all that's bothering you, forget it. I got nothing else to do. This isn't just a lark for me. I really enjoyed it today. We could make it together without getting in each other's way. That's the way I feel, anyway. And if you're worried about me getting tired of all this, maybe you're right. But I'll promise you right here that if I decide to leave, I'll tell you so and I'll stick around until you find somebody else. Give you my word. That's the best I can do."

Pickett stood silent for a moment. He looked at Lenny, his face bleached blue in the pale street light beneath which they stood. Lenny had worked hard. He had hefted his share of the load and he had not complained. Moreover, long hair and all, he had not been such a bad companion in the cab. He was a fighter but he knew who was boss of this operation.

"Okay," Pickett said. "I'll give you a hundred fifty a week to start, till you learn to drive. Then I'll jump you up to two twenty-five, maybe more. I'll pay you only when we're workin', but maybe I can juggle my books so you don't lose half of that in taxes and such.

"That sound okay? Good. Uh, there's just one thing I got to get straight kid. You ain't, um, any sort of dope addict, are you?"

Lenny looked into Pickett's eyes and tried not to laugh.

"J.W.," he said. "Not everybody with long hair has to take a shot of heroin every twelve hours."

"Okay, okay," Pickett said. "I don't know why, but I've got a thing about it, is all. I pop a few pills now and then to stay awake, but I figure it ain't the same."

"Of course not," Lenny said. "Of course not."

So it began. After a week, Pickett decided that Lenny had

54

watched and listened long enough. On a long, open stretch of road in Montana one day, he stopped the truck, dismounted, switched seats with Lenny. They spent three hours on that part of the road, Lenny jerking the truck along, Pickett lecturing, berating, praising, and trying not to act uncomfortable when the gears ground under Lenny's untrained touch. But he learned. Pickett gave it to him in steady doses, three hours that day in Montana, a couple of hours a day later in Oregon, four hours later that week when they passed through Nevada. And, as Lenny had promised, he learned quickly. By the end of the summer, he was ready for his California trucker's exam. That test is one of the most extensive screenings a trucker faces in the country. With that permit in his wallet, Lenny was ready to drive any rig anywhere. And Pickett felt relaxed enough even to sleep when Lenny took over the driving.

Lenny never expected the driving to be a problem. He wasn't sure, however, just how he would go over with the rest of the country's truckers. He decided he would not cut his hair, not right away, at least. He wore his faded jeans and his workshirt, so that he looked like nothing less than a wandering militant student activist as he strolled into truck stops. His salvation was that Pickett was never far behind, and that was good enough for almost anybody, not necessarily because they feared Pickett but because that established Lenny's credentials as a trucker. Once they knew Lenny as a truckin' man, he was tolerated and accepted, because the truckers' fraternal loyalty runs deeper and stronger than the most deeply ingrained prejudices.

That first year, he went home for Thanksgiving. After dinner, his father motioned him into the study. He poured cognac for them both and they sipped this silently until his father cleared his throat and asked, Lenny, what is it about this job that you seem to enjoy so much?

Lenny knew it was coming. He had played the conversation over in his mind a dozen times. And, still, until that moment, he was not sure how he would answer that question.

Lenny swished the cognac in the snifter. He looked into his father's face. And the words began to come.

First thing, Lenny told his father, you have to understand that this is not so much a job as it is a way of life. A trucker does not simply drive trucks; he is a member of a society. A society of the road, a society with its own customs and culture and art.

His father smiled at that.

"You don't believe me?" Lenny said. "You ought to buy a Citizens Band receiver and listen to the way truckers talk on there. You'll never understand them, but you'd better believe they understand each other. Or spend a few hours one day at one of the big truck stops. Watch the way the truckers congregate together. They can spot each other in a second. I don't know, there's something about the way a man walks or the way he slumps his shoulders and cradles his warm coffee cup in his hands after he's been on the road all day and half the night. And you notice they always sit together. They don't want anything to do with the guy who's got his kids in the station wagon for a Sunday drive. It's snobbishness, but it's more than that. The trucker and that guy in the station wagon are in two different worlds. The only person who really understands a trucker's problems is another trucker."

His father nodded.

"Or look at the way truckers admire some shiny rig with tons of chrome and a slick paint job. They don't know shit about Rembrandt or Picasso, but they can appreciate a beautiful, good-running machine. For them, that's style, art, status.

56

"And if you spend enough time in enough truck stops all around the country, you begin to realize something else about trucking. It's one way, maybe the only way, to really stay in touch with what's happening in a country this big. You talk to people in one state, maybe some kid pumping fuel in Missouri. A day later, you're talking to a sixty-year-old waitress in Georgia. They've both got their own problems, their own outlook. Or you might be sitting at a truck stop in Arizona, and here beside you at the table is a trucker from Arkansas who's telling you what he saw in Massachusetts, and across the table is a trucker from Oregon who's bitching about what a hard time he had yesterday in Texas, and maybe you've got a story to tell about the time you passed through South Dakota a couple of days ago. All I know is that after six months in that truck, I'm beginning to learn about this country. For the first time in my life, I can say that I'm starting to grasp just how big this country is and how different it is, the land and the people, from one part to another. And how beautiful it is and how ugly it is, too. You don't get that by flying over it in an airplane. You don't get that from watching the network news, either. But a trucker can."

His father nodded. He could understand that, he said.

"Maybe," Lenny said. "Maybe. Sometimes, though, you have to be there to see it. There was a night, a couple of months ago, when we pulled into a truck stop about midnight near Phoenix. We were just walking into the diner when we heard this yelling, shouting inside. Some trucker was going berserk. He saw the waitress coming up to take his order and he thought she was a gorilla. He was freaking out, as bad as I've ever seen it. They calmed him down and somebody there knew what rig he was driving, so a couple of truckers went to get his log and his papers. Well, his logbook was three days behind, but he had bills of lading that

57

showed he had hauled a load from L.A. to Chicago, then turned right around and hauled another load right back to L.A. All this in about three days, getting wired every six hours, never sleeping, not a bite to eat, just staring at that damn centerline until you either collapse or crash the truck or get smart enough to pull over to the side and sleep for about a day."

And that doesn't scare you, his father said.

"It scares me," Lenny answered. "It scares me to think that one day, sooner or later, I'm going to run into a patch of glare ice going around some turn or maybe going over a narrow bridge and there won't be a damn thing I can do about it. If I'm lucky I'll slide right through and if I'm not I'll jackknife and that'll be the end. If I'm taking those chances, then so are about three hundred thousand other guys like me out there. So I feel like I'm part of them. They're good men. Truckers are the best damn friends you can have. Truckers have signals, you know, with their headlights. With their CB sets, they don't have to use them as much now, but everybody knows what they are. I can be driving down a highway and when I come to pass another semi, I move out into the fast lane and blink my lights, just once, so he knows I'm there. And after I've passed him, I just watch my right-hand mirrors for him to blink me once. That means I'm clear of him, that I've got room to pull back into the lane. No guessing. I *know*. Okay, it's a little thing, but it means a lot. We're communicating. We're strangers, but we understand each other. And if I see a semi coming the other direction flash his lights twice, then I slow down and watch, because I know that in a mile, or two, I'm going to come up on a patrol car behind a billboard, or the Smokies, the cops, with their radar box set up on the side of the road. That guy may never see me again. I'll never know his name, but he just saved me maybe a hundred bucks and a trip to the Justice of the Peace."

Lenny asked: "Can you understand that?"

Yes, said his father, he could understand that.

"Then," asked Lenny, "can you understand why I do what I'm doing?"

His father raised the snifter to his lips, touched his tongue to the cognac and felt the liquid warm his tongue. Then he said: No, son, I don't understand.

Lenny was gone the next day, gone to help Pickett haul a load to New Orleans.

Chapter 7

Daylight catches them hauling across the Great Salt Lake Desert. They are naked and alone and although Pickett is holding a steady sixty-five, they seem to make no headway, no headway at all, through this incredible expanse. Pickett is driving straight into rising sun, wearing sunglasses and hiding behind the shade from his windshield visor. And still, the glare from the sun on the sand and the salt keeps him squinting, looking at the road through his eyelashes. And it is bright enough, too, to turn the blue corduroy curtains of the sleeper box into a glowing, translucent veil of aquamarine into which Lenny stares as he slowly awakens to the light and to the familiar road sounds. He has learned not to part the curtains without some preparation. So he blinks, yawns, puts his left arm across his eyes and draws back the curtain with his right.

"Morning, Pickett. Got my sunglasses?"

Pickett finds the glasses, hands them back, and Lenny turns his back to slip them on his face. Then he climbs down into the seat. And, *Jesus,* he yells, the sun is bright.

"What time is it? About seven out here? Pickett, you drove hard."

"Stopped to take a leak up at the top of Emigrant Pass. Straight through except for that. We'll fuel up near Salt Lake."

"Okay. You tired? Hungry?"

Pickett is neither. When he stopped at the turnout near Emigrant Pass, Pickett also popped a Hummer and washed it down with a cup of coffee from the Thermos. That has set him to grinning even as he plunges headlong into the white glare of a rising sun splashing across flat desert sands.

In the panoply of chemical energy that these truckers store in their tackle box, no single stimulant is more prized than the Hummer. It is the size, shape and color of an aspirin tablet, not a capsule but a solid, with a glazed surface that gives it the look of alabaster. Few truckers know of Hummers and fewer can find them; Pickett sometimes begs a dozen from a line driver in Stockton who has a cousin in Denver who has a friend who is the assistant trainer for a professional football team. Pickett swears that the Hummer should be taken with a caffeine kicker, either from coffee or a cola.

The pill creeps into the consciousness, like a sexy woman slipping into a strange bed in the middle of night. Its effect is a hearty *Gemütlichkeit,* a glowing warmth for fellow man, a general contentment with life and the situation at hand, no matter how shabby that may actually be. The Hummer is not a stimulant in the true sense, not compared to the violent rush of, say, a Turnaround Special. It is mellow without inducing sleep. It is warm without suggesting drowsiness. The

60

feeling is simply so pleasant that you cannot imagine closing your eyes or relaxing your attention for fear of missing one moment of this beautiful existence. One chats amiably, endlessly. One beams with sunny good cheer. And suddenly one realizes that one has just spent eight hours grinning like an idiot without once blinking his eyes. Pickett has never understood how the football team's trainer uses such a chemical, but he knows that it sure as hell comes in handy for a morose trucker who drives all night across a bleak, dark desert.

Pickett has found one drawback to this miracle of modern living. That is, the fall from these ecstatic heights is so sudden and so jarring that the victim is liable to seek deep and immediate sleep in concession to an overstressed cerebrum and as refuge from jagged reality. But Pickett is not there yet, and he knows when the end is coming. Now he is gliding through the desert and practically pulling the rig behind him. He is so happy to have Lenny beside him in the cab again, to talk to Lenny, to inquire of Lenny's health, to rhapsodize about the glory of sunrise over the magnificent openness of the desert, yes, to squeeze Lenny's hand, Lenny such a good and faithful friend, to tell Lenny, by God but this is the best of all possible times in the best of all possible places, to be here doing what we are doing, and isn't it a great morning?

"Pickett," says Lenny, "you must have popped a Hummer somewhere along the way."

"I did," Pickett says, "and it was a hell of a good idea, let me tell you."

"I don't suppose you're hungry. Or very tired, either."

"Well, Lenny, boy, I'm not, to tell you the truth. But I know you like a big breakfast. So we'll stop up near Salt Lake. Oh, I might have an orange juice or somethin'. And I sure could take another leak, too."

So they wing across the salt desert, and the sun begins to angle mercifully higher, and they see the uncompromising gray granite of the Lakeside Mountains begin to take form to the northeast. Pickett decides he must have music, so he punches up the volume knob on the AM radio, twirls the tuner until he hears a splash of sound slide past on the dial. He zeros in on the music. It is a bubble-gum Top 40 station in Salt Lake. Pickett, who is not in much of a mood to be discriminating, whistles the monotonous, ringing chords, and Lenny knows that Pickett must really be spaced this time.

They settle into a truck stop outside Salt Lake, one of the standard fifteen-acre blotches of asphalt, upon which is perched a sprawling artifice of plastic, flashing neon, multicolored tiles, Formica, and chrome. It has been built to resist the smudges of diesel exhaust and the stains of sweaty hands. Lenny believes that in a century it will still have its artificial patina, still proclaiming to the passing world its chain-managed origins. At least, there is room for parking.

When they are inside, Pickett shambles off to the men's room. Lenny orders from a frumpy waitress, and when Pickett returns, they talk.

"Pickett, what's going on? I know you've got something on your mind. Something bugging you?"

"Oh, hey. No big thing. I, uh, I just hadn't told you. Doris is havin' a baby. She's four months pregnant. Can you believe that? She doesn't show it."

"She sure doesn't. Hey, Pickett, that's good, real good. I'm happy for you. You sure take your time between babies, old man. John William must be eleven by now."

"That's right. Eleven."

"I'm happy for you two. Way to go, Pickett. I guess there's life in you yet. But I don't know why that should get you so upset. John William ought to be happy with a brother. Even a sister."

"Yeah, well, I'm not upset so much, Lenny. It just . . . kind of comes as a surprise. Sort of takes us unawares, you know. You get settled into a rut, thinking life is goin' to be one certain way, and it takes a while to adjust when matters change so quick."

Now Pickett is toying with his coffee cup, looking intently at his hands as he cradles the cup in his fingers. Lenny knows that something is wrong and that Pickett will give out with it if he is played right.

"Pickett, are you sure there's nothing else? Nothing else bothering you?"

"No, no, nothing like that, Lenny. I mean, everything's fine. It's just that, shit, I'm forty-nine years old. I'm goin' to be sixty-five if I keep drivin' until that kid is just sixteen years old. When was the last time you saw a sixty-five-year-old trucker? I mean, most people are smart enough to quit before then, and the ones that are too dumb to do that don't last much longer. I mean, look at me. I feel like sixty-five already, sometimes. I was hopin' to spend some time at home with my wife and kid before I kick off."

"I can see a point there, Pickett. I don't know how you feel about this, but they've got a very lenient law in California. If a woman doesn't want a baby, there's doctors, hospitals and such that'll . . ."

"No, no, Lenny, no way. I don't like that. Anyway, the doctor says she's too far long, especially at her age. Too much risk. Besides which, I couldn't ask Doris to do that. There's reasons, things I can't really explain to you, but that's out of the question. From any angle."

"I'm beginning to understand, Pickett."

"Not really, kid, not really. You ever had somethin' you really wanted? Somethin' that you kept seein' ahead of you for days, weeks, months? Somethin' you couldn't do without, somethin' you knew was worth workin' your tail off for?"

63

"You better believe it. I always liked cars, you know, but the summer I turned seventeen, I'd crashed one car and I needed wheels and I was looking for something real sharp. One day I saw an ad in the classifieds, some guy in Laguna Beach selling his sports car, this little white sixty-one Alfa Romeo, for two thousand bucks. You know the model I'm talking about. Sexy lines, fast as hell, and this car was all tricked out. Competition headers, hot cam, beefed-up suspension. Man, I wanted that car *so* bad. My parents could've gone out and bought it for me right there, but the best they'd do was, they said they'd match whatever I could save if I went out and got a job. So I went out and got a job pumping gas, nights, Saturdays, Sundays. My social life went straight to hell, but I was getting the money together. Every other week, I'd call the guy, make sure he still had the car, tell him I was getting closer to buying that thing. And the week I saved up my share of the money, and my parents said they'd come up with the other thousand, I called the dude and found out he'd sold the car for sixteen hundred to a girl in Westwood. Man, that hurt."

"Uh-huh. Well, multiply that by about twenty years, and you get some idea of what I'm talkin' about. Ever since I got married I've been figurin' that one of these years, I was goin' to put some money together, buy me a really great truck, work like hell for a couple of years more, save all the money I could and then go off and live like normal folks with my family. Shit, you know me. You know how I spend my money. It's taken me a few more years than I figured, but now I'm finally close to that truck. I've been thinkin' on it for a good while, and I know what I want. Man, that's goin' to be some truck."

"Pickett, tell me about it. I want to hear about this."

Now Pickett talks with the relish and reserve of an adolescent boy describing his first love.

64

"Man, I've got this down to every detail. If a trucker is really a trucker, if he loves what he does and knows he is goin' to spend a few years at the job, he keeps in mind the rig he'd buy if he had unlimited money. You know, you read the ads in the truckin' magazines, you see a certain paint job on the road that really turns you on, and you think, damn, it would be nice to have this or that. And you change details here and there as time goes on, when you hear about this trick new clutch or some other hot setup. Sometimes a man will stay in the business just 'cause he thinks that if he works hard enough, he'll own that dream rig one day.

"I know just what I'd do if I had forty thousand dollars. How many people can say that, tell you right off the top of their head, exactly what they'd do, down to every detail, if you put forty thousand bucks in their hand? Not many, I bet. Well, I can. What I would do is, I would walk into that Peterbilt dealership, the one in Oakland, and put my money down on the counter. I would tell the man that I want a top-of-the-line cab-over tractor, twin-screw six-by-four, with an eight-hundred-fifty-two-inch Detroit Diesel Vee-Twelve turbocharged. I seen a brochure on that engine once. That's five hundred and twenty-five gross horsepower, buddy-boy. 'Course, with an engine that big you wouldn't need any twenty-speed gearbox. Just something strong and reliable. I figure a thirteen-speed Fuller Roadranger would do just fine. With that kind of power you could *fly* right up any pass in the country with a full load. You wouldn't *never* get passed by nobody, not a truck, not even a four-wheeler. No more hearin' station wagons and sports cars honkin' at you as you're tryin' to crest some ten per cent grade.

"'Course, a rig like that would shoot your fuel mileage all to hell, so you'd have to order it with twin hundred-gallon tanks, at least. Maybe even hundred and fifty. And you'd want air conditioning, temperature gauges on every component, deluxe air-ride seats, torsion bar suspension, extra-large sleeper box, plus Citizens Band to go along with stereo and AM-FM.

"Sound neat?"

"Pickett, it sounds like a dream. What a truck."

"Yeah, well, there's more, too. I figure black Naugahyde tuck-and-roll upholstery. Maybe a TV in the sleeper box, one of those little color sets. Chrome everywheres. Tanks, air horns, air-cleaner cap and air intake, muffler and pipes, the rims around the headlights, driving lights and clearance lights, chrome bolts on the bumper, chrome lug nuts on aluminum wheels, chrome grille, and all the rest of the trim. Shit, when that truck is polished, it'd blind you in the open sun.

"I thought for a while about my paint job. You know, I never owned a red truck before? So I figure red. I figure maybe even a special candy-apple paint job, but with a broad silver stripe, maybe eighteen inches wide, running right up the middle of the cab. Shee-yit. That would be the ultimate. 'Course, you couldn't just find something like that on the lot. There'd be a good six-month wait for a Peterbilt like that. But when I finally got the truck and drove it home, I'd be drivin' the sumbitchinest tractor that ever rolled out over the road. You know, I could drive that baby into any truck stop in the country, any place, any time, and I'd know damn well that there couldn't be a rig on the lot that would come close. I'd know without even lookin'. That's the kind of truck that can make you feel like you haven't wasted your time, bustin' your ass for thirty years."

"Pickett, don't tell me you've already ordered the truck."

"Not quite, Lenny, but I'm thinkin' hard about it. Doris and me have been talkin' about it, makin' plans, savin' money. I've been tryin' not to spend money like a fool, but bad habits are hard to break. We're close. I don't have no forty thousand dollars, but I do have a few thousand in the bank, and this sorry-ass Mack is still worth a good eight thousand in trade. I went to the loan company, the one that financed my Mack. My credit's good. I could buy that Pete with four thousand down on a five-year loan, but the interest and the payments would be murder. I've seen too many guys kill themselves tryin' to keep up with payments on a rig they couldn't afford. You've got to have a decent down payment or you'd better just forget it.

"So, I was thinkin'. I could order that Pete and let my lease with Mercury run out just about the time I took delivery on the new tractor. Then I could hire on as a line driver, spend five or six days a week haulin' chemicals, maybe, from Oakland to L.A. Those guys do all right for themselves if they're willin' to put in the hours.

"You follow me so far?" Pickett says.

Makes sense, Lenny says.

"Well, a line-haulin' job like that is practically nine-to-five work, as far as truckin' is concerned. If I made three round trips a week, that'd be twenty-four hundred miles a week with a full load, assumin' they give me a load to back-haul. The good thing about a job like that is that you know you've always got a load to haul. You never worry about loadin' and off-loadin' your cargo. You just drive to the plant and hitch up to some tanker or reefer and you hit the road. I'd have a lot more time to spend at home. Hell, even if I was doin' San Fran to Denver couple times a week, I'd still have most of my weekends and even a night or two a week to spend at home. I've never done that before.

"I figure I'm entitled to that. It used to mean a lot to me, bein' gone and on the road, but I've had that feelin' and it doesn't do so much for me any more. I'm more interested in puttin' away some money and spendin' some time with my boy before he's a man.

"You got me talkin' now, Lenny, so I'm goin' to tell you somethin' now. Don't ever get married when you're on the road. Don't ever do it. I'm not sayin' that against Doris. She's more woman than you'd ever hope to find in one place, and I love her. But somethin' happened a couple months ago that made me think. I come home from a trip, the one when we finished with that load from Miami to L.A., and Doris is all flustered. Bad news, bad news, she says. Got to have a talk with John William. She caught the boy playin' with himself in the bathtub and she doesn't know what to do about it. I thought about that one for a while. It doesn't seem so long ago that I brought home that boy's first pair of shoes. He couldn't have been more than a month old. Now, all of a sudden, the kid is gettin' a hard-on and I'm still doin' the same thing, still on the road, still spendin' most of my life behind the wheel. Everythin's changin' except me and this damn business. And even that ain't true because I'm gettin' older and this business is gettin' tighter. Sometimes I think there's a new kid wearin' John William's clothes and sleepin' in his bed when I come home from a trip. I think, man, how long have you been away? That's depressin' as hell, lemme tell you.

"So, I figure I've got to get out, and I figure maybe the best thing is to ease myself out. Buy that Pete that I've been dreamin' about so long, work steady as a line driver and try to spend as much time as I can at home, make the payments on the tractor and still put away as much money as I can until I can make my break."

Until now, Pickett has been grave, discouraged. But as he talks about this he begins to smile, and Lenny feels good for him.

"Then, after five years, I own the tractor free and clear. I'd be fifty-four, fifty-five, which is not a bad age to think about gettin' off the road. And on top of the money I've saved, I would still have a cherry Peterbilt worth a good twenty, twenty-two thousand. I might have a nice stash to settle down on. Maybe sell the place in Antioch, buy a little business, somethin' I could work on and live at home. Doris and I always liked Nevada. Hawthorne, Fallon, Tonopah. That's not such bad country around there. Sounds good, huh?"

Yes, says Lenny, it makes sense.

"It did, until this baby comes along. Let's suppose that I have enough money to pay for the hospital and all that crap and still put a good down on the Peterbilt. I doubt it, but let's suppose. Let's say I sign on with some line and drive till I pee red. It don't stop after five years because what have I got? I got a five-year-old kid and another that's just sixteen. Forget retiring. Forget about sendin' John William to college. None of that, no sir. So I drive until the baby is sixteen, that's a minimum of sixteen, which makes me all of sixty-five years old.

"Presumin' I last that long.

"And now what have I got? Add it up. By this time, John William is twenty-seven and he's long gone, married, prob'ly got a couple kids of his own. Maybe I even get the time off to go to the weddin', but prob'ly not. And what else? Another sixteen-year-old kid who don't even know me, a broke-down old truck that ain't worth ten cents, and a woman who's maybe left me because she finally got tired of bein' a part-time wife. And I'm sixty-five years old and not worth a damn for anythin', because you know the way truck drivin' takes the life out of a man.

"And that's it, Lenny. Am I talkin' to you? I know it's harder'n hell to see when you're young. I seen it happen myself a hundred times but I never learned the lesson, never thought I'd be in that fix myself.

"Lenny, dammit, it's a bad business. It'll suck the years out of you just quicker'n you know. It'll put you into a hole and then it'll take away the ladder that you spend half your life buildin'. The fuckin' thing is, I had it beat. I had that ladder, I had the plan, and I was goin' to sneak out real quiet, before it knew what I was up to. And then this baby comes along. God *damn*. I just don't see a way out. I got obligations and the only way I can meet 'em is by truckin'. I've got nothin' else. I got no other way to pay my dues, 'cause there's nothin' else I can do. I can see it now. I'm goin' to die truckin'.'"

Pickett is drained. He has spilled more than he ever intended. He has put his premonitions into words, and he sees by the look on Lenny's face that they are true. The Hummer has done the job, has spurred him into an uncommon eloquence, and now it is setting him down, not gently.

They eat breakfast. Lenny leaves the table to drive the truck to a pump. He is signing for the oil with a bank card when Pickett walks from the restaurant, climbs into the passenger seat. He is worn, haggard, with a stubble of beard and a harried look about him.

"Pickett, I'm fresh. I'm good for a few hundred miles. You owe yourself some sleep."

"Okay, kid, I'll sleep. But not right away. I think I'll just crash here in the seat for a while."

Then they pull out of the lot, chug slowly around a cloverleaf, and pull back onto the highway, Interstate 80. They cut through the southern section of Salt Lake City and almost immediately they are in the mountains, threading through the Wasatch Range.

"Music?" Lenny asks when they reach the open road.

"No thanks, not really, kid."

"Okay. This scenery's somethin', huh, Pickett? Just about my favorite part of the trip along 80. Though, I don't know, the Ruby Mountains are awfully nice at sunset, too. What do you think?"

70

"Don't know, Lenny. Hard to say."

"Yeah," Lenny says. "Pickett, I know you're feelin' shitty, but don't brood. Shitfire, these assholes can wait a day for their furniture. Remember that cowboy bar in Cheyenne? The one with Hank Williams on the jukebox? Remember? We played 'Honky Tonkin'' about a dozen times when we went there before. Pickett, it's about that time. Time to get tuned up. Time to get a little crazy. We got to get with the program. This trip is starting out much too solemn. This isn't the way it's supposed to be. What do you say?"

Pickett is beginning to smile. Lenny is trying so hard to cheer him that Pickett can hardly let him down. Besides, Pickett has this thing about Hank Williams and cowboy bars.

"Okay, kid," he says.

So he sleeps while Lenny drives on into Wyoming. North of Flaming Gorge he passes, over the Green River. He crests one, then the other of the twin forks of the Continental Divide. Then into Rawlins, into Laramie, to Cheyenne before five in the afternoon. Outside Cheyenne, he wakes Pickett, and they watch herds of pronghorn bound beside the truck, swift, aloof, and graceful even in the crusty first snow of the season that blankets the open range land. Close to Cheyenne is a massive truck stop, itself a community, an almost legendary gathering place for truckers. Here, they shower. They visit a barber for shaves. They eat thick sirloin steaks with fresh vegetables. When he has finished his meal, Pickett goes to a pay phone and calls collect to his dispatcher.

"Pickett here," he says. "I'm in Cheyenne. Havin' a little engine trouble, is all. Got to get tuned up, ole buddy. You understand. Yeah, I knew you would. So we'll be a day late to Boston, y'hear?"

Chapter 8

She waits.

She hears her mother's morning sounds. Even before the smell wafts upstairs, she hears bacon crisping in angry grease. She hears the padded shuffling of her mother's slippers on the linoleum floor of the kitchen. She hears bathroom sounds, splashing water and a ghastly gargle. She hears an ancient toaster belch forth two more charred slices of bread. Then the eating and sipping sounds are followed by the squeak of weary hinges on her mother's bedroom door, the bump of wood on wood and the resolute click of the lock. Mother must be dressing, she thinks.

Mother dresses quickly. The bedroom door squeaks open again and the sounds are more determined, more direct. Gone are shuffling footsteps. Now the footfalls are sharp and quicker-paced, heavy heels banging out a staccato declaration that the day has begun in earnest. The footsteps become louder as her mother walks to the foot of the stairs.

"Mynette," her mother says. "Time to get up, girl. I know you caught your alarm before it had a chance to ring. Here it is Thursday and you still haven't been around to see Eb Thomas down at the grocery store about that job. I promised him on Monday that you would be around to see him and you haven't done it yet. Don't go making a liar out of me, girl. Do you hear me?"

"Yes, Mama," says Mynette Hancock.

"Good," her mother says. "Now get moving, honey. I left

some Cream of Wheat warming on the stove for you, but it's going to lump up if you don't get down here quick. You've got a big day ahead of you."

Oh, Mama, if you only knew, Mynette thinks.

"Yes, Mama."

Mynette listens for the footsteps to trail out across the living room, over the carpet. She waits for the turn of the knob in the front door, the shake of the venetian blinds and the solid thump as the door is opened wide and slammed shut again. She listens for the click of the wide heels of those sensible black oxfords on the flagstone walk, and when she is satisfied that those shoes are truly bound for another day beneath a teacher's desk at Eureka High School, Mynette Hancock takes her mother's advice to heart and begins to move. It is the last maternal command she intends to obey for a long time.

Mynette moves with a swiftness and a sureness born of determination. She knows what she is doing. She is leaving home, fleeing to Boston just as her best girl friend did a year ago when she followed her lover East. Perhaps she will stay with them. Or, she may call her cousin, a girl six years older who will be sympathetic. Mynette will make out somehow. She will survive. She will be a small-town girl no longer.

Already, the clothes for her big day are set neatly on the chair beside her bed. Mynette pulls a sweater over her head and slips into a comfortable pair of denim slacks. She has considered, but rejected, a more feminine skirt and blouse. When traveling, she decided, comfort means more than vanity. So she opted for the denims.

She bounds downstairs, barefoot, and eases open the door to her mother's bedroom. On a shelf high in the closet sits a suitcase, a black suitcase with brass rivets at the corners. Mynette feels like an intruder as she pulls the suitcase from the shelf, but she sees no other way. She needs luggage.

Upstairs with the suitcase. She knows already which blouses, which shirts and sweaters, which slacks are to go and which she must leave behind. Her slim hands work quickly, deftly, pulling the select articles from the dresser drawers and leaving the others piled neatly. She moves to a closet. She will take one dress, a deep blue double-knit with a fine white belt across the waist. She likes that dress. The others she will leave. She decides she must have room for her only pair of high heels. Yes, they will go. So, too, will the tiny jewelry box, a gift from her father a year before he went away to live in Arizona. Mynette hesitates over her mementoes box. It is black, lacquered, with oriental characters brushed in delicate gold strokes on the cover. Will Martin gave her that box the night they finalized their almost-engagement. She filled it with sad and silly bits from her childhood and her adolescence: ticket stubs from her dates with Will, love notes scribbled in study hall and passed secretly across the room, a strip of four photos, she and Will mugging behind the drawn curtains of a dime store camera booth, a small chip of rust-colored sandstone she had slipped into her pocket during a family trip to Texas one summer. It will hurt to leave these things. But, she thinks, she has decided to leave this life and begin another, so hurt it must. She lays the box carefully aside.

Now she is nearly ready. She pulls on her slim suede shoes and laces them tight. She looks into a mirror above her dresser, runs a brush through her blond hair for half a minute and then ties it into a pony tail. Then she stares at her reflection, studies it as she has often done since she was a child.

She is beautiful, easily the most beautiful female in Greenwood County. In a world of flaws, hers is almost a freakish beauty. Her teeth are straight and white, her nose in perfect symmetry with the soft ridge of her brows and her high, spare cheekbones. She straightens before the mirror so that the image of her torso fills the glass. Her slacks and cashmere sweater are filled out exactly as some designer must have hoped. Somehow, she has escaped puberty without a blemish, with breasts that are full but not ponderous, with hips lean yet not bony, with thighs and calves and ankles that flow in a single, sinuous, sculptured curve.

She breaks her gaze from the mirror and moves to her desk. From under her dictionary she pulls a savings account book and a letter to her mother over which she labored past midnight last night.

She tried to say so much to her mother. She tried to explain that she was tired of watching the world through books and magazines, that she was ready to see and do things not to be found in Eureka. But everything she said sounded clumsy or ungrateful. So she began another letter and this time she did not explain. Instead, she reminded her mother that her eighteenth birthday was already a month behind her. She promised to write home as soon as she is settled and secure in her new home. She did not say where that would be. Then she closed by apologizing to her mother for any hurt, and giving her love. "And," she added, "if Daddy should ever call, please tell him I love him, too."

Downstairs she goes, leaning from the weight of the suitcase. Her letter to mother she props against a glass on the kitchen table. She thinks, she really must get something to eat, but the cereal cooling in the pan is now a grainy, lumpy conglomerate. Poor Mama. Suddenly, for the first time, she wants to cry. No, no, none of that. She is determined. She brushes her teeth in the bathroom, wraps the brush in a plastic bag, and stuffs it away in her purse. She forces herself into the pre-trip ritual on the toilet, because she dreads having to visit a restroom on the bus.

Nine fifty-seven, says the clock on the kitchen wall. Her

timing is perfect; the bus to Topeka will pull away from its daily stop at Johnson's Drugs at ten thirty-two. She must not spend too much time waiting there or walking down the street, swinging that black suitcase. Eureka is a small town in so many ways; people will surely gab about Ruth Hancock's daughter taking a bus out of town, and the gab might spread fast to the wrong places. No, Mynette must get out quickly and with little fuss. She wants nothing to stop her.

So, at nine fifty-eight, she walks out of the house, chin up, trying not to let the suitcase look too heavy. She goes down Maple Street, taking care not to slip on the wet leaves that plaster the sidewalk. The morning is gray and bleak. Down Maple she walks to Fourth Street, down Fourth to Main, down Main to the ponderous façade of Eureka Federal. She puts her suitcase down by the door and walks up to the teller's cage.

"Hello, Miz Atkinson," she says, smiling sweetly.

"Hello, Mynette," says the spinster lady. "You going somewhere?"

"Visiting my cousin in Topeka. She's ill and her husband can't stay home to watch the kids. So I'm going up to help out. I'll need my savings for bus fare and emergencies."

Miz Atkinson squints at the book through bifocals.

"How much do you want to withdraw, Mynette?"

"All of it, Miz Atkinson. My cousin's husband is going to pay me back, but I need the money right now."

"Mynette, I'm not sure that's such a good idea. Your credit rating in later years is influenced by both the size of your accounts and the number of years they have been active. You can keep your account open by leaving in just five dollars."

"Maybe I'd better do that, then," Mynette says, still smiling. She can definitely use every penny, but she does not need a fuss now.

Miz Atkinson counts the money into her palm. One hundred fifty-two dollars and thirty-three cents, including interest. She earned the money behind the counter of a cafe on Route 96 the summer before her senior year of high school. That is to say, she truly earned it. She folds the money into a hidden pocket of her purse and checks the clock behind the teller's grille before she picks up her suitcase. Ten-twelve.

One block back up Main is Johnson's Drugs. In the back, behind the soda fountain, Johnson runs the local agency for the bus line.

He is wiping glasses behind the fountain when she walks in.

"Going to visit my cousin in Topeka," she says before the question comes. "She's feeling bad, and I'm going to help take care of her kids. I want to catch the next bus out."

Johnson is in his mid-fifties, thin, proud of the thick thatch of salt-and-pepper hair that he has managed to retain.

"Topeka," he says, "that would be the ten thirty-two. You're just on time. That's eighteen dollars, forty-four cents for a round-trip ticket."

"Oh, I should've told you, Mr. Johnson. I'm not sure when I'm going to be coming back. And, anyway, my cousin's husband will be paying for my return ticket. So I'll just need the one-way."

And she reaches into her purse for a ten-dollar bill before he can say another word. Ten seventeen. She has time for a doughnut and a glass of milk. She gobbles that, looks quickly at the rack of paperbacks, decides that she cannot spare the money and that she probably will be too excited to read.

Now the bus is outside, drawing up with a hiss. Mynette gallops outside, tossing off a thank you to Mr. Johnson, and she stands, panting, as the driver checks her ticket.

77

"Topeka," he says. He pulls open the door to a luggage compartment and shoves the suitcase out of sight. She steps lightly up into the bus, walks down the aisle to a pair of empty seats so that she may be alone. The driver is ready. The door closes, and Mynette must stifle a moment of panic. No, she assures herself, she has not forgotten any of the essentials and, no, she is not a heartless ingrate. She is doing what she must do.

The bus pulls away from the curb, and the shops and homes so familiar to her pass in a steady procession. Then Mynette wants to cry, and she decides she will allow herself a few tears. She holds a handkerchief up to her face until the bus leaves the town limits and picks up speed. Now it is behind her and she sees only flat, open pasture land, without special significance, nothing to prick her sentiment. She does not need the handkerchief any longer. Instead, the rush of the fields past her window has begun to excite her. She is gone, off and away, and her life is just beginning.

Chapter 9

"What night is this, Lenny? Thursday night? Hell, that's fine. Thursday night is about right. See, these Cheyenne bars are too much on Fridays, Saturdays. Packed full of horny cowboys who can't get the smell of horseshit out of their clothes. But Thursday night ought to be just about right, I figure. Thursday nights, you get those hard-core drunks and all the good-time ladies who can't wait for the

78

weekend to start. That's the kind of company we need to-night."

They are tooling down an old two-lane blacktop, a secondary road that has been bypassed by a wide, modern highway three miles away. Once this was a main route. Now they pass boarded-up shop fronts, used-car lots, a feed-and-grain store in a building that once housed a movie theatre. The marquee reads:

BUD CALF STARTER
VITA-GROW FEED
BARB WIRE SPECIAL THIS WEEK

Two miles outside the city limits, Pickett brings the Mack to a frantic, shuddering stop.

"Missed the goddamn turnoff," he says, and the brakes hiss as he releases the pressure and slowly backs the rig down the highway. Then he pulls off the road and wheels into a gravel parking lot.

The place is easy to miss. It is a stubby, small building of unadorned gray cinderblock, dark except for a flickering OLY sign in one small window and a naked bulb that casts a cold light on the sign outside.

Wander Inn Lounge, it reads in flecking red paint.

They clamber down from the cab. It is a frigid night, the coldest of the season so far, and Pickett beats his arms against his chest as they stride toward the door, puffing breath into the chill air.

Pickett pushes open the door and a few faces turn in mild irritation at the wind that gusts through the place. Then Lenny steps through behind him and the faces follow him as he takes his seat at the bar that stretches the length of one side of the building.

Burnished hardwood with an honest-to-God brass rail, the

79

bar itself is a masterpiece. It is a proper bar, a leaning-on-your-elbows bar, a solid, substantial bar. It is also the only spot in the building that has been rescued from the pervasive coat of grime that has built up everywhere else, on the veneer paneling of the walls, on the rough hardwood floor, on the plaster ceiling. The grime is the product of years of tobacco juice, spittle, smoke, handprints, flyspecks, spilled drinks, road dust tramped in from outside and even an occasional splattering of blood. The grubby patina suggests a murkiness that not even the brightest fluorescent fixtures could dispel. As for the shaded forty-watt bulbs at the corners of the room, they are far overmatched. Like candles flickering before a coffin, they do not truly shed light, but, rather, merely illuminate the gloom. The barkeep, with his ceaseless wiping and polishing, has kept the treasured bar surface spotless. Everything else has long ago fallen victim to the relentless growth of filth, a process as irresistible as erosion in this place.

"I remember," says Pickett, "when they used to have a big picture window at that end of the bar. But they finally bricked it up about eight years ago. Saturday nights, the ranch hands would get drunk and start fighting, throwing bottles, turning over tables. That damn picture window was always the first to go. Somebody was always heaving a chair through it, just for the hell of it."

Now the spot where Pickett points is just as dank and smoke-stained as the rest of the place. Hanging from the wall above the bar, are game heads—deer, pronghorn, a cougar—with lifeless black orbs peering out from the eye sockets, the fur showing bare in spots. A fading poster on one wall hypes a boxing card from 1962, the results and principals long since forgotten. A plastic Hamms sign on another wall shows an angler in hip boots yanking a steelhead from a gleaming azure lake while a huge mug of beer towers above him. Above the jukebox is a 1957 John Deere calendar. That is the extent of the decor. This is a no-nonsense place with a devoted clientele attracted by the barkeep's adamant refusal to mix a shot of whiskey with anything but another shot of whiskey.

"Canadian Club for me, a double," Pickett tells the bartender. "Make it a bourbon for my friend, water back. And change a dollar for the juke, too."

Pickett fishes through his pockets, comes up with two quarters.

"This'll do for a start," he says. "You know what I want to hear, Lenny. See if they've still got 'Hey, Good Lookin'' and 'Honky Tonkin'.' Scruggs is okay, and so is Bill Monroe. But I don't need Roy Acuff, not tonight."

Lenny bends over the Wurlitzer juke and reads the titles through a haze of stains. He punches up Merle Haggard, Dave Dudley, decides to skip Charlie Pride, picks both sides of a Hank Williams disc, Charlie McCoy doing "Orange Blossom Special" and a Chet Atkins instrumental. When he returns to his seat, Dave Dudley is booming through "Six Days on the Road," Pickett is working on his second double, and the bartender is wondering how long this crazy trucker can hold off without cracking his barstool over a convenient head.

Because Pickett is very disturbed.

"Son of a bitch," he says. "I finish off my first drink, order another, and this bartender gives me the eye and says, you guys planning to stay long? I tell him we might just stick around until we get good and shit-faced. So he says, we've got regular customers here and they might not be too happy about drinking with your hippie buddy there. And I don't want no trouble in my place."

"Sorry, Pickett."

"Sorry, nothing. I told the asshole that there was going to be real trouble if anybody tried to stop us from doing what we came here to do, which was to have a few laughs and drink a lot of booze. And that's just what we're going to do."

So they drink and they laugh. They stare in open admiration at a cowboy with a sunburned face like a relief map of the Grand Canyon, who lines up three shots of booze and a draught beer, and methodically consumes them all in less than a minute, tossing down a shot, swallowing a mouthful of beer, tossing down another shot, gulping some more beer, throwing down the third shot and draining the glass of draught. Then he pulls a red bandanna from a hip pocket and burps, just once, as he wipes his mouth.

"Awesome," Lenny laughs, and they order another round. They hoot about the aerospace engineer whose furniture now is jammed into their van. His wife had watched anxiously as they carted piece after piece of expensive and fragile furniture down the stairs and into the trailer.

"Be careful. Oh, do be careful. You will be careful, won't you," Lenny says, trying to imitate her piping voice. "Christ, can you imagine what she'd say if she walked in now and saw us? She'd have a shit-fit. She'd lay an egg, right on the floor. Oh, Christ. Whew. Bartender, another round."

Now Lenny is seeing things through a murky haze, and he suspects that it is not just the bad lighting and the smoke that is beginning to collect around the ceiling. He concentrates on putting one foot in front of the other when he walks over to the jukebox with a hand full of quarters, and he has trouble with the buttons. The damn things will not hold still. He feeds the coins into the machine and then hobbles into the men's lavatory. There, he squints and turns his face away from a startling bright bulb hanging bare from the ceiling. He starts for the urinal and bumps against a man in gabardine working clothes who leans over the sink, splashing water on his face. The man glances into the mirror.

"You," he says, in a voice as weary as it is angry. "Tell me something. I want to talk to you. Hey, you."

Lenny, who is calling on all his powers of concentration to reach the urinal without falling on his face, barely hears the man shouting into his ear.

"Me?" he says, turning toward the man. "Me. You wan' talk t'me?"

Lenny blinks his eyes, as if to clear them. The man's face is red. His gray, bushy eyebrows arch when he speaks. His hairline is receding toward the back of his skull and the bare scalp shines with the glare from the light overhead. Lenny watches, fascinated, as water beads up on the man's forehead, courses down his cheek, poises on his chin and then drops onto his shirt.

"You," he says. "You got to tell me something. You got to tell me what the hell you're trying to prove, wearing your hair like that and smoking dope and all that crap. Can you tell me that?"

Lenny turns away, steps toward the urinal, unzips.

"Tell me," says the man. "Tell me and maybe I'll understand. What are you trying to do, just tear down everything you get your hands on? I got a kid, you know, about your age. A good kid, never any trouble, but about three years ago he starts letting his hair grow down around his ears. I try to tell the kid that he looks like hell, he's going the wrong direction. But does he listen? No. Hell no, he wouldn't listen to me."

Lenny cannot follow the man. His head feels heavy and he is having enough trouble keeping it from listing to one side. And he is tired, so damn tired. He zips up. He does not

83

want to turn around to face the man who is ranting behind him. He turns and looks at the man.

"No, he wouldn't listen to me, not to me. He's got to go off and live in Oregon, someplace. Tell me," he says, now almost pleading, his right hand reaching out to grab the sleeve of Lenny's jacket. "Tell me what I can do. Tell me where to go, what to say. He walked out of the house a year ago, told me he hated my guts, that he never wanted to see me again. I just want to talk to him. You're his kind. You can tell me what to do."

Lenny stares at him, as through a fish bowl.

"Mister," he says, "I'm so drunk I can barely find my pecker to pee with. How the fuck am I going to make your son love you?"

He jerks his shoulder free, walks to the door, and turns back to the man.

"Look, fellow, I'm sorry," he says. "I hope you get together with your boy. But I'm no expert about what's happening to us, no more than you are."

The man sighs and his eyes begin to moisten.

"He's a good kid. I know I could've spent more time with him, but his mother died when he was twelve and I was working two jobs," he says, but Lenny is out of the door and back into the bar. He hears Pickett's voice, calling him from the other side of the room.

"Over here, ole buddy," says Pickett. "I decided to move to a table. Been spending too much time sitting at that bar."

And Lenny sees why he has decided. He is sitting with two women and a young cowboy who seems to be thinking of the thousand other places he could be visiting at this particular moment. And the look on his face says that every single one of them would be a better bet than what he's got now.

84

Lenny threads his way toward a table.

"Sit down, Lenny. Sit right down and meet my friends. This is Claudine," he says, patting the blond hair of a woman who sits at his right. Claudine is what Pickett would describe as a very healthy girl. She wears heavy mascara, lipstick liquid and red as fresh blood, with nail polish to match. She draws deep on a cigarette, distorting her cardigan sweater into bizarre configurations. She exhales and nods at Lenny through the cloud of smoke.

". . . And this is Emily. Say hello to Emily, Lenny."

Emily is small, thin, brown-haired, with the beak and general appearance of a sparrow. She holds out a bony hand to Lenny.

"Pleased, I'm sure," she says.

". . . And this fella's name is, uh, dammit . . ."

"Bob," says Emily.

"Right. Bob. How the hell could I have forgotten old Bob?" Pickett says, and the two women laugh. Bob tugs on the lapels of his blue cotton jacket and stares at the ceiling.

Lenny sits to the left of Pickett, beside Emily. He watches Claudine lean over to Pickett, murmur in his ear.

"That's an awful big truck you fellows drive," Emily says in a reedy voice. "Sure must be exciting, driving all over like that."

"Mostly hard work," Lenny says, and he thinks: Pickett did it again. Midnight on a Thursday night in Cheyenne, Wyoming, and Pickett has done it again.

"Oh no," Emily says. "You must be awful brave to drive a truck like that down the road. I know all about you truck drivers, all the chances you take. That takes real nerve."

"Sometimes," Lenny says.

"That's right," the girl says. "Truck drivin' is a real man's job. Claudine and Bob—he's kind of a friend of mine—we

85

was just on our way home from this club downtown when Claudine saw that big rig sitting outside the Wander Inn. Well, we just had to see what kind of fellows would be driving a big Peterbilt like that."

"It's a Mack," Lenny says, as he watches Claudine lean even closer to Pickett, follows her hand as it drops under the table. It's happening again, Lenny thinks. It is another manifestation of that phenomenon Pickett mentioned the first month they rode together.

They had been stopped at a traffic light in Atlanta when a redheaded woman in a convertible pulled up on the passenger side. She looked up at Lenny. He smiled. She smiled. She pursed her mouth in a mock pout, ran her tongue over her lips, and laughed when she saw the look on his face. Then she hiked her skirt up until he saw the white of her panties. She cocked her head, watched his eyes, and then accelerated away as the light turned. It was the most lascivious exhibition Lenny had ever seen. He could not believe it. He almost stammered when he told Pickett about it.

"Is that right?" Pickett said. "Good looker? Well, that's your first, kid, but you can bet it won't be your last. I couldn't believe it when I started truckin', either, but there are lots of women around who think truck drivers is just about the biggest studs to come down the pike. Sometimes they give you the big come-on right on the street, where they know you can't do anythin' about it, but sometimes they're serious.

"Fact is, kid, that a truck driver don't have any trouble gettin' laid. You can always pay for it. They've closed down a lot of the big houses in Peoria, Gary, Seattle, but when you've spent some time on the road you know where to find professional pussy.

"But that's just if you've got a few extra bucks in your

86

pockets. Some guys don't like to pay for it. And if you don't, you usually don't have to wait too long before some little honey comes along. Don't ask me why, but there's a lot of women who really have a thing for truck drivers. I guess they take one look at the big rigs and that gives 'em ideas. I don't know. But I do know that you can spot 'em fast. Hell, they spot you faster. I'm not sayin' that every trucker in the U.S. goes around constantly pussy-whipped, but bein' on the move doesn't mean you've got to be horny, neither."

When he was a younger man, Pickett had accepted the availability of the truck-stop Annies as a matter of course, a convenience, a pleasure no more or less than a good cup of coffee or a wide-open stretch of highway. He neither pursued nor avoided the diversion they provided. Perhaps because he approached it so routinely, it was a pleasure that he saw no reason to forego after he had married. He saw no harm done and he enjoyed the brief human contact, especially during those years when he drove alone. His obligation to his wife was to take the proper hygienic precautions, he felt, and this he did with pride and smugness. He has never caught a dose and he does not intend to.

On this particular night, the ache of responsibility, the problem of his wife's pregnancy that had obsessed him all week at home, has receded into a nagging discomfort once he got on the road. He is not drunk, but pleasantly buzzed, and he has decided to ignore his problems tonight. The big blonde is his for the taking, if he wants her. Pickett savors this situation he has engineered: Lenny, almost incoherent, trying to cope with the mousy brunette; the young cowboy squirming in his chair, trying to get one of the girls—which one? Claudine? No, couldn't be Claudine, has to be the other—trying to connive chirping little Emily out the door and into his pickup before she makes a fool of herself over this hippie trucker.

Pickett stretches his legs, arches his back in the chair, and folds his hands behind his head. The blonde is doing something nice to him, her left hand busy under the table while she lifts the glass to her lips with her right. Lenny, poor Lenny, is trying to sort out what is happening around him. And Emily is trying to get his attention while Cowboy Bob fusses with his string tie and chews vengeance on a stick of gum.

"Cowboy," Pickett says, "you work on a ranch? A big ranch?"

"Yes," says Claudine, "he works on one of the big spreads east of town."

"No foolin'," Pickett says. "Must be cattle, right? What kind? No, let me guess."

He leans across the table and sniffs.

"Must be, uh, Charolais. Am I right? I thought so. That damn Charolais smells worse than any animal on the road, even pigs. Ain't that right, Lenny? You pull into a truck stop in the Midwest, all you got to do is stick your nose out the window and you can tell if somebody's stopped there while he was haulin' Charolais."

"Thass true," Lenny says.

"Bob," says Pickett in a voice laden with concern, "ain't you worried about them new absorption tests?"

"No, I ain't worried about that," the cowboy says. "Nothin' to worry about there."

"You know what I'm talkin' about, then, don't you?" Pickett says.

"Sure. I think so."

"Sure you do, Bob. I heard it was a federal law that any rancher grazin' Charolais had to post the notices on the wall of the barn and in his bunkhouses."

"Yeah, I think I seen that."

88

"You must've," Pickett says. "It was all over the newspapers a couple of months ago. Damndest thing, Lenny. You know how the government is always spendin' millions of dollars on these crazy experiments and such? Well, some scientist with a government grant discovered that Charolais manure is just like garlic and alcohol. It goes straight into your bloodstream and you exhale it with every breath you take for the next day or so."

"I never heard of that," Bob says.

"Me neither," says Lenny.

"Listen, dumbfuck," Pickett says to Lenny, "how are you goin' to hear about it? You can't read."

"It's disgraceful," he says to the girls. "Poor kid was orphaned at age eleven, had to go to work to take care of his eight brothers and sisters, all younger than he was. Got a job washin' sheets in a cathouse. Never made it out of fourth grade. A real sad story."

"But you kept your family together," Emily says, "I think that's beautiful."

"Not really," Pickett says. "A few years ago, he went on a TV game show and won a trip for eight to the Caribbean. Naturally, Lenny didn't go himself. The trip was just for eight and Lenny didn't have the heart to leave any one of the kids at home while he went himself. So he stayed at home. Would you believe? The cruise ship went down with all hands aboard. Not a single survivor."

"You poor thing," Emily says. "What a tragedy for you."

"I don't know, he sounds pretty lucky to me. After all, he wasn't on the boat," says Claudine, tossing back the dregs of her drink.

"That's one way of lookin' at it," Pickett says. "Anyway, Bob, these scientists discovered that Charolais shit—pardon the expression—just goes straight into the bloodstream and

89

comes out in your breath. How do you think I knew you worked on a ranch that raised Charolais? And you don't have to eat it or drink it like you do with garlic and alcohol, neither. Just be around it."

"I never heard of that," Bob says.

"It was in the papers," Pickett says. "But that's not all. They also discovered that the smell is, like, contagious. Somebody who's got it can give it to somebody else just by kissin' 'em or even by touchin' his skin to theirs. It travels right through the pores."

Now Emily is trying to move her chair, ever so discreetly, out of arm's reach from Bob. Pickett goes on.

"But that's not the worst part," he says. "They haven't finished their tests on this yet, but it looks like, if you spend enough time around Charolais manure, your body builds up reserves of the stuff inside. So, even if you move away from the ranch, years later, your breath and your sweat still smell like Charolais. It's as bad as coal minin' and Black Lung disease. I hear the government is ready to declare Charolais ranchin' a hazardous occupation."

"I think that's a bunch of bull," Bob says.

Claudine laughs. Pickett nearly chokes on the drink he has raised to his lips.

"No, cowboy, not just any bull. It's got to be Charolais."

"You goddamn truckers think you're pretty smart," Bob says. "Well, we don't need you around here. No sir. This is a goddamn good bar and we don't need a bunch of hill-billies and hippies around here."

"Ordinarily," Pickett says, "I would take you apart for that. But I'm havin' too good a time to spoil it by bustin' up my knuckles on your face. I guess this is your lucky night. As a matter of fact, I'm gettin' tired of smellin' Charolais shit, myself. So I think my buddy and I are pullin' out.

90

Emily, you was talkin' about that big truck outside. You ever ride in a big semi? Here's your chance, girl. Why don't you and Claudine come along for a ride? How 'bout it?"

"I'm with you," Claudine says in a low voice.

"I don't know," Emily says, looking at Bob, glancing out toward the truck, looking back at Bob. He is standing, hands on hips, snapping his chewing gum as he looks at her.

"You're not thinkin' of leavin' with these bums, are you? You are. I never would have believed it. I thought you were different than that, girl. Well, let me tell you somethin'. You leave with them, you can just give me back my school ring before you do."

"I will," she says. "If you don't trust me any more than that, I will give you back your ring."

Bob is alarmed. His bluff has been called. New tactics are in order. He sounds suddenly sympathetic.

"Emily," he says, "I'm sorry if I hurt your feelin's. I didn't mean to. You know how much I care for you. Look, honey . . ." and he reaches out his hand to grasp her left arm.

"Go away," Emily squeals. "Don't you touch me. I don't want to smell like any Charolais."

"Pickett," Lenny says, "I don't feel so hot."

"Sure, kid, you need some fresh air, is all. Come on girls, let's go. Time to move out."

"I'm *going*," Emily says. And she does, wrapping her right arm through Lenny's left, marching him out the door as Pickett stands aside, grinning, one arm tight around Claudine's waist.

"Tough luck, cowboy," he says. And they are out the door and into the chill of the night. Lenny and Emily are huddled, shivering, outside the cab, waiting for Pickett and his key.

He reaches up, turns the lock, opens the door, steps back down.

"Gettin' up is easy," he says. "One foot here on the step, the other a little bit higher and you just lift yourself up. Nothin' to it."

Claudine tries it. One foot, the other. She tests her weight, tentatively.

"Watch your skirt," Pickett says.

"You watch it," she answers, and she shows a stunning expanse of fleshy thigh as she hefts herself into the seat.

The room inside the cab diminishes with amazing speed as they climb, one by one, into the compartment. They shift positions, elbows digging into ribs, rump tight against rump, and the women finally find perches more or less in the laps of the two men.

"Kind of close in here," Lenny says. "I think I need some air."

"Don't you *dare*," Emily squeals. "It's cold out there. You wouldn't want me to freeze, would you, Larry?"

"Lenny," he says. "No, I guess not."

"Wow," she says, "look at this thing. All the dials and things. It looks like an airplane. Or a spaceship, maybe. You sure sit awfully high in these things."

"Sure do," Pickett says. He is beginning to wish he had not been so hard on good old Cowboy Bob.

Pickett prods the truck to life. Diesel engines can be balky in chilly weather; diesel fuel takes on the consistency of molasses. Pickett concentrates, plays with the accelerator, then relaxes as it catches and roars again.

"Where to, ladies? Any scenic attractions we ought to see while we're here in Cheyenne?"

"There's a nice dark road about five miles north of here. It's on the way home. Nobody to bother us there," Claudine says.

"I don't know," Emily says.

"Right," says Pickett. "Five miles north. You show it to me."

They heave onto the highway and rumble north. Pickett is not hurrying. No, he is cool, very cool, concentrating on his driving even as Claudine goes to work doing the most incredible things to his ear. And Emily, ahh, she is loving it, soaking it up, bouncing on Lenny's lap. Then there is Lenny. He is absolutely unmoved by the good cheer all around him. He feels like hell. Something is going to happen to him soon and he accepts it with sad resignation, the way some bad gamblers watch their money vanish from a craps table. He knew this was going to happen, he knew it from the way his last bourbon coursed down his throat, as though it were full of jagged glass and rusty razor blades instead of good sour mash. What always happens when Lenny quits one drink too late is about to happen now. Claudine points them off the highway and they turn down a rutted dirt road.

"Pickett," he says, "how about pulling over for a minute?"

"Kid, I know you and Emily got the hots over there, but you might as well wait till we get a little farther down the road."

"Pickett, I don't think you understand. If you don't stop the truck right now and let me get out, we're going to have a hell of a job, washing off the side of this truck tomorrow."

"Oh. I think I understand, Lenny. Well, Mercury doesn't need that kind of advertisin'."

He brakes, gears down, stops beside the road and flicks off his headlights.

"I won't be long, Pickett."

Lenny climbs down from the cab and lurches off into the darkness.

"Hell of a note," Claudine says. "What a dumb stunt."

93

"What are you bitchin' about?" Pickett says. He sounds harsh; he does not like her tone.

"I mean, this is a hell of a thing to happen, him going off like we didn't have anything better to do than wait around for him to puke," she says.

"Nice," Pickett says. "Real nice. I can tell I've fallen in with a real nice lady tonight. Why don't you go kick him in the stomach? Maybe that would hurry him up. You've got a real heart, lady."

"Shove it," she says. "You're getting particular at one in the morning? You're a real prize yourself, you are."

Pickett and Claudine are heavyweights at this sort of verbal brawling. And while they slug it out, Emily sits back in her seat and wonders whether she might not have made a bad mistake in treating Bob so badly. Truckers do seem to be a little, well, coarse.

"I think I want to go home," she says.

"Hell, we just got out here," Claudine yelps at her. "What's the matter?"

"I ought to call Bob. He'll probably be home by now and I ought to apologize. Maybe he'll give me his ring back, if I treat him nice."

"He's a loser," Claudine says. She reaches for her cigarettes, scratches a match, and they all wince as the flare lights the darkened cab. "Look, my place isn't so far away from here. We can go there and you can call him from there. Then you can have the rest of the night to yourself without worrying."

"I don't know," says Emily. She thinks about the familiar, comfortable bench seat of Bob's Chevy pickup. She wishes she were there now.

"Emily, you couldn't be more right," Pickett says. "Old Bob is not such a bad fellow and I did pull his leg pretty good. I think you ought to call him up, maybe have him come over and pick you up at Claudine's, make up with him right away tonight."

"I think you're right," Emily says.

"That would solve a few problems," Claudine says. "Then your long-haired friend could sleep in the bunk and J.W. and I could spend the night inside."

"Oh, I don't think so," Pickett says. He is beginning to tire of this woman already and, besides, his heart has not really been into that sort of fun tonight. "We've got a long way to go," he says. "Ought to get on the road."

"That's beautiful," Claudine says. "I wish to hell you'd told me that before you sat down."

Lenny, meanwhile, is recovering. He does not do this sort of thing very often, but when he does, he always manages to discover just how miserable a human being can become in just three or four hours. He has been to the depths and he will be on his way back up just as soon as he can find some water to wash the nastiness from his mouth and blow it from his sinuses and his nostrils.

He hears the trickling of a stream nearby but he cannot make it out in the sheer blackness of the grassy field. He sets off through the shin-high grass. The night is not quite chilly enough for the dew to have turned to frost. His boots are wet. His pants are damper than just damp. He hears the stream burbling so loudly that it must be, yes, just at his feet. He kneels in the moisture-heavy grass and drinks from the stream. It is cold, cold and wet. Good. He spits the first mouthful across the stream, swallows the next. He rises, wipes the water from his face with the sleeve of his shirt, sets off back to the road, toward the dim outline of the van.

Inside, he finds that the chill is not only in the weather.

"Thanks, Pickett," he says. "I feel a lot better now. Where we going?"

"We're going to Claudine's. We're going to drop off the girls there. They've got things to do. So do we. Boston is still a hell of a long way off."

"Guess you're right," Lenny says.

Claudine lives at the end of the rutted dirt road, seven miles away. The home is a contractor's joy, a rambling ranch-style place with wings jutting off in all directions, with asbestos shingling and aluminum siding. It sits alone in the middle of a wide, circular drive.

"Quite a place," Pickett says.

"You ought to see the twenty-six hundred acres that go along with it," Emily says.

"That's none of their business," Claudine snaps.

"You run this thing by yourself?" Lenny asks.

"Oh, her husband helps," Emily says. "Don't worry, he's off in Texas, buying cattle, right now."

"That's none of their business, either," Claudine says.

"Still, you'd better not go all the way around the drive," Emily says. "You wouldn't want to wake the kids."

"Thanks a lot, bitch," says Claudine. "Just wait."

Lenny opens his door, climbs down and the two women follow him.

"Nice," Pickett says. "Real nice. Want to thank you for a real fun evening."

He waits until Lenny is in the cab, door shut. When the two women are inside the house, he guns the diesel and hits the air horn, shattering the stillness with two long, excruciating blasts.

Then all is silence again, and the silence is painful. Pickett laughs, gears down, heads back toward the highway.

"You must've woken those kids up," Lenny says.

"I hope so," Pickett says. "Wait till they tell Daddy about the big truck that was honkin' away in front of their house in the middle of the night."

Back to the pavement, back toward the massive truck stop along the highway. There, they know, they will find a meal. They are both hungry again.

"Bring the log with you," Pickett says when they leave the cab. "We've got to bring that sucker up to date before we get stopped."

The logbook is government issue, designated Form MCS-59 in its upper-left-hand corner. Here, in slide-rule style, the trucker's twenty-four-hour day from midnight to midnight is marked off in fifteen-minute increments. The driver marks his time as either off-duty, or driving, or sleeping, or on duty (not driving). The driver totals his hours in each of the four categories, and he is in trouble unless he can somehow make his driving and on-duty totals fall within the maximums prescribed by the Department of Transportation. Today because they have not been on the road since late afternoon, the job is easy for Pickett and Lenny.

"Total miles. About nine hundred? That's about right, I'd say. And the date. Let's see," Pickett says, "Monday was the twenty-fourth, Tuesday, Wednesday . . . Thursday was . . . I'll be damned. Thursday was the twenty-seventh of October."

"Yeah?"

"Yeah. My birthday. Today is my birthday. *Was* my birthday. I forgot all about it. I've had so much on my mind."

"No shit? Forty-nine?"

"Fifty. Fifty years old and I forgot all about it. Too late now to worry about it."

"Not really," Lenny says. "It's still Thursday night in Hawaii. Happy birthday, Pickett."

"Thanks," he says.

An hour later, they are on the road, and Pickett celebrates with Johnny Cash in his earphones and two Big Reds before his cup of coffee as they wing across Nebraska.

Chapter 10

Her bus rocks on, through Batesville, Yates Center, Burlington, and Carbondale, towns with names that suddenly sound bucolic to her ear. By the time the coach wheezes into the terminal, Mynette Hancock has decided that she already is thinking like a city girl. She feels that she is ready for Boston; she has no way of knowing that she is not even ready for Topeka.

Her ticket for Boston takes a major chunk out of her savings. She could have saved six dollars if she had bought her connecting ticket to Boston in Eureka, but that would have been all wrong. No, she did not want to leave tracks. So her trail ends in Topeka, as far as anyone knows. She thanks the ticket clerk, shoves the ticket into her purse, and finds a seat in the waiting room to mark time, impatiently, until her connecting bus to Boston arrives.

Until now, Mynette has been smart and lucky. Her luck runs out when she takes the empty chair just ahead of Harry Stapleton and carelessly places the purse under her seat. Harry is a hustler, a grifter. Ordinarily, he is not the sort of man who makes a habit of boosting a few bucks from ladies' purses in bus terminals, but on this particular day, Harry is in tough straits. He is sitting in the Topeka bus terminal when Mynette Hancock takes the seat directly in front of him and puts her brown leather purse under her chair, practically right at his feet. He cannot ignore the invitation.

There are four rows of chairs in the waiting room, euphemistically labeled "the lounge." The chairs perch on metal stems set in the floor. Mynette sits in the middle of the second row of chairs; Harry is in the middle of the third, so his movements are perfectly shielded. He works in almost total privacy. He shifts in his seat, moves his left leg under Mynette's chair and hooks his foot through the loops of her purse. He crooks his leg, and the action automatically drags the purse back toward him, within arm's reach. He is casual and his movements are entirely natural. Just to be sure, he drapes his overcoat over his left knee so that the purse is lost in the folds of fabric. He glances at his wristwatch, surveys the scene around him, then bends down as if to tie his left shoe. There he gets his first look into the purse. Mynette's wallet and her ticket to Boston are near the top. How convenient, Harry thinks. He glances at the ticket. He can convert that to cash in thirty seconds. Harry deftly picks through the wallet. He is ready to pull the sheaf of bills from the wallet when he is struck by the merest glimmering of conscience. No sense being greedy, he decides. So he leaves Mynette a ten and a five.

Then he straightens up and slides the purse back under Mynette's seat. He is off to the ticket counter to get cash for the ticket. Five minutes later, he is gone. Mynette knows nothing of this. She is full of anticipation an hour later when she hears that her connection to Boston has arrived from Salina. But when she arrives at the gate and begins thumbing through her purse for the ticket, she discovers that something is wrong. She runs back to her seat, thinking that the ticket must have dropped from her purse. She searches the floor. She is frantic, ready to cry, when she hears the last call for her bus. Then it pulls from the terminal, on its way East. She is left behind, kneeling on the floor to peer under seats in the waiting room.

Finally, she knows that it is gone. As an afterthought, she

checks her wallet and then she knows that the ticket did not fall accidentally from her purse. She sits down again, this time clutching the purse to her stomach. She considers her options. She still has bus fare back to Eureka. She could be home again before her mother returns to find the note. But, no, her mother may have come home for lunch. Besides, she would hear sooner or later about her daughter's one-day excursion to Topeka.

No, she has thought and planned this too long to quit now. There are other ways of getting to Boston. She walks outside the terminal and walks two blocks with her suitcase to a busy street. She stands at a corner, takes a deep breath and sticks out her thumb. Her mother would kill her. But she has got to get away.

Chapter 11

Doris Pickett is alone in the house, washing the breakfast dishes, when she feels a fluttering beneath her stomach. Her hands grasp the sink. She tries to steady herself.

My God, she thinks, the baby is kicking. First time. My baby is kicking. This must be how it feels.

The idea staggers her. She walks unsteadily to a chair and eases herself into it.

Baby, baby, she thinks. You're coming and we're not ready for you. You're coming and there's nothing I can do to stop you. You don't know what you're getting yourself into, she thinks. We're trying, baby. We're trying to change things but it ain't easy. What's it going to be like for you? We're unhappy before you even get here.

She bites her lip and begins to cry.

Child of woe, she thinks. Child of woe.

Chapter 12

Roll, roll on. With Lenny asleep behind him, Pickett sits hunched over the wheel, staring ahead as the truck's high-beams gouge into the dying, lonely, last hour of darkness. This has always been a tranquil, easy time for Pickett. The highways are clear of traffic and the smudge of light of the eastern horizon has always meant that he has outlasted yet another eternal night. But today, there is no peace in this moment for him.

His mind is weary with the weight of his concern. He has resisted it, but it will not leave him. It will not be ignored. It shrilly demands a solution, and Pickett knows that he is solving nothing as he herds thirty tons down the highway toward Nebraska.

Pickett has no solutions, and there is no escape from this worry. Doris, John-William, the unborn child, the Mack, his fantasy Peterbilt, even road-hungry Lenny, who reminds Pickett so much of himself . . . all of these are part of Pickett's problem. All figure in his dilemma. His mind finds no respite in any of them, nor even in the road itself. Always before, Pickett could forget his problems on the road, his soothing, understanding mistress. But now even the road is part of his problem, and there is no getting away from that.

He could not lose his worry in Cheyenne, and he cannot lose it on the highway.

Pickett sets his lips and clutches the wheel. I'm going to do something, he thinks. I'm going to do *something*.

Chapter 13

"Jackie? Jackie Ellis? This is Billy-Frank. Billy-Frank Freeman. Right, the dude with the antique store. Right. Hey, baby, how they hangin'? Good, real good. Hey, I've got a business proposition for you. I'm looking for a reliable dude to haul a shipment for me, here to San Fran. Pay's good, real good. I thought you might be interested. I knew you did some work a couple of years ago for Red Chenier down in New Orleans. Yeah, sure, I know Red. We do business now and then. He tells me you always played it like a pro, so I figured I'd give you a call, see how you're looking, the next few days. No. No, I didn't. No shit? Probation? No, man, I never heard. Three years. Pretty stiff, huh? Tough luck. I could've used you. No, no. I can appreciate that. That's cool. You already got your neck in a noose, you don't want to jump off the scaffold. I can dig that. You have any other ideas? I don't mean some joker, but somebody who knows his way around, somebody can be trusted with a fairly major haul. Alex Boyd? That English doper? No, I don't need them problems. He'd shoot up half the shipment before he got it to the Coast. No, I need somebody professional. Okay. Okay, baby. Right. See you later."

Well, *damn!* Billy-Frank cracks the receiver down in its

cradle. He has been standing in a telephone booth for more than an hour and a half and his feet are beginning to get numb from the cold concrete floor. He has fed nearly two rolls of dimes into the slot. He has run through his list of prospective couriers for his hot stash of cocaine, and when he exhausted those possibilities, he began reconsidering his rejects. Now even jerks like Jackie Bates are finding excuses for staying away from the coke. Word does travel fast in these circles, Billy-Frank thinks. Word gets around that Billy-Frank Freeman is sitting on a hot load of coke and nobody wants to get near him, not even for ten big ones.

Billy-Frank's prospects all fear the law; in the rampant paranoia of this underground profession, they see a hundred undercover agents ready to swoop down and smite them with swift and unyielding justice the moment they try to move a shipment. In this case, they are not far wrong. Billy-Frank knows that will happen to himself, too, if he does not get rid of the stuff soon, but he has another worry. If Rivera does not get his shipment soon, Rivera is going to be upset. But if Billy-Frank picks the wrong courier, and if Rivera is caught holding the shipment because of that mistake, Rivera and his friends are going to come down hard on Billy-Frank. And, unlike the law, they are not going to bother listening to his side of the matter. He will not even get a free phone call. Thus, Billy-Frank's haste to get rid of his load of cocaine is tempered. Somewhere, Billy-Frank thinks, there must be somebody who needs ten grand for an easy week's work, somebody who will do the job like a pro, somebody who can keep his mouth shut, somebody whose face does not set off bells and flashing lights in the head of every narc in the country.

Forget it. Billy-Frank decides he will go home and think about it for a while. Annie is going to want to know why he has been standing in the phone booth on the corner when he has a phone in his own living room. Well, Annie, you see, I have this expensive chest of drawers I need shipped special across the country and I didn't want to tie up our phone. Right. Annie will go for that. Annie Jenkins will go for anything.

And, of course, she does. She even fills a tub with hot water and tells him to soak, and then she dries him with a towel and begins massaging his back with confident, sympathetic fingers.

"You shouldn't get so worked up," she says. "After all, it's just business. Those antiques have been around a long time, and nobody's going to get too upset if they don't get shipped right away.

"Don't worry, baby," she says. "You'll find somebody to take good care of that chest of drawers. I just know it."

"I sure hope you're right," says Billy-Frank.

Chapter 14

Mynette has been standing on the street corner in Topeka not fifteen minutes when she hears a woman's voice hailing her from the second lane of traffic stopped at the light.

"Come on," the woman's voice says. "This light isn't going to stay red forever."

Mynette grabs her suitcase and runs toward the voice. The woman is leaning from the window of a VW bus hand-painted in crude red, blue, and yellow enamel stripes, gleaming white stars sprinkled at random over vents, under windows, between door and wheel well. The side windows of the van have been painted purple, and one of them bears a hand-lettered sign that says:

"Don't laugh, redneck, your daughter might be inside."

Still, it is friendly-looking in a raffish sort of way, and the woman smiles as she motions Mynette into the back seat. So Mynette steps in.

"You're lucky. Don't you know the cops'll chase you right off the streets for hitchhiking around here?" the woman says.

"I guess I didn't," Mynette says, as she looks about her.

The driver is a young man with red hair, long red hair, and a thick beard. Mynette cannot see his face. The woman is turned half in her seat to talk to Mynette. She is pretty, Mynette thinks, but she ought to take better care of herself. Her hair is black and beautiful, but kinky and dirty, too. She wears a small gold earring in her left lobe.

Mynette has found a space on the first back seat. It was the last empty spot. On the seat beside her are two nylon backpacks fastened to aluminum frames. Behind her, Mynette has caught a glimpse of dirty clothes piled in a heap, dishes and pans piled into a dusty box. Sleeping bags, duffle sacks. Mynette wonders what else is stuffed back there.

"Where you headed?" says the driver.

"Boston," says Mynette.

"Boston!" the woman yells. "Good luck, sister, you got a long way to go. No, we're not going anywhere near there. We're headed for home, up near St. Joe. That's only about seventy-five miles."

"Sorry," the man says. "That's the best we can do. We spent the whole summer out in New Mexico and in the mountains up in the Colorado high country. Now it's getting cold up there. I've got to find a job to finance our next expedition."

"You ever been to Boston before?" the woman asks.

"Never," Mynette says.

"You'll like it. Lot of mellow people up there," the man says.

They are warm and open, though Mynette cannot help feeling like an intruder in their excitement at returning home. Still, she feels much more optimistic about her trip by the time they drop her at the Twenty-eighth Street interchange with the advice that she hitch north to Interstate 80. There, they assure her, she will find a ride headed straight to the East Coast.

This time, Mynette does not even stick out her thumb. She is still standing on the sidewalk, trying to get her bearings, when a 1967 Plymouth Barracuda squeals rubber to stop beside her.

"Looking for a ride?" says the boy inside.

Mynette thinks about it, but not for long. All day, she has been breaking new ground, finding hidden resources of boldness. Now she is ready to take a ride from a black-haired stranger in a red 'Cuda with megaphone glass-pack muffler, foot-wide mag wheels, and a Confederate flag sticker fixed to one corner of his rear window.

"Maybe," Mynette answers him over the burble of his exhaust. "Are you going north?"

"Going to Minneapolis," the boy says. "I'll drop you anywhere along the way, anywhere you want."

"Okay," Mynette says, and then she is inside and the boy is popping the clutch, bombing up the freeway ramp before she has time to close the door.

"Do you always drive this way?" she asks. The motor is roaring, the exhaust rap of the engine booms throughout the car and Mynette has to shout to be heard.

"Why not?" says the boy. He grins at her.

He is handsome, Mynette thinks to herself. He is, maybe, nineteen. His hair is razor cut, flopping over his ears and

106

nearly into his eyes in a gentle shag. His torso fills out a print double-knit shirt very nicely and his pants are modishly tight. In fact, Mynette could be interested, if only his approach were half as appealing as his body.

"How far north?" the boy says.

"What did you say?"

"How far north are you going? Where do you want me to drop you off?"

"Oh. Interstate 80. Wherever that is. I'm traveling to Boston."

"Interstate 80. That's up by Des Moines," the boy says confidently. "We've got a good three hours of driving before we get there. We might as well get friendly," he says, and he switches on his headlights to brighten the road ahead in the deepening dusk.

"Not too friendly," Mynette says.

"Come on, what do you take me for, some kind of maniac? I might drive crazy, but I'm as reliable as can be. Mister Nice Guy."

"Good," Mynette says.

Mynette spends the next two hours pushing him away, trying to be coy, pleading with him, threatening him. None of this works. She cries, and that she does not have to fake, because she is beginning to feel depressed and frustrated. Even that ultimate defense has no effect.

"Who are you kidding with that crap?" the boy says. "I've had that pulled on me before. That might work on some other guys, but not on me. I've been around."

"Admit it," he says. "You want me. You want it as much as I do, but you're ashamed to say so. Look, it's a long night. We can get a room, have dinner, get some sleep, have some fun. You'll be good and rested on your way to Boston in the morning. You aren't catching any rides to Boston after dark.

Nobody's going to stop, not even for a girl. Play it my way. It's a lot smarter."

"I hate you," she says. "I think you stink. I wouldn't want to sleep with you for a thousand dollars, and if I did, I wouldn't ever admit it."

"That kind of attitude is never going to get you anywhere," the boy says.

Mynette decides that it is time to take another chance, and if he calls her on this one, she may have to give up.

"You let me out of this car," she says, "or I'll jump out. You think I'm kidding? You'll find out. I'm crazy. Don't you realize that yet? Think about it. Would any normal woman be hitchhiking to Boston from St. Joseph, Missouri, all alone? You've got to be crazy to do that. And I am. I'm opening up the car and stepping out if you don't let me out, the next town we come to."

"Love to see you try," the boy says. Then he laughs.

Mynette yanks up the lock button on the door.

"I'm waiting," the boy says. He grins at her, in a way that makes her want to retch. She stifles the urge.

"You know," she says, "those people driving behind us are bound to get your license number and call the cops when they see me fall out of the car."

The boy glances into the mirror at the headlights behind him. His grin begins to fade.

"And if you're thinking of running away, you'd better ditch my suitcase," she says. "You didn't forget that, did you?" Then she yanks on the latch and pushes the door with her shoulder.

He reaches out and grabs her left arm, pulls her away.

"You'd do it," he says. "Crazy bitch."

He stops three miles down the road, at the exit for a small town north of the Iowa line. Mynette does not look at him as she climbs out. The car's rear tires throw gravel and

108

chirp on the pavement as he roars off. Mynette watches his red tail lights recede and disappear in the darkness. I could have liked you, she thinks. Mynette is tired and hungry now, but mostly she needs to be alone, to end this day that has already gone on too long and too hard. She cannot take any more setbacks today. She sees a neon motel sign fluttering down the side road. She trudges with her suitcase down the rocky shoulder of the road and into the motel office. It is an auto court, with two rows of off-white stucco buildings stretching from the central office. Mynette steps inside and the woman watching a portable television on the counter takes off her glasses to watch her.

"I need a room, ma'am, a cheap room," Mynette says.

"We don't have any cheap rooms," the woman says, "but they are inexpensive."

"Well, that's the kind I want," Mynette says. "The more inexpensive, the better. I don't have a lot of money."

The woman turns to look at the keys hanging from nails on the wall.

"I've got one for five," she says. "It's clean. No TV, of course, not for that price. Does that sound like what you're looking for?"

"If that's the cheapest—I mean, the most inexpensive you've got, then that's the one I'm looking for," Mynette says.

The woman squints to look at her, to take another look at this girl with her denim pants and the strong edge in her voice.

"That bad, is it?" the woman says.

"I guess so."

"Tell you what. This is the off season. We don't rent too many rooms, anyway. I'll give you the room for two dollars if you promise to take the cot out of the closet and sleep on that. There's blankets up on the shelf. It isn't worth it to me if I've got to change the bed, but if you promise to be out early and to sleep on the cot, then it's yours tonight for two dollars."

"I promise," Mynette says, and she pulls the money from her purse.

She sleeps a fitful, troubled sleep, a fever sleep of strange dreams. When she wakes, it is with a start. She bolts from her bed and wonders, for a moment, how she has found herself in this strange bed in a strange room. Then she remembers, and her sense of unswerving direction fills her again. She brushes her teeth, showers, changes into fresh clothes. Sunlight is beginning to fill the room. She knows, then, that she should be back on the highway, hustling for a ride. She carefully folds the blankets and then replaces the cot. She is ready to walk outside when, on impulse, she puts down her suitcase and opens the writing desk in a corner of the room. Inside is a ball-point pen and a sheet of stationery.

"Thank You. Thank you very much," she writes. She leaves the paper on the desk. Then she is gone.

Across the street is a bake shop, nearly empty except for a fat man in overalls who is talking with the waitress when Mynette walks into the shop.

Mynette smells the sweet odors, the fresh and inviting bakery smells. She checks the price list on the wall, asks for a bowl of cereal, and milk. The waitress walks to the far end of the counter to pour Mynette's cereal into a bowl and the man in overalls still talks, now bellowing down the counter at her.

"Old man Pulaski's got me goin' again," he says. "Goin' up to Des Moines right now. Then I gotta be back before three to help 'im unload a shipment of grain. Sheesh. That old bastard keeps me running."

Mynette turns to take a good look at the man. He is no slick operator, not like the boy last night in the Barracuda. In fact, his overalls are streaked with dirt and his undershirt looks almost gamy. He needs a shave, Mynette notices, and the flab hangs on him everywhere, from his arms, his chin, his jowls. His butt spills over the stool on which he sits. Mynette walks to him.

"Excuse me, sir, but did you say you were going to Des Moines?"

"That's right. That cheap flint I work for got me up at five-thirty this morning to go to Des Moines. And that's jest the beginning. Oh, he is a real bastard."

"Is there any way I could get a ride with you? To Des Moines? Interstate 80?"

The fat man looks up from his coffee, turns to look at her.

"A ride? Naw, I don't think so. Old man Pulaski would have my hide."

"I'd really appreciate it, mister. I've got to get to Interstate 80 real bad."

"You do? Well, don' know. I guess old man Pulaski don' have to know about it. Okay. It's a deal. But I'll tell you right now, I'm not much of a conversationalist."

"That's okay," Mynette says. "I'm obliged. But I've got to eat my cereal first."

"Take your time," the man says, turning back to his coffee. "The old man ain' given me time to eat a proper breakfast yet, either. Oh, my name's Jones. Ernest Jones. You can call me Jonesy."

"Pleased. I'm Mynette Hancock. And I'm really grateful."

Jonesy's proper breakfast would stop a horse. Mynette tries not to gape at the prodigious amounts of food the man consumes. He sails through three chocolate-covered doughnuts. He cruises through a double stack of pancakes. He destroys a plate of fried eggs, stabbing the yolks with a fork, attacking the whites, cleaning his plate with a slice of bread. When he is finished, he pats his stomach.

111

"Man can't get started without a decent breakfast," he says. "You finished? Good, I'm parked around back."

Around back is a truck. At least, Mynette thinks it is a truck. It has four wheels and a cab and a flat-bed body, just like some of the other farm trucks she has seen in Kansas. But this one is covered with a cackling, white-feathered, mass of life form that has attached itself to almost every square inch of the vehicle.

"Chickens," Jonesy says. "Old man Pulaski raises chickens for one of them fried-chicken take-out stores. I'm bringin' a shipment up to Des Moines."

The chickens are everywhere, angry in their crates. Crates of chickens are eight feet high on the flat-bed, secured by ropes. They are tied atop the cab, too. Jonesy opens her door and she steps inside. When Mynette looks out the rear window and into the side mirrors, she can see nothing but chickens.

The truck is a twelve-year-old Ford medium-duty, but its makers would disavow its origins if they could see it now. Springs are popping out of the seat like columbine dotting a mountain meadow in spring. When Jonesy turns the ignition, the engine groans, turns over languidly, then begins firing as if from habit, nothing else. The gears grind as Jonesy moves the long shifter on the floor.

"Des Moines, here we come," Jonesy says. "Somebody wake up them chicken-pluckers."

Jonesy is true to his word. He is not much of a conversationalist. In fact, Mynette cannot get a word in; Jonesy talks from the moment he jams the truck into first gear, as they bounce and heave down the highway, the motor whining, until they ride beneath an underpass near Des Moines. Overhead, cars and trucks whoosh by.

"Interstate 80," Jonesy says. "If you're looking for a ride, you might's well head over to that truck stop over there.

Those guys are okay. You'll find somebody headed in your direction soon enough."

Mynette climbs out of the cab, slams the door with a loud metallic rattle, and waves at Jonesy as he grinds away. The truck stop is busy enough, she thinks. There must be a hundred big rigs. She crosses the road, walks toward the restaurant. How does one go about this, she wonders. Walk up to them, I suppose. Walk up and smile and ask them, real nice, excuse me, sir, would you happen to be going anywhere near Boston?

Nothing to be gained by waiting, she thinks. She rehearses the line in her head three more times, then draws up her nerve to approach a trucker who stands outside his cab, gabbing with the attendant who is pumping fuel into the truck's tanks. The truck is painted in the colors of a moving company, and just before Mynette opens her mouth, she catches the man's name on the side of the door:

"J. W. Pickett, Antioch, Calif."

"Excuse me, sir," Mynette says, "but would you happen to be going anywhere near Boston?"

Chapter 15

Doris Pickett is in the basement, sorting laundry, when the news comes. She hears the telephone ring once, twice, three times. She hurries up the stairs to pluck the receiver from its perch on the kitchen wall before it can ring a fourth time.

"Mrs. Pickett?" says the unfamiliar voice on the other end.

"This is Miss Williams, in the principal's office at the elementary school. I'm afraid I have some bad news. Your son has been hurt, ma'am. He was hurt in a playground accident. We've already called an ambulance. He's on his way to Delta Memorial. I'm sorry."

Like that, Doris' day is jolted, her life turned upside down. Her mind simmers with questions. How did this happen? And why? Why now, with the baby and all, why me?

"Is he hurt bad?" she says.

"We can't be sure," says the voice, but Doris Pickett knows better, just from the way she answers.

"All right," she says, and when she hangs up, she leans against the wall to breathe for a minute, to think. Then she hurries, half stumbles toward the door. Her keys are in her corduroy coat, hanging in the closet. She pulls the coat from a hanger, and then she is gone, banging the door behind her.

Already, even as she runs to the car, her son has been lifted from the ambulance stretcher onto an emergency-room gurney. He is wheeled behind a screen, where an intern pulls on rubber gloves, ready to get to work. The intern sees that this one is bad, very bad. The ambulance attendant has told the admitting nurse that the boy has not moved since they stretched him out on the pallet. The intern knows his limits; he calls for help without putting a finger on the boy.

John William Pickett has always been his father's boy. From his adolescent parody of a man's swaggering walk to his brash talk, there is nothing to betray his genetic secret, nothing to suggest that J. W. Pickett is anything but his true father in every way. Young John William has been his father's joy and his mother's constant worry, because he has always seemed a little too eager to do things that should have scared him. When he was eighteen months old, hardly big enough to walk without stumbling, Doris used to take him to the playground nearby. There, he would claw his way up the stairs to the top of the slide, climbing on his knees because his legs were unsteady, crawling on his knees and pulling himself up with his pudgy little fingers. Doris tried, just once, to stand behind him and steady him with a hand on his rump. But, no, he would have none of that, no mother hovering nearby. She had to stand away, nervous, while he climbed to the top of the slide and then flew down the slick surface to land in the sand.

So that is the way it has always been, and that is how he has gotten himself in this trouble. John William, like the rest of his friends, rides a bicycle. But none of his friends rides a bike the way John William does. This afternoon, after school, they set up a racecourse around the school playground, over the asphalt parking lot, through the grass of the school's playing field, circling the playground equipment and cutting through the middle of the basketball court. There were a dozen of them, and John William was ready. He rode hard, just as he always rode. His strong legs pumped. He skidded the bicycle around the turns and he slid in the dirt, keeping his balance with his left leg skimming along. It was a fine autumn afternoon and he felt as though he could never tire of this, as though he could pedal like this for an hour and never feel breathless. The heat of the summer was gone, replaced by just the suggestion of a chill, just enough crispness to make a boy's chest tingle with the excitement of life. Naturally, nobody could catch him. Then it happened suddenly, as these things usually do. As he cut a turn, perhaps a bit sharply, on the cement basketball court, his front wheel slipped and buckled under him. John William was pitched over the handlebars. Even before he hit the ground, his head smashed against one of the thick metal uprights of the chain link fence surrounding the courts. He lay there motionless, as in a deep and untroubled sleep. Blood began to spill from the gash atop his head. He lay that way until the ambulance came, and he lay that way in the ambulance until he was wheeled on the gurney into the emergency room.

Doris Pickett knows none of this as she turns the ignition of the car and starts for the hospital. She knows only that her boy is hurt, that he needs her, that she must be close to him. In ten minutes she is there, there in the emergency room. The intern who saw her boy first is stripping off his gloves, coming to speak to her as the nurse from the admissions desk points her out, whispers in his ear.

"Mrs. Pickett? I'm Dr. Davies."

"My boy," she says. "How is he? How did he get hurt?"

The intern is human. He takes the easy one first.

"Apparently he fell from a bicycle. He struck his head on something solid. He's alive and breathing; his vital signs look okay. But he's still unconscious. He's got a bad concussion, I'm sure of that. And he had a nasty cut. That's easy enough to take care of. But, frankly, Mrs. Pickett, we're worried that he hasn't regained consciousness yet."

She is numb. She feels her hands jumping and she clutches the sleeves of her jacket.

"But . . . what does that mean?"

"Well, we're not sure at this point. We'll have to take tests, X rays. I'm sorry, you can't see him now. There isn't much for you to do except wait. I guess you'll want to wait here?"

"Yes," she says. "I've got to wait here."

"Good," he says. He puts his arm on her shoulder and feels her trembling. "Just find a seat over there. You've got to calm down now. You don't want your boy to see you so worried when he comes to. I'll have a nurse bring you a tranquilizer."

She sits in a folding metal chair, and for the first time,

116

she sees, hears, smells the place. There is the standard antiseptic hospital scent, but more than that, a sense of disaster, of fractured lives whose steady flow has been halted abruptly by some crisis or another. There is a young mother, younger than she, who holds a baby boy distractedly while she peers down the corridor. Doris hears a child's weeping somewhere, the crying of a boy younger or less proud than John William, who would never sob unabashedly that way. Not him. She hears metal instruments ringing as they are dropped into an aluminum pan behind a screen. The nurses and doctors in their white tunics are intense, joyless.

There is no happiness, no comfort here. Doris feels alone, ready to cry, but she knows that she cannot break down now. There is no one else to take care of things if she cannot.

Pickett, she thinks. Damn you, Pickett. I need you and you're gone. Where are you, what the hell are you doing, now that I really need you?

Chapter 16

Lenny is double-timing it out of the restaurant, Thermos and a bag of sandwiches in his hands, feeling much better after a few hours' sleep and full breakfast. Pickett, inexhaustible Pickett, has driven straight through from Cheyenne to Des Moines, 490 miles with no more fuss than if he were driving to the store for a loaf of bread. Not only has he driven straight through, but he has allowed Lenny to sleep until well past nine, while they rolled through Iowa. Now he has stopped for breakfast, and he has sent Lenny to the

117

men's room to soak his head in cold water and wash his face and generally try to clear the effects from last night's over-indulgence.

So now Lenny feels fine. He bounces out of the restaurant, up to the service island where the truck sits.

"Ready to roll?" Lenny yells at the pump jockey.

"Full up," says the man.

Outasight, Lenny thinks. Look out, highway, 'cause here we come. Boston is practically over the next hill.

"Thanks a lot, Pickett," he calls up into the cab as he opens the door. He puts his foot on the lower stirrup of steel, lifts himself up to the second.

"I was in bad shape there for a while, but I'm ready now."

He is about to swing his leg around the seat when he looks across the cab.

"Hello," the girl says, in a voice that somehow makes Lenny want to lean over and kiss her feet. "My name's Mynette Hancock."

"Lenny Lewis," he says. "I must be dreaming."

Pickett's voice rumbles from behind the sleeper curtains, somewhere near Lenny's ear.

"This nice girl is from Kansas, not far up the road from Bartlesville. She's a good girl and she's ridin' with us to Boston," Pickett says. "If you don't mind. Now see if you can get in a couple of hundred miles without runnin' off the road while I'm asleep. You think you can do that?"

"No sweat, Pickett. I'll take it on through to Toledo, maybe even Cleveland. I could drive all day."

"I'd settle for just a couple of hours till we get to Daven-port. Wake me up when you get tired."

Lenny notches the truck into gear and they crawl through the parking lot, then onto the highway. Lenny turns and smiles at Mynette. Lenny is struck. He cannot

118

stop looking at her. She is shy, a little awkward in this situation; to Lenny, that sets off her good looks perfectly.

"He seems like an awfully nice guy," she whispers.

"Pickett? He's tough, but he's a good man," Lenny says. "You don't have to worry about talking. He's asleep already, I'd bet. In this business, you've got to take advantage of every minute of rest that you can get."

"It was good of him to give me a ride. I might have spent a whole day there trying to find somebody else who was going to Boston."

"I don't think so. Not you. You'd have found a ride soon enough," he says.

"That's nice. I can hardly believe it. I'm really on my way to Boston. I wasn't sure I was going to make it, for a while. I'm sort of running away from home, except that I'm legally old enough to do what I want. So I'm not really a runaway. How far is it to Boston?" she asks.

"About thirteen hundred miles. Twenty-six hours if we average fifty miles an hour. From here, it's freeways and turnpikes all the way, so we'll do better than that, even stopping for fuel and a meal or two. Limit's fifty-five now, but that usually doesn't bother truckers. No way we can make money at fifty-five. It depends. In Illinois, Ohio, Pennsylvania, you watch your mirrors real close. You're taking a real chance any time you go over the limit. Those guys are always on the prowl and they'll nail you for fifty-six in a fifty-five-mile zone."

"Twenty-six hours. You say it like it's nothing. I think it's incredible. I feel like we're sitting here in this box and Boston is moving toward us. This time tomorrow, I'll be looking out of this window and I'll see Boston roll right up toward us."

"Just like that," Lenny says.

"Just like that? Do you know what you're saying? We're just going to sit here and cover almost half the country in one day. And you do it all the time, all over the country," she says.

"You sound impressed," he says.

"I am. I spent eighteen years in the same place and it seemed like the town got smaller every day. I decided I had to get away, I felt like I was strangling. It's no way to live."

"It doesn't bother everybody," he says. "Sometimes I wonder whether I'm not a little strange. I rent a place in a small town called Bolinas. It's a few miles north of San Francisco, but quiet and secluded. Right on the ocean. It's a beautiful spot. Most people would be happy to spend the rest of their life there, but I couldn't. To me, no matter how beautiful a place is, it's still a prison as long as you're stuck there."

He stops and moves his left arm in a sweep across the dash that takes in the flat landscape and the concrete of the highway.

"Now this," he says, "is not what you would call beautiful scenery. It doesn't start to compare with Bolinas. But I'd rather be here, right now, than there. At least, I'd rather be in this truck, wherever we're headed. That way, when we do go home, I can feel like I'm seeing Bolinas all over again. But a lot of my friends will never understand why I would choose to be here, instead of there."

She beams across at him. Lenny likes the way she smiles at him. Now she is sitting with her legs tucked under her, back to the door, facing Lenny. He drops down a gear, snaps on his turn signals, and twists the wheel smartly to pass another truck. He hopes she notices how deftly he handles the big rig. He is not ashamed to be showing off.

They ramble on through Iowa, past Davenport before noon, and past Chicago before rush hour, Mynette kneeling up in the seat to look over Lenny's head at the faint, hazy skyline to the north. They are through South Bend and making time toward Toledo when Pickett begins to wake with a satisfied grunt. Lenny realizes that he has driven nearly nine hours, a good five hundred miles, yet he is not the least sick of it. He is just as fresh as ever after drinking in the natural goodness of this country girl, soaking her up and liking everything he feels. Lenny likes her even more now; she has made the time pass quickly and that is a precious gift to a long-haul trucker.

Pickett pulls open the shades, peers out.

"It's getting late. How long did you let me sleep? This is Indiana, for Chrissakes. You're makin' good time, Lenny. Must've missed rush hour in Chicago."

"Timed it just right," Lenny says.

"Good job. Let me shake myself a minute and I'll be ready to drive."

"No hurry, Pickett. I'm in a good groove now. No sense in rushing things. You might as well rest as long as you can. You can take over later and bring her straight on through into Boston."

Pickett is about to make a smart remark about Lenny's conscientious working habits when he notices, oh, maybe it is the way the girl sits in the seat, closer than she should be to Lenny. Or maybe it is the way she is smiling, or maybe it is the way Lenny sits straight up in the seat, really straighter than he should after eight hours of driving. Oh-ho, Pickett thinks. Lenny, old boy, what are you letting yourself get into?

"Sure," Pickett says. "I can always use the sack time. Want to pass me up a sandwich? Got a ham and cheese left in there? Good. Sure, Lenny, you're doin' fine, just fine. Don't forget we'll be needin' fuel in a couple hundred miles. Maybe

121

we can get a decent meal then. Okay, kids, papa's goin' back to sleep just as soon as he eats his sandwich."

They roll onward, into the night. As they drive away from the setting sun, darkness arrives suddenly and almost without warning. The shadow of the truck lengthens in front of them by the minute. Then all is shadow and Lenny must flick on his low-beam headlights.

"Do you notice how different it feels," Lenny says, "when it gets dark outside and you turn on the lights? There's nothing to distract you. You realize that this cab is your world, just this little box of steel and glass."

"Kind of cozy," she says. Then she leans over in the seat to kiss him on the cheek. Lenny feels his chest swell. They drive on, past Toledo, past Cleveland, feeling closer all the time. Finally they swoop into a truck stop outside Erie, Pennsylvania, when the indicator needle on the second fuel tank begins dipping low.

"Pickett. You awake? Pennsylvania, Pickett, you've slept clear through to Pennsylvania."

"Uhmm. I'll be God-*damned*. So I have. You been haulin', buddy-boy. How you doin' there, Miss Hancock?"

"I couldn't be better," she says, and still she smiles. Pickett knows then that Lenny has gotten himself into something, all right.

"Enjoyin' the sights, I guess? Good. We'll be in Boston early tomorrow mornin'. Just a little over five hundred miles from here. We'll do that in no time. Well, I guess you two must be ready for dinner, huh? How's a steak sound?"

"Pickett, I don't know what it is," Lenny says, "but I don't have that much of an appetite. I've been hitting that bag of sandwiches pretty hard. Maybe, uh, maybe I could ask you to bring me back a hamburger and a milkshake."

"A hamburger and a milkshake," Pickett repeats. "Whatever you say. You want a chocolate milkshake?"

122

"Sure, chocolate, that's right," Lenny says.

"Well, you're comin' to eat with me, ain't you, young lady?"

"Oh, I guess I've been eating quite a few sandwiches myself," Mynette says. "Maybe just a hamburger and a milkshake for me, too."

"A hamburger and a milkshake. A chocolate milkshake?"

"Chocolate would be fine, Mr. Pickett."

"Sure, I understand. You must be tired. You ought to at least get out and stretch your legs, though."

Lenny opens the door, climbs down, making room for Pickett. Pickett is behind him, yawning as he lowers himself down from the cab, still yawning as he trundles off toward the restaurant. Then he turns back, turns back as Lenny takes Mynette down the steps to the asphalt.

"That's right, stretch your legs, you two. Lenny, you did such a good job, we're a couple of hours ahead of schedule goin' into Boston. No sense gettin' to Worcester before eight. We can't off-load that first bunch of stuff till then, anyway. I figure I might as well take my time eatin', maybe even take a shower, relax in the lounge for a while. Or shoot a game of pool. I haven't done that in quite a while. But only if you can wait for those hamburgers."

"Thanks," Lenny says. "We'll wait."

He turns to Mynette.

"They've got showers in these places. And TV sets, pool tables, just about everything. He'll probably be in there an hour, hour and a half. Maybe more."

"Oh," she says, "it's quiet, all of a sudden. That truck can be pretty noisy."

Compared to the truck, the night is, indeed, quiet. Traffic whines on the highway and trucks growl and grumble in the parking lot, but that is nothing like the incessant rumble

123

of the Cummins. Lenny reaches out to her, and they kiss. They do not feel the stiffness in their legs, nor do they hear the buzz of the traffic.

"Let's go back up," he says.

"To sit?"

"No, I don't think so. I think we're ready, don't you?"

"I shouldn't be," she says, "but I am."

She goes up the steps before him and she is waiting, nearly hidden in the sleeper box when he crawls in there.

"Before anything," he says, "I want you to know this isn't something that happens all the time."

"I could say the same," she says. "But in a way, I hope it wouldn't make any difference."

No more talking now. She is warm, she drops her reserve by precious degrees and Lenny can only respond. He can see dimly. He knows that she is beautiful. And, like the moment, exquisite. Lenny thinks that this is one of those times that makes life worth living. He thinks that this evening is something he will remember well for many years. Then he does not think at all, because things are happening. There is no thought, but there is emotion, yes, and feeling. It is good, God it is good, and her voice becomes lower by almost a half octave when she pants her love-making sounds.

They lie together, breathing in syncopation. Lenny can feel it through his chest. They are in harmony. They are finished with their love-making, silent, but still breathing in rhythm. Then their hearts fall out of step, just slightly, and she leans away to grab the blanket and spread it over them. Their magic ebbs away, but not their joy. Then Mynette begins to crab about in the dark, reaching out for clothes, socks, underwear.

"What are you doing?" Lenny asks. "Pickett won't be back for a while. He knows. He won't bother us."

"I know that. But I have to find a place to stay. I've got a cousin in Boston and my best friend lives there, too. I've got to call one of them and let them know I'm coming."

"Okay," he says.

"When I'm finished," she says, "can we sleep together back here tonight?"

"Uh-huh."

"Good." She reaches out to kiss him. Then she climbs down from the bunk, onto the seats, and feels her way down the steps to the asphalt of the parking lot. She walks into the cafe, squinting in the bright light. She finds a telephone booth. From her purse she retrieves a scrap of paper with two telephone numbers. She fingers the paper. Time for a decision. She wonders how her cousin will react. They never were especially close, and they have not seen one another in three years. She *is* flesh and blood, Mynette thinks. Family ties *do* count. But then Mynette thinks of her friend. Mynette knows how she will react. They were always like sisters. She even sort of invited Mynette to come. Mynette is suddenly anxious to see her, and that decides the matter.

She drops a dime into the telephone and dials the operator.

"I'd like to call Boston," she says. "A collect call from Mynette Hancock."

Mynette hears the ringing on the other end. She hears the familiar voice accept the charges.

"Mynette?" says the voice.

"Annie, Annie, it's really you," Mynette blurts into the receiver. "Annie Jenkins, you're not going to believe what I have to tell you."

Chapter 17

How long, how long? Doris Pickett sits in the folding metal chair, watches the clock, follows the interns and nurses pacing busily past her, sees the faces in the emergency room come and go, new miseries and illnesses. But she is constant, she and her pain. The doctor has gone and has not returned. Tests, he said, tests and X rays, and meanwhile, her boy is lying hurt somewhere beyond those walls, perhaps on the other side of this partition. She wants to reach out to him, to hold his hand and ruffle his hair even though he cannot know that she is there.

She is numb, lost, so deep into herself that the doctor must tap her twice on the shoulder before she looks up and focuses her eyes on him. This is another one, older.

"Mrs. Pickett, I'm Dr. Rodrigues. I've been treating your son since he was admitted. Your boy is in very serious condition. He needs surgery. It's terribly involved, but I'll try to explain the situation the best I can. Your son should have regained consciousness not long after his accident. His concussion was bad, but not that bad. The reason is that his fall against the post ruptured arteries around the brain. A blood clot has formed and it's creating pressure in some critical areas of the brain. This epidural bleeding is most serious. Unless the pressure is relieved, your boy has very little chance of regaining consciousness."

"How? You mean you want to go into his head?"

"That's correct. The condition is too severe to treat chemically. We want to cut into the boy's skull, and actually drain the clot. Hopefully, that will alleviate the problem. We can't be sure of that, but he hasn't much chance unless we do it."

"Is it . . . dangerous? Can you do this here?"

"It's not an uncommon procedure, Mrs. Pickett, but it does have its risks. And I won't perform the surgery. There's a man at Stanford, an expert at this. We're equipped to do the surgery here; I've asked him to drive up. I explained that it's an emergency, and he is already on his way."

"There's nothing else you can do?"

"Nothing, Mrs. Pickett. If there were, we would try that first. We need your consent, Mrs. Pickett. I'm going to have a nurse bring you the release forms."

"All right, Doctor. If you say that's the way it has to be."

He strides away, leaving her with her mind bobbing on a choppy sea of uncertainty. She thinks bitterly: This is how life is. Four hours ago I was doing the laundry. Now I'm going to sign a paper that lets some man cut open my son's head. For the first time in hours, she is aware of the fetus inside her. For one moment, she wishes she could kill it right there and spare it this life.

Chapter 18

Incredibly enough, it is the silence that rouses him.

The Mack rocks gently to a stop; Pickett cuts the engine and the rumble dribbles away to nothing. That is enough to wake Lenny this morning. Pale light against the blue corduroy sleeper curtains. A faint wheeze, Pickett leaning across the seats. The rattle of their tackle box, the lid squeaking open and then snapping shut with a click. Mynette stirs and smiles as Lenny pulls his right arm from under her head.

Pickett turns to see Lenny's face poking between the curtains.

"Mornin' kid. Pleasant night?" he says quietly.

"I've had worse."

Outside the window, Lenny sees a thick stand of pine trees, black and lacking definition in the haze of these early hours. Then the hum of a car ends the quiet and Lenny knows the place. They are parked in a rest area along the Massachusetts Turnpike, not far from Worcester.

"Time to wake up our engineer friend," Pickett says. "He's stayin' in a motel in Worcester. Supposed to have flown in yesterday morning. We got a lot of carryin' to do today."

Lenny nods, yawns. Pickett lays the tackle box on the passenger seat, stuffs the wrapped rolls of dimes and quarters into his breast pocket, and leaves the cab.

Lenny feels her arms wrap around his waist. They are thin, warm, gentle. Her face is against his back. She holds him for three heartbeats before she relaxes and draws back. For the first time in their new intimacy, they look at each other in the light of day. Lenny knows the uncertain, shifting ground of these morning-after encounters, and as he moves his glance around her face, then fixes on her eyes, he hopes that this one will be different.

In less time than it takes her to smile, he knows that it is. Perhaps the uncommon passion of their love-making has carried through the night, or perhaps it is simply the narrow confines of the sleeper box, its spare dimensions refusing to countenance anything but intimacy. Whatever the reason, the artificial barriers have no chance between them this morning. He reaches across, holds his right hand at the nape of her neck and runs his thumb across her cheek. They kiss, and then Lenny knows that they have lost nothing from the night before.

"Not far from Boston," he says. "We drop off our first load in Worcester, about thirty miles from the city. The other two are in Newton and Needham. They're just outside Boston. We'll be working all day. You can get a bus from Newton, if you're anxious to see your friend."

"If I stay in the truck, I won't be in the way, will I? Maybe I'll just call Annie later and tell her I'm on my way. That way we can have dinner together, if you want."

"That's good," he says, "but it's going to be a late dinner. We'll be working all day. We're lucky that all three homes are pretty close together on this load. Otherwise, we'd be spending all our time chasing back and forth."

"What do you do," she asks, "when you're finished with this load?"

"Back on the road. We might rest a day, but I don't know. I think Pickett's got the inside line on another full load, and he won't have time to fool around. Work can be pretty scarce this time of year, so he's not going to turn that down, even if it does mean missing a day off."

"Then you might be leaving soon. Maybe even tomorrow."

"Maybe so. I'm sorry. I wish it weren't that way."

"Don't be sorry. I knew what I was getting into last night. And I don't regret it a bit. It was beautiful."

"It was," he says. They kiss again.

Then Lenny tells her to slide down into the passenger seat. He will drive, giving Pickett at least a half-hour break before they go to work. Their job will not be as time-consuming as the loading. There are no inventories to be compiled, and it will be the homeowners' job, not their own, to search the goods for scratches and chips. If all goes well, unloading the van will be a job of nine, ten hard hours, if each client is there at the door, waiting with the payment and knowing where the furniture is to be carried.

Mynette is brushing her hair, combing out the ponytail and letting it hang to her shoulders when Pickett walks up to the tractor, hands jammed into his pockets. Lenny has climbed down to wait for him outside.

"We ready to roll? Any hang-ups in Worcester?" Lenny says.

"Nope. The guy's ready. He couldn't believe we're on time. Place isn't far off the turnpike. Directions are easy."

"Good. The sleeper's all yours. I'll wake you up when we get to the city limits."

The engineer's home in Worcester is expensive and nondescript; disappointing. Lenny wants to tell the man that he has made a bad move away from the sunny hillside in Corte Madera. As he lifts crates from the floor of the van and walks them mechanically into the house, Lenny has time to think. It is a job that has made the man do this, he decides, but then he corrects himself. No, not a job, but an outlook, something in his perspective that will not allow the man to turn down a raise so that he can live in a home and a town that he truly enjoys. Surely he hated to leave that funky brown-shingled home on the hillside in Corte Madera, Lenny thinks. But he is locked into this obsession with . . . what is the phrase? Upward mobility. Yes, that is it. The engineer seems like a genuine nice guy with a fine family. Lenny feels sorry for him, but he says none of this aloud; he merely nods and smiles at the man. The engineer will never be able to take seriously the sympathetic advice of his moving man.

Meanwhile, Pickett works as though he had slept through the night. He bends over to lift crates alone, without even a grunt. When they guide a bulky chest upstairs to the second floor, Pickett takes the downstairs side, shouldering the brunt of the job. And each time, after they have muscled

their load inside and lowered it gently to the floor, Pickett
turns and steps quickly back toward the van, back for
another armful.

"Pickett," Lenny says after two hours of this, "time for a
break, huh? Don't burn yourself out. We've got a lot more
carrying to do yet today."

"No problem," Pickett says. "I figure I'll pop a couple of
Specials when I start draggin' this afternoon."

They lean against one wall of the van as they talk.

"That ought to pick you up," Lenny says. "Then your
only problem will be falling asleep tonight. You won't
come down for a long time."

"If that's all I've got to worry about, we're sittin' pretty
good, buddy-boy. And speakin' of problems, what are you
plannin' to do about that honey of yours in there?"

"I was going to ask if we could bring her into the city this
evening. She has a friend to call. I thought we might at least
bring her to her friend's house."

"Sure. That's fine. You've got all night, far as I'm concerned. But I got to call the dispatcher this afternoon. I
want him to commit that full load to Dallas. I can always
use that, specially this time of year. But if he gives me that
load, we'll have to move on it. Like tomorrow mornin'. You
know that."

"I know it."

"Okay, I just wanted to tell you. That girl in the cab ain't
goin' to be too happy about it. She's really got it for you."

"I like her. She's a very nice girl."

"I told you so. Didn't I? Didn't I tell you so?"

They are finished in Worcester a few minutes after noon.
From the satisfied look on the engineer's face, Pickett knows
that if the man ever moves across country again, Mercury
will get that rarity of rarities in the interstate moving business, a repeat customer.

Pickett's mood carries him through lunch. When they have eaten, he leaves his seat to call home for the first time since they left, Wednesday evening. His face is clouded when he returns to the table.

"No answer. I even had the operator try it twice. No answer. What is it, ten-thirty back there?"

"That's not too early, Pickett. John William gets up early, doesn't he? Maybe he's gone somewhere and Doris had to take him in the car."

"Maybe. I'm not sure exactly when they do wake up. Maybe you're right. I'll try it this evening."

But Pickett's fragile good mood is broken now. He is quiet when Mynette leaves the table to phone her friend in Boston.

But Pickett thinks. He thinks: That is depressin'. I really can't say for sure what time my wife and my boy wake up on Saturday mornings.

Chapter 19

The jangling of the telephone catches Annie Jenkins and Billy-Frank in the middle of another argument. Things have not been so smooth for them lately. Annie cannot say exactly what has been wrong, but Billy-Frank has been an absolute bear. He has not been putting in his hours at the store and he has been listless, sitting alone and, even worse, turning on alone. This bugs Annie. Billy-Frank will shut himself in the second bedroom, turn up the stereo, and sit. And then, in a few minutes, she will smell the sweet-musty odor drifting out from the room, drifting out from under the door, and then she will get awfully put out. And it is not as though she can go off by herself in the city, go away and leave him to his ruminations. She does not feel safe, walking alone in their new neighborhood and, in fact, she does not much enjoy Boston without Billy-Frank at her side. He is comfortable in the city; she is not. She has written cheerfully about the city to Mynette back in Eureka, but the truth is that she would not stay if Billy-Frank were not here, for she has no friends except his friends and she ventures nowhere unless it is with him.

She has been reading him out for his reclusiveness, telling him just what a lousy mate he has been for the last week or so, and he has told her that he needs none of the bullshit she has been handing him, and she is telling him that she has tried to be considerate, but she has just about reached her limits . . . when the phone rings.

They welcome the diversion. She flounces off to answer the telephone.

"Billy-Frank," she says, "it's for you. It's a long-distance call."

Amazing how Billy-Frank's attitude can change. No longer is he sullen and snappish, no longer peevish and put upon. He clears his throat and—oh, this frosts Annie Jenkins—he even smiles as he speaks.

"Hello," he says.

"Freeman, my name is Collins. I'm an associate of a business acquaintance of yours. You met this man several days ago at Logan International. Do we understand each other?"

"Yes," Billy-Frank says.

"Good," says the voice. "My associate has come to terms with you on a business transaction, I believe. Now he is very anxious to know whether you have planned the logistics to complete this transaction."

133

"I've been working on it," Billy-Frank says, his voice becoming husky.

"I'm sure that you have. But my associate is very anxious to have the goods that you discussed. You see, his buyers are impatient people and my associate is in a position to make a considerable profit. I'm afraid he is going to be very disturbed that you seem to be reneging on your agreement."

"I'm not doing that," Billy-Frank says. "I want to make the deal just as much as he does."

"I'm pleased to hear that, Freeman, and I know my associate will be, also. However, time is running quite short. My associate and I must set a twenty-four-hour deadline for you to make suitable arrangements. Otherwise, we will be forced to take appropriate action."

Billy-Frank does not want to even imagine what horrors might be couched behind that fine phrase. He simply says:

"I'll have something by then. Call me this time tomorrow."

"I was already planning to do that, Freeman. Make it good, for your own sake."

Billy-Frank's mind is somersaulting as he turns away from the telephone. He had not expected Rivera to get that impatient. He had figured on at least another two days. Just as well. He cannot count on the law holding off much longer. He had damn sight better come up with something tonight, he thinks, or his ass is in a sling. This is the line of his thinking when Annie walks up to him and puts her arms around his neck.

"Let's not argue any more, huh? C'mon, honey," she says, "let's go make up, like we usually do. You know what I'm talking about. How about it, lover?"

"Not now, not right away," he says. "I've got some serious thinking to do."

"You do? Well, maybe I do, too. Is this the way it's going

134

to be tonight? Billy-Frank, you are being just terrible. My best friend calls on the telephone and says she's going to come visit, and you go into a big snit. I told you I was going to invite her to visit, and you said that would be fine, just great. Now you're going to spoil the whole night if you don't change your attitude. This is important to me. I want to show off our house to my friend. I want to show that I can put together a nice evening."

"Ah, shit, girl, would you shut up? Just shut the fuck up? Listen, I've got things, real important things, to think about. I don't need this kind of grief now. Go ahead and have your damn dinner, I don't give a good God damn. But don't bug me, okay? Just leave me be."

"Okay, Billy-Frank. If that's the way you want it, that's how it's going to be. But you could talk to me about it, you know. I'm not a stranger in this house. You could tell me what's got under your skin. Are you still worried about that chest of drawers? Because if you are, I know how you can take care of it."

Only one thing keeps Billy-Frank from walking away in disgust. It is her confident, sincere way of saying that, of *course,* she knows how he can get that chest of drawers shipped across the country.

"How?" he says.

"If you'd been listening, you'd know. I told you Mynette hitched out here with a couple of truckers. Real truckers, and they're from San Francisco. I bet they'd be glad to carry that old chest across the country. They're furniture movers, silly. They know how to take care of valuable junk like that. I don't know why you didn't think of a moving company before."

In fact, Billy-Frank thought of a moving company as he scrabbled for a safe, reliable carrier for his cocaine. The idea struck him then as too risky, too outlandish. He would have to explain why he was moving only one piece of furniture across country. Moreover, he would need an address for delivery, and Billy-Frank knew without asking that Rivera would never go for that. Rivera would not want any traces of the transfer. Still, Annie has put him on another track, and for the first time, he begins to see a way out. The truckers would have to know exactly what they are doing. He could not make the proposition to just anybody, but he knows, by vague reputation, that long-haul truckers tend to be loose and less than conventional. The right man just might like the money, hang the risks and take the job. Could be. He would have to talk to these guys tonight, try to get an inkling of their attitudes. He is not about to jump to conclusions, but Billy-Frank Freeman thinks he may have found his answer.

"I've been a creep," he says to her. "Let's go make up, just like you said."

Chapter 20

Lenny can feel it as they chuff haltingly through the streets of the city: this is a night of clashes, a night of conflict and of ugly moods, a night when words better left even unwhispered will be shouted loudly and defiantly. He can feel it in the cab, an unhealthy compound of vibrations. Pickett with his nerve endings frayed by fatigue and an afternoon of hassles on the job, silent with worry because he has not been able to raise an answer at his home in Antioch, snaps the gearshift lever forcefully, laying a heavy

foot on the accelerator as they follow the directions Mynette has taken over the telephone. This is not like Pickett, to
abuse his tractor so; Lenny suspects that it is because he has
badgered Pickett into coming along to dinner with Mynette's friend. As if that were not enough, Pickett is riding
a fierce wave of chemical energy. He popped two white
Specials after lunch, so he licks his lips mechanically and
clenches the wheel tightly as he searches for street signs.
Pickett is wound tight.

Mynette, too, is hyper. But this is naturally induced and
she shows it another way. Lenny tries to figure her as she
sits beside him in the passenger seat, leaning against the
engine compartment, intent on the sights that stream past
the windows as they roll on. She is giddy at her arrival in
Boston, but Lenny wonders whether the giddiness is not a
makeshift mask for her panic at being here, being on her
own, and seeing him leave so quickly after opening herself
to him so easily and so completely.

Nor is Lenny at his very best. He feels the two of them
tugging at him from opposite directions, each challenging
his allegiance, each silently but surely invoking obligations and precedence. It began when Mynette asked him to
dinner with her friend, Annie. Lenny wanted to go, but
Pickett did not. All well, except that Pickett, without actually saying so, clearly did not want to be alone this night.
From his eyes, Lenny could tell that Pickett was not about
to sleep tonight. The Specials have carried him through the
day's labors, but now they bring into painful focus his worries about home and the general depression that he has not
completely shaken since they left California. He wants Lenny
near for talk, for encouragement, perhaps even for compas-
sion. He could not say these things, of course, but he was
miffed when Lenny seemed ready to desert him for the
night. So Lenny has been on a tightrope, stepping lightly

over the physical and psychological dilemma of being around them both, telling Mynette that, yes, he does care and that he will be sorry to leave and assuring Pickett that, no, he is not so struck with this girl that he is going to neglect his old friends when one such friend might not be in such great shape. This, too, is unlike Pickett. His demands rarely exceed the minimal: driving relief, a fair share of the heavy work, and amiable companionship. So Lenny knows that Pickett is hurting, to ask this much of him.

And Lenny? Lenny is coping. He feels the strain, but stress has never been strange to him. He has sought it out and he thinks it has made him a better man, whether it came from diving deep into a corner at Ascot or cramming desperately for a midterm in his statistics course at UCLA. He enjoys the trucking life because it has always provided that feeling of living close to the edge. Maybe it is his familiarity with the manic, unstable sides of life that has given Lenny this nose for trouble, this sense that tips him off: This is going to be a wild one.

The close quarters of the cab do not make any of this easier. They all feel relieved when Pickett turns down the last street on Mynette's list of directions. Pickett coaxes the truck against the curb, the van blocking a fire hydrant. He has no alternative; legal parking space for tractor-trailers is just too scarce in a city. Pickett scribbles a note and slides it beneath a windshield wiper blade and they walk to the house. It is one of an unbroken series of row houses on that block; a dirty, brick-faced two-story in a neighborhood that, at its best, was never more than a lower-middle-class workingman's ghetto. Pickett follows Lenny and Mynette up the cast-iron steps to the door. He is not happy about this. He is not even trying to pretend.

Mynette rings the bell. She scrapes her right foot nervously as she waits and when the door opens, she puts out her arms to embrace the small, chestnut-haired girl inside the corridor. She breaks to make the introductions. This, she says, holding the right hand of the girl, is her best friend from Kansas, Annie Jenkins.

"Billy-Frank," says Annie, "is in the living room."

She leads them down the hall.

Lenny sees that Pickett will not like this a bit. Billy-Frank and Annie have set up housekeeping in a free-form, post-Haight fashion. They keep cats, and the cats are not housebroken; the powerful odor that assails the visitors is prima facie. Photos of rock stars, mostly has-beens and neverweres, Lenny notes, are tacked to the walls of the main hall. There is a full-color poster prominent among these. It shows a man with his long hair streaming in the wind as he sits astride a full-dress Harley chopper. He is wearing fringed buckskins, and the snarl on his face is even more belligerent than the middle finger he flashes to the world passing by.

"Half a peace sign," Lenny says in a whisper to Pickett as they pass the poster. Pickett does not even grunt.

They walk toward the living room, and another smell replaces the odor of the feline droppings. It is . . . almost grass, Lenny thinks. Incense. Then they turn the corner into the living room and Lenny hears the ringing strains of a sitar and the insistent thump of a drum. It is an Indian raga, and the sound comes from floor-to-ceiling speakers hooked to a massive bank of electronic equipment. Lenny thought Ravi Shankar and incense went out with Wesson Oil group-grope sessions. Then he remembers Mynette telling him that Billy-Frank is not so long off the farm himself. What Lenny sees around him now is a grotesque and dated parody of the hip ideal as it was seen, preserved and finally brought to life by these two Kansas farm kids. Lenny senses that Mynette too

139

is uneasy about the surroundings. He credits her with natural good sense; instinctively, she knows that things are badly out of kilter here.

Billy-Frank is sitting cross-legged on the bare hardwood floor when they enter the room. He opens his eyes slowly, smiles beatifically, and rises without haste to greet them.

He says hello to Mynette. He gives Pickett a pleased-ta-meetcha. He reaches for Lenny's right hand with his own and clasps it in the locked-thumb grasp.

"Far out," he says.

What a load of crap, Lenny thinks.

They sit around the floor to talk. Pickett squats into a vinyl-covered chunk of foam rubber contoured like a chair. They talk, and Lenny notices that Billy-Frank is full of questions about trucking. He is more than a politely curious outsider. He gets specific about inspection stations and bills of lading.

Over dinner, he asks: "You guys pretty much have freedom of the road, right? I mean, you've got a destination and you can take side trips and pick your own routes. You don't have cops pulling you over to search your cargo, do you? Nothing like that?"

"That," says Pickett, "is about the way it works in our end of the business."

"I figured so," Billy-Frank says. "That's about the way I thought it was."

Billy-Frank sends the girls into a bedroom after dinner.

"I think I've got business to talk with these guys," he says.

"Go ahead," Pickett says, "but I've got to tell you that we hire agents and salesmen to take care of the paperwork and estimates."

"I don't think there's an agent who can take care of me on this one," Billy-Frank says. "I think I'm better off dealing direct with you."

"I don't know why," Pickett says.

"The truth is, J.W., that what I want transported isn't exactly kosher, if you know what I mean."

"You mean it's illegal," Pickett says, not as a question.

"It is, yes. But before you say anything else, let me tell you that there's good money in it. Ten thousand dollars. Five on this end and five when you get it to the West Coast."

"I don't think I even want to know what it is, if you're talkin' that kind of money," Pickett says. "No way. I don't want any part of it. I don't know what you're talkin' to me for. I'm just a workin' stiff. I may cheat on my logs and pop a few pills, but I've never done nothin' seriously illegal, and I don't plan to start."

"Is it dope?" Lenny says.

"It sure is."

"Grass?"

"Uh-uh. Nothing that bulky. This is in a nice, small package. Nothing conspicuous. I've got a perfect cover."

"Ah, fuck you, asshole. I ain't touchin' it," Pickett says. "I ain't gettin' near it, if you're talkin' about drugs. Not this country boy. I don't want to get mixed up in it."

Billy-Frank smiles and refuses to be headed off.

"You don't have to get mixed up. Just pick up the stuff, bring it to the West Coast, and drop it off. Nothing suspicious. Nothing out of the way. I've got it in a piece of furniture. What could be more natural than that for you guys?"

"Interesting," Lenny says.

"Horseshit it is, Lenny. What are you talkin' about? Man, don't we have troubles enough as it is? No sir. I refuse to even talk about it any more. You're crazy for even considerin' it seriously."

"It's your truck," Lenny says. "It's your decision to make."

"And I just made it," Pickett says.

"I wish you'd think about it a little bit more," Billy-Frank says. Pickett glares at him, and Lenny senses that it is time to take Pickett away from this.

"Let's go outside for a few minutes," he says to Pickett.

"I'm ready to leave for good. You stay here tonight if that's what you want. I've had enough of this dump."

"Okay, Pickett. You wait for me a minute out there."

Pickett stalks out, his boots thumping heavily down the hall.

"What is this shit you want us to carry?" Lenny asks.

"Forget it. If your buddy there doesn't want the deal, then just forget I ever said anything, okay?"

"If that's how you want it."

"Sure. No hard feelings, huh?" Billy-Frank says. "You splitting? Let me lay a little something on you before you go."

He walks toward the kitchen and returns with three expertly rolled joints, thick and tight. Big bombers.

"Very good stuff," he tells Lenny. "Jamaican. *Ganja*. Dynamite shit."

"Thanks," Lenny says. He is ready to walk into the bedroom to say his good-bys to Mynette. He knows now that they will both be better off if they do not linger over an all-night farewell. He hears her laughter and he does not want to spoil her evening.

"Tell Mynette I said good-by," he says to Billy-Frank. "I really ought to be getting along. Tell her I'm sorry I had to leave so early."

Then he walks down the hall and opens the door. Pickett is sitting inside the cab already, waiting. Lenny shuts the door of the house behind him.

"Some nerve that fucker had," Pickett says when Lenny climbs inside. "Do I look like some dope pusher? I wouldn't do that, not for any kind of money."

"The money was awfully good."

142

"So what? I ain't haulin' dope. That's all. It's wrong. I wouldn't do business with that creep if he wanted me to haul feathers, so I definitely ain't haulin' dope. That stuff is bad. It fucks up kids, screws around with their minds. Look, Lenny, if I thought some dope pusher was tryin' to get within a hundred yards of my boy I'd bust his fuckin' head. You know that. But how can I justify that if I take a job carryin' the shit across the country? Answer me that."

"Pickett, don't be a hypocrite. You're flying higher than anyone else tonight. What do you think the cops would say if they looked in your little medicine chest?"

"I ain't proud of them pills, but that's different. What the fuck kind of a livin' would I make if I didn't pop pills? I wouldn't own this truck long, that's fuckin'-aye sure. Anyway, what are you doin? You was takin' that guy's side in there, and now you're givin' me a hard time. What you want to get out of this?"

"Ten thousand is a lot of money," Lenny says. "But I wouldn't want any of it. That'd be yours. I just think it would be a gas, something out of the ordinary. It's been a long time since the idea of doing something pumped me up the way I got when I heard that guy's proposition."

"You're jokin'. No, you're not jokin', you're serious, dead serious. Is that what it comes down to? Forget right and wrong, it just sounds like it would be fun to do, huh? Well, buddy-boy, that's real interestin' to hear. God damn, that's a kick in the stomach for me. I trusted you, I treated you right, and I figured I got to know you pretty good. Then you come up with somethin' ridiculous like that. Maybe I don't know you so good at all. I see everythin' pretty clear now. You're no different from that good-for-nothin' creep in there. You're both cut from the same cloth. You've got marshmallows for brains, but more important, you got a big blank space when it comes to right and wrong. The word is morality, buddy-boy, and you ain't got it. Oh, you're smart and you're educated and all, but somewhere along the way, somebody forgot to tell you that when you go through life, you've got to have some idea of what should be done and what shouldn't. And you should stick by what you believe and kick the rest in the tail. Shit. You got all the conviction of a jellyfish."

"Save it, Pickett. Save it and shove it. Or maybe somebody should write it on your tombstone. Something like, 'He died driving the straight and narrow road.' Because that's what you're going to do. You're going to keep driving a rig till you drop dead. You're never going to get out of it. You're going to be a stranger to your wife and kids but you'll keep on driving, because that's all you ever knew how to do.

"You had a chance up there tonight. With that kind of money, you might've salvaged all those dreams you talked to me about. But you didn't, and I know why. Not morality, none of that bullshit. Nope. You were just scared, plain scared. I saw it in your face when the guy started talking. You saw your big chance there and you were too scared to reach out and . . ."

The back of Pickett's open right hand flashes across the cab, an angry, impulsive, jerk.

Pickett is a strong man and his hands are quick. The movement is so rapid, so unexpected, that Lenny cannot begin to raise his hands in defense, and the thick, callused edge of Pickett's right palm cracks into the bridge of Lenny's nose.

Lenny feels the blow as a terrific impact, followed by a searing pain that burns white in his skull. He feels Pickett grabbing him by the shirt, but there is no anger in his grasp this time. Then it comes: thick, dark and warm. Lenny feels the blood flowing down his face from his left nostril. But something is disconnected. He cannot make his arms raise to halt the bleeding.

"Come on," Pickett says. "Shit, I'm sorry, Lenny. I've got a handkerchief. Here, take it."

The connection is restored. Lenny reaches for the cloth, seeing it on the very periphery of his vision as he rests with his head thrust back to slow the streaming fountain.

"You okay?" Pickett says.

Lenny nods carefully. Lenny has always bled easily from this nostril and past experience tells him that this one will be memorable. He knows that there is nothing to be done except to relax, hold a rag to his nose and keep his head back. He feels the blood trickle down his throat. A clot begins to thicken and the trickle becomes a drip. The coagulated blood is forming a wet streamer down his throat. Tentatively, he pulls the bloody handkerchief from his nose. No drip. He straightens his head.

"Okay?" Pickett says.

"Okay."

"I'm sorry, Lenny," Pickett says.

Lenny shakes his head, dismisses that with a wave of his left hand.

"I mean it," Pickett says. "I just lost my head, some of the things you said. You really shouldn't have said some of that stuff. Even if it is true. I guess we both did a lot of flappin' in the breeze."

"I guess. I'm sorry, too, Pickett."

"Yeah. Good enough, then. Your shirt's all bloody. Hold on, I'll get you another one. Sit still. Unbutton that one. Take it off easy. Here, this one's dirty, but it'll do."

Pickett is stuffing the bloody shirt into Lenny's gym bag when he sees the hand-rolled cigarettes in one pocket.

"Don't tell me. You get this from that asshole?"

145

"Yeah. I know you don't want to have it around. I'll shit-can it."

"No, no, that's okay," Pickett says. "I'll take care of it. You just sit back, old buddy. What do you say to a steak sandwich? That vegetarian crap tonight just didn't do the trick for me. Okay? You can wash up in the restaurant and I'll call home. It's eight back there now, and I know they've got to be home."

Lenny nods. His face hurts and he does not want to speak. He knew this was going to turn into a miserable night. He knew it all along.

Chapter 21

"Yes, operator, I accept."

"Hello, Pickett," she says.

"Finally got you," he says. "Where you been all day?"

"I haven't been home. Pickett, I got some bad news. You ready? John William got himself hurt real bad yesterday afternoon. Real bad, God, it was bad. I been to the hospital with him ever since. Don't get excited. He'll be okay. But it was bad there for a while. It was just horrible."

That is how Pickett gets the news, standing outside the men's room of a chophouse in Boston, with diners passing by, brushing past him, uncaring.

Pickett listens to the details. A young bus boy hurrying to the kitchen notices him, watches this broad-shouldered old dude dressed like a Country & Western singer slump visibly

146

against the wall, his shoulders sagging, his legs looking like they cannot support him.

"No," Pickett says. "No. All that goin' on and I knew nothin' about it. He could've been dead and I would never have known. You should've called the dispatcher or somethin'."

"For a while, I was just too wound up to think like that," she says. "Then I figured there was no use in telling you until we knew one way or the other. Pickett, there's nothing you can do three thousand miles away."

"I should've been there," he says. "My boy needed me. You needed me."

"We did all right," she says. "We did okay, me and John William. He understands. He knows why you wasn't there. When he woke up this morning, he never even asked. He just wanted to know if I'd told you yet. I told him I had and that you said you'd be here as soon as you could."

"I will," he says. "I'll catch a plane in the mornin'. You can pick me up at the airport and I'll be at the hospital by tomorrow afternoon. You tell him that tomorrow mornin'."

"Pickett," she says, "I don't want you to do that. He's okay and he can only get better. The doctor says he needs rest. He'll be in the hospital a long time. So you've got plenty of chance to go visit him. He'd be better off if you didn't show up, anyway. You'd just get him all excited.

"I'm hanging on okay, too. I got neighbors over here, fixing me dinner and helping me out. The worst is over. You don't have to fly, but I hope you can get back here in the truck soon as you can."

"I'll do that," he says. "I'll start now. I'll start right away. I guess they won't let me call his room, huh? Okay, you just tell him I'm comin'. You tell him his daddy's comin', you hear?"

He is shaken, his face drained of blood, when he returns to the table.

"Pickett? You okay? Did you get your call through?"

Pickett is silent. He breathes shallowly, unevenly. He reaches for the coffee in front of him and the cup clatters as he lifts it from the saucer.

"Lenny," he says, "I'm gettin' out. I come to the end of the line. I don't care what it costs me, I've hauled my last load. John William damn near died yesterday. They had to bring in a brain surgeon from Stanford to save his life. Ain't that a bitch? And what am I doin'? I'm haulin' people's furniture across the country while my boy lays on the operatin' table. This has been comin' on me for a long time. Tonight, just right now, I made up my mind. I'm finished with truckin'. It ain't gettin' any more of me."

"I understand."

"Funny. I always thought you'd be the one to run out on this job. Never figured it could be the other way around. Sorry, kid."

"You said it to me an hour ago, Pickett. A man has to do what he feels is right. I can't argue with that."

Lenny pauses to choose his words. This is important.

"There's just one thing. If you're getting out of trucking, it'll take money to get into something else," he says. "At least, that's if you're planning to go to work for yourself. I can't see you taking orders from some foreman. You know your affairs, but you've got to consider doctor bills and living expenses. You probably won't have any money coming in for a while. I know we went over this before, but . . ."

"I know," Pickett said. "It came to my mind pretty quick, too. I sure won't like to do it. You sure as hell know how I feel about that crap. And that Billy-Frank, he makes my skin shrivel. I don't want to help the guy. I'd rather grab him by his long hair and beat his head into the wall. But you're right. We've got little enough saved as it is, Doris and me. With that shitty Mercury hospitalization, the hospital would eat up that little bit before I get a chance to even think about drawin' a pay check. You're right about somethin' else, too. I wouldn't last a day in a normal job. I'd blow up, and I can't afford to do that, not at my age. I don't know what else I can do, but I've got to get out of this damn business. So I guess that's that. I hate to say it. It makes me sick to think about it, but I guess we're goin' to haul Billy-Frank Freeman's dope for him. He says we're gettin' ten. How much do you want?"

"I told you before. This one's for you, Pickett. You and John William. You keep the money. It's your truck, right?"

Chapter 22

"Well, hot damn. Look who's here. Damn if it ain't the truckers, come to pay Billy-Frank another visit. Social or business? Don't tell me. Let's see, it's after midnight. Considering my line of work, it's time for business. Am I wrong?"

"We want to talk to you," Lenny says. Wordlessly, they have decided that this is the way they will do it, he and Pickett, for Pickett is filled with hatred of the job, of Billy-Frank, and mostly of himself. Lenny can think and act with some detachment, so he will talk to Billy-Frank.

"Come on in for a minute," Billy-Frank says. "If we've got serious talking to do, I want to get my coat and my car keys. We'll talk in my car. I don't want anybody listening in."

They walk inside, and Lenny sees Mynette standing at

the foot of the stairs. She is wearing a football jersey and nothing more that Lenny can see. Her hair is tousled; it hangs free down to her shoulders. For the first time, Lenny sees her legs in the light, and he sees that they are excruciatingly lovely. As she stands, graceful and shy as a half-tame doe, she seems to Lenny the personification of every man's fantasy of the way a woman should look when she rises from sleep.

"I was in bed," she says softly, "when I heard your truck outside. Maybe I shouldn't have come down, but I did. Hello, Lenny."

"Hi," he says. He takes a step forward, then two. She smiles. She does not retreat. This doe will not approach, but she is not backing away as he comes closer. He faces her now, just a foot away, and he feels his pulse pounding against his head. He wants her even more now than he did last night in Erie.

"I wasn't running away," he says to her. "You just seemed to be having such a good time here, I didn't want to spoil it by saying good-by. You understand?"

"Sure," she says. "But why did you come back?"

"We've got business with Billy-Frank."

She does not understand, but she does not question him. She looks at him—Lenny sees that her irises are a soft hazel in this light—and she smiles again, a slight, wistful smile. And Lenny, who has been guilty not only about deserting her, but also about leaving her in the house of this viper, has decided he must take steps.

"Mynette," he says, "I don't want you to stay here tonight. I can't tell you why right now, but we can talk later. Get your stuff. Put some clothes on, fast as you can, and meet me outside. Please do what I say."

"Lenny," she says, "I've got a room upstairs . . ."

"I can't stay here tonight and I don't want you here, either. I'll explain it to you later, but I don't have time now."

Mynette looks at him, frowns, but whispers "Okay" as Billy-Frank walks back into the hall.

"Ready, boys? My car's parked outside. We'll talk there."

"We're ready," Lenny says. He steps toward the door, then turns to where Mynette stands, uncertain, on the stairs.

"I want you to be there," he says.

Billy-Frank's silver Jaguar is parked across the street. They are silent as they cross over to it. They squeeze into the convertible, Pickett folding himself into the tiny back seat, nothing more than an upholstered ledge. Lenny sits beside Billy-Frank in the front.

"I presume you guys are ready to do the job. You are ready, aren't you?"

"We're ready," Lenny says. "We've got some questions to ask, first. We don't want to just carry a load of dope right out in plain sight. You got some way of hiding it?"

"You think I'm dumb? I've been hiding it all along in an old chest of drawers. I own an antique store in Cambridge. It's a perfect cover. You guys can carry the chest out into the truck and nobody would ever know the difference. I don't care who's watching or how smart they are."

Pickett speaks for the first time: "Watchin'? Who's goin' to be watchin'? You in hot water with this?"

"No, no, man, nothing like that. But in this business, you've got to be prepared for everything. You have to presume that you're being watched. If you're that careful, you stay out of trouble. Like, I never keep any shit in this car. Never let any dope near it. I've known a half-dozen guys, personally, who got sent up because they were carrying dope around in their cars. Nobody knew about the shit, but one day, they were a little stoned, or maybe they were just careless, and they did something dumb. All you've got to do is make an illegal left turn. Whoops. The cop sees you've got long hair, so he pulls you out of the car and starts looking around. All of a sudden, this routine traffic ticket has turned into a three-to-ten. So, like, you can't be too careful. Same with home. I keep a little grass around for social purposes, but that's it. Nothing I can't flush down the john in about fifteen seconds. It doesn't pay."

"Okay," Lenny says, "the chest of drawers sounds good. What about the rest? Who are we supposed to see and where are we supposed to bring this stuff?"

"All I've got for you right now is a phone number in San Francisco. You call them when you're a day away and they'll fill you in. I ain't telling you that number unless you say we got a deal. I ain't saying any more unless I know we're doing business and you're in tight with me."

Lenny looks back at Pickett, and Pickett nods his head once.

"You've got a deal," Lenny says. "Now talk."

"All right, all right. Ten minutes after nine tomorrow, that's just after we open, you show up at the store. I'll give you the address tonight. I've got a man there. He knows what's up. I'll call him tonight, tell him to expect you. He knows the chest and he has the five grand. You'll get 'em both and you'll be out of there in two, three minutes. He'll also give you the phone number on the Coast. That's it. It's out of my hands then. You make your arrangements when you call the man in Frisco. He'll tell you where to be and when. He'll have the other five big ones when you make the transfer. Nice, clean, and simple. You're not risking any more than a strained back when you try to pick up that big chest. It's a heavy motherfucker. Solid oak. Really built."

"What are we hauling?" Lenny says.

"It doesn't matter. That shouldn't bother you, just so long as you know it'll fit into a chest of drawers. Far as you're

152

concerned, it's just another load. 'Course, it is sort of special. I know there's a word you guys use. You know, when you're carrying some illegal cargo that has to get through right away, something out of the ordinary? What do you guys call that?"

"A hot load," Pickett says.

"Right," Billy-Frank says, slapping his knee. "I knew that was it. A hot load. Well, boys, I guess that's about the word for what you're picking up tomorrow. A real hot load."

Billy-Frank laughs at that. He feels fine now, just fine. He congratulates himself for handling this problem so coolly. Rivera will like this, he thinks. Rivera will have to sit back and take another look at him. Yes, Billy-Frank will definitely command some respect now from Rivera after coming up with this magnificent ploy.

"That about covers it," he says. "Here's my card, with the address for the antique shop. It's easy to find, right off Prospect. Make it ten minutes, maybe a quarter after nine. Store won't get crowded until after ten. And thanks, boys, thanks a lot."

Billy-Frank lopes back across the street and up the stairs to his house, feeling the burden of his predicament disappear.

The two truckers wait inside the cab, talking.

"I asked Mynette to come back with us. We'll find a room somewhere, until the morning. That okay with you, Pickett?"

"Sure, kid, I understand. She's a good girl. She shouldn't be mixed up in all of this. Christ, I hope I'm doin' the right thing. This goes against everythin' I've always known to be right or wrong, but I know just the same that it's wrong for me to leave my family any more."

"I'm not a moralist, Pickett. But it does seem as though one good can get in the way of the other. A man just has to decide which is more important. I know we'd better do this right. I've been running it over in my mind, trying to get the details straight. It seems easy enough, but if you overlook one little thing, you could be up shit creek.

"Hey, I almost forgot. You better get rid of that grass you took out of my pocket. We don't need that complicating things."

"I already got rid of it," Pickett says. "I put it under the seat of that sports car."

"What the hell for?"

"He started talkin' about how careful he was to keep any kind of dope out of the car. I don't know. I just reached into my pocket, pulled out them hand-rolleds and stuck 'em under his seat, the driver's seat. He never saw me. He was too busy talkin' to you.

"I can't say why, exactly, 'cept that I feel sick about what I'm doin'. I feel like I'm helpin' that creep out of a real jam. He must have been in bad shape to hire us to do somethin' like this. I don't want to help him out. I don't know if there's some way I can use that grass to screw him, but if there is, I'll do it. I'd just feel better about everythin' if I did."

"Pickett, you're amazing."

"Thanks, buddy-boy. You better open up the door. Here comes your honey and that old suitcase of hers. She looked awful nice tonight. There's just one thing I want to get straight. You sure you don't want any of this money we're goin' to be gettin'?"

"Not for me. But I've been thinking about Mynette. If you could let me have about five hundred for her, just something to help her get started so she doesn't have to take anything from Billy-Frank, I'd appreciate that."

"It's yours. I've got that much with me already. I'll give it to you in the mornin'. Hey, you better open the door. She's goin' to freeze out there."

Mynette hands up her valise, then climbs up. She bangs

154

the door shut and Pickett turns the key to cough the engine alive again.

"Here I am," she says, "although I'm not sure why."

"I'll tell you all you need to know," Lenny says. "We've got a lot of talking to do tonight."

Chapter 23

Strange, Lenny thinks. Mynette does not seem surprised to hear that her best friend's lover deals dope. She is naïve and untrained in many ways, Lenny thinks, but she is sensitive to what happens around her and she is sharp, quick, empathetic. She is nobody's dummy.

"I don't know what I'm going to do now," she says. "I don't have any place to stay. I don't have any leads on a job and I don't have any money. Pretty bad, huh?"

No, Lenny says, he wants to help her out. He tells her that he has some spare cash, that he wants her to take it to start her new life.

"No way," she says. "I haven't asked for anything from you and I don't want anything."

She is sitting in their bed in a motel room. Real beds are an indulgence for Pickett and Lenny, but they splurge because they expect to drive non-stop back to California beginning in the morning. This will be their last real sleep for more than two days.

"I won't take it," she says. She crosses her arms over her chest. "That wouldn't be right. I know that much."

"Why? Because you're a girl and we made love last night?

Because we might do it again tonight, if we ever stop talking? That has nothing to do with it. Would you be so bullheaded if you were a man, just a regular friend of mine, and I wanted to help you out? Don't you think it's possible that I just care about you and I might like to see you make out okay? Did you ever consider that?"

"Maybe," she says. "But you've only known me two days. Do you give money away to all your casual friends like this?"

Lenny is kneeling at the other end of the bed, sitting on his heels. He leans over to her and takes her hands.

"No," he said, "but you're not just a casual friend. I can't totally explain the way I feel, except to say that when I was your age, I felt a lot of the same things that brought you out here. The difference was that I never stopped to understand them and I never got brave enough to do what you did. I just languished. I stayed out of the Army by going to school, but those years couldn't have been wasted any worse if I'd spent them in the service, doing nothing but peeling potatoes and standing at attention.

"But you're luckier. You're just barely old enough to leave home legally and here you are in a strange city, two thousand miles from your home, looking to start your life all over again. I admire that. I admire you. I'd like to help you. So, one day, you'll be a politician, maybe. Or a great actress or a song writer. And I'll be able to say that my five hundred dollars helped give you a start when you needed one."

"I still don't think I can take it," she says.

"Okay, how about a loan? That will give me an excuse to look you up every time I come to Boston. So that I can check on my investment, you understand."

She considers this, lips pursed.

"Maybe," she says "under those conditions . . ."

Their love-making this time is, by turns, fierce and gentle, sudden and lingering, familiar and strange. Her range of passion astonishes Lenny. It inspires him, too, and she draws from him things he never knew he had to give. She is a novice at this, but she brings to their coupling a rare gift of abandon. She has the unabashed sensuality of a mature woman and the eager, tender touch of a young girl who does not love in small ways. The glow lingers in them after they have broken apart, after they lie staring into the darkness above them.

She is silhouetted against the moonlight that seeps around the window shades. Her face in profile is without a single harsh line, yet he knows there is firmness and true character there. Her breasts are two lush hillocks of darkness outlined by thin, sharp, coronas of light. Her waistline is trim. Yet, even as she lies supine, there is a certain fecund slope at her abdomen, from hip to hip.

He reaches across the expanse between them, finds her right hand, and holds it.

"That was the way it's supposed to be, isn't it?" she says without looking at him.

"That's what I thought last time," he says. Her cheeks rise when he says that; he knows she is smiling again.

Reluctantly, they gather the blankets around them and they sleep.

Pickett's knuckles on the door awaken them.

"Past eight," he says. "We've got some movin' to do."

Lenny thrashes out of bed, stumbles to the bathroom, picks through the clothes on the floor to find his own. She is awake. She watches him without blinking as he pulls on his pants, buttons his shirt, bends at the waist to stretch his socks over his feet and finally jams them into his scuffed, Western-style boots.

"I'm not running out on you," he says. "You don't have to get up. I want you to know that if I didn't have this obligation, well, I could stay here with you for a long time, that's all."

"Don't say that," she says. "You love what you do. Don't let me make it a prison for you, like it is for your friend."

He nods. He tells her that he must see Pickett for a minute, that he will be back to say good-by.

Pickett is waiting a respectful distance from the door with the five hundred already counted and waiting in his hand.

"Here we go," he says. "We ain't got a whole lot of time."

Lenny returns to the room. She is sitting with her back against a pillow, leaning against the wall.

"Leave the money on the dresser," she says. "Write down you address, too. Then kiss me, okay?"

Pickett is in the cab, waiting, when Lenny closes the motel door behind him and walks into the sunlight of this New England autumn morning. A good day for loving, he thinks. A bad one for going back on the road. But Pickett gets him thinking like a trucker when he turns the ignition, teases the accelerator to bring the engine around, and then asks Lenny to unfold the Greater Boston street map for directions.

Lenny thumbs through their atlas.

"All the way down Mass Avenue," he says. "Across the bridge to Prospect. Right on Prospect. The cross street isn't listed here."

"We'll find it," Pickett says.

Traffic is light. They find the street. It is lined with trees, now stark and bare. They double-park the truck. Lenny feels the paranoia of his doping days tighten in his chest. He decides to wear Pickett's cap, part of his Mercury uniform. He tucks his hair under the hat. Straighter the better, he thinks.

They walk inside the store, and a thin black man with his hair coaxed into a bulbous Afro steps from behind a desk.

"You want the chest, right?" he says. "Here. In back."

"The money first," Pickett says. Pickett has a talent for firmness. When he gets serious, the tone in his voice and the stance of his body suggest that this is a man who cannot be swayed.

"It's in the cashbox," the clerk says. He walks back behind the desk, pulls a small, nickel-plated key from his pocket, and uses it to open the box. He takes a legal-sized business manila envelope from the box and hands it to Pickett. It is not as bulky as Pickett has expected.

"It's in hundreds," the clerk says. "Don't count it out here, though, man. At least wait till you get a block or two away. Be cool."

"Don't worry about me," Pickett says. His voice does not begin to quiver and betray him.

"I've got a dolly here," the clerk says. "You'll need it. This bitch is heavy."

The chest is more than heavy. It sits in a storeroom behind the shop. A thin layer of dust coats its finish. It is the color of strong German beer in a clear glass. The stubby legs are carved flawlessly into a thick, ample shape that resembles a globule of honey lapping from a jar on a frigid morning. It is substantial, ponderous, conservative. It is the last place anyone would expect to find twenty pounds of mind-numbing contraband. But Lenny knows it is there, sequestered somewhere in the three roomy drawers.

Lenny walks outside to open the side door of the van and fit the metal ramp into place.

"No dolly," Pickett is telling the clerk when Lenny returns. "No hand trucks, either. That's too much trouble. We'll just pick it up and walk it outside. Clear an aisle for us. Get that umbrella stand out of the way. Shove that chair off to the side, too."

"I'll help," the clerk says.

"We're better working alone," Pickett says. Together, he

and Lenny count to three. They lift, strain, then hold the thing in position at knee level.

"Easy," Pickett says, talking Lenny out because Lenny is backing out toward the door, stepping blindly. Sweat beads up on Lenny's head. He arches his back to take some of the strain off his arms. And that is how they do it, one short step after another, Pickett heaving but keeping his balance as they walk the chest up the ramp and the fullness of the load shifts down toward him. They let the thing down in the back recesses of the van and they shove the chest back into a corner. They bind it with a thick strap which they secure to one wall of the van. In motions that are automatic by now, Lenny folds the ramp back into the van and locks the door while Pickett climbs into the cab and turns the diesel over.

Without a word, Pickett finds a gear and when Lenny drops into his seat, they roll away from the store, perhaps more conscious than they have ever been of the load they drag behind them.

Chapter 24

Detective Sergeant Salvatore Zanalotti of the Boston Police Department has no way of knowing, of course, that the source of his immediate troubles is none other than Miss Wilhelmina Barrett, the white-haired lady who holds down the midnight-to-eight shift on the PBX board of one of Boston's less distinguished hotels. Even if Detective Sergeant Zanalotti knew, he probably would not be able to pacify his wife, who knows only that Detective Sergeant Zanalotti is ninety minutes late coming home on the morning when they and their three children are supposed to pile into the sergeant's 1971 Chevrolet station wagon to visit the sergeant's mother-in-law in Barnstable.

"Sal," she bleats at him into the telephone, "we get how many Sundays off? Three, maybe four a year. I know you don't work a normal job with normal hours like most men. But when you do get lucky enough to know you'll be off all day Sunday, can't you at least get home on time so we can get away for a day? Do you realize what the traffic is going to be like going down to the Cape? Do I need to tell you, of all people? I don't understand, Sal, I really don't. Maybe I'm dumb. Maybe I'm dense. So tell me, Sal, tell me how I am going to tell our three lovely children that their father, whom they barely recognize, is going to be too busy again today to take them to the Cape to visit their grandmother? Tell me, Sal, how am I supposed to break that news to them?"

Detective Sergeant Zanalotti sighs and breaks off a piece of stale prune Danish that is left over from yesterday's breakfast. He curses Special Agent Alfred J. Wheeler of the Drug Enforcement Administration, New England division. He curses this woe-begotten assignment. He curses the stale prune Danish. And, if he only knew, he would fire off a couple of special zingers toward Miss Wilhelmina Barrett. While he is at it, Detective Sergeant Zanalotti curses his own lack of judgment in marrying an Irish girl. Of course, he keeps that cursing to himself.

Detective Sergeant Zanalotti has been spending twelve hours a day for the last ten days in this cramped third-floor garret of a rooming house in Cambridge. He has been maintaining surveillance on—that is to say, he has been watching—the antique shop across the street from the rooming house. Detective Sergeant Zanalotti has the boring shift, 7 P.M. to 7 A.M., during the store's off hours. He has been assigned to watch the front door of the antique shop. If anyone had tried to open the store during off hours and remove any part of its contents, Detective Sergeant Zanalotti would have been right on the hot line to headquarters. No one has been near the store during Detective Sergeant Zanalotti's ten days on the job. Naturally, he has gotten the shit end of the stick in this "co-operative surveillance." But from seven in the morning until Detective Sergeant Zanalotti relieves him at 7 P.M., Special Agent Wheeler holds forth in the third-floor garret of the rooming house. Now, that is different. Special Agent Wheeler has a nifty pair of Bushnell binoculars and a motorized Nikon camera with a 1,000-millimeter telephoto lens. The Nikon's servo motor allows Special Agent Wheeler to fire off as many as five frames per second. It is a hell of a gadget. Special Agent Wheeler trains the binoculars on everyone who enters the shop. He is familiar with most of the known drug dealers in the Boston area, and if a suspicious face passes through the doors of that shop, a face that strikes an off-key chord in the cataloguelike brain of Special Agent Wheeler . . . zip, zip, zip, that face is recorded on the roll of Tri-X film in the magazine of the Nikon, the telephoto lens catching every mole, every dimple. Each day, Special Agent Wheeler detaches the magazine from the Nikon and leaves it at the Department of Justice photo lab. In such a way, the Drug Enforcement Administration and the Boston Police Department hope to get a line on what happens to the twenty pounds of cocaine which, they are sure, now reposes in Billy-Frank Freeman's antique shop.

This co-operative stakeout worked well enough until Miss Wilhelmina Barrett intervened. Last night, Special Agent

Wheeler got lucky with the new redhead in the Department of Justice steno pool. Special Agent Wheeler and the redhead both have roommate complications. They decided to retire about midnight to the second-rate hotel where Miss Wilhelmina Barrett holds down the midnight-to-eight shift. Wilhelmina, to fill the quiet hours at the switchboard, has over the years become addicted to late-night movies on television. Last night, she was watching Jimmy Cagney blast it out with the cops from atop a gasoline tank in the climax of *White Heat* when Special Agent Wheeler phoned down to leave a six o'clock wake-up call. That, he had decided, would give him plenty of time to shower, dress, and pick up his favorite breakfast of prune Danish and hot tea before he relieved Detective Sergeant Zanalotti. Wilhelmina listened to Special Agent Wheeler and even repeated it back to him: "Mister Wheeler, Room Three-Two-Seven, at 6 A.M." She repeated it but she did not write on her list of wake-ups because she could not bear to take her eyes from the TV screen during the big shoot-out scene. And when that gasoline storage tank blew all to hell with Jimmy Cagney on top, calling for his mother, it was more than Wilhelmina could stand. She forgot about Special Agent Wheeler's six o'clock wake-up call.

That is the reason Special Agent Wheeler is still asleep in bed beside the redhead from the Justice Department steno pool. Which, in turn, is why Detective Sergeant Zanalotti is still on the job in the illegal third-floor garret across the street from the antique store. That, sequentially, is what has piqued the wrath of Mrs. Kathleen Zanalotti to the point where she is scolding her husband over the pay phone in the hall outside the illegal third-floor garret. And that, finally, is how the two men in their movers' uniforms were able to drive their Mack truck up to the store, double-park, carry out their huge oak chest of drawers, and drive away again without ever having been detected.

Not that the distraction made a lot of difference.

Detective Sergeant Zanalotti doesn't know how to work a Nikon, anyway.

Chapter 25

Back on the road and balling down the highway. Westward through Holyoke, through Albany. Westward past Syracuse, past Rochester and Buffalo. They speak but little. Each nurses his private ache of the soul and they respect that in one another. They have no stomach for small talk, not today, so the hours dissolve and the mile markers approach and recede in a seemingly infinite procession.

This evening, they drive straight into the sunset. Lenny likes that. The colors seem brighter and less fleeting this way, spread out in front of the truck. The windshield becomes a movie screen for the spectacular show. The sun is a shimmering wet orange orb with a diameter that widens as it slips behind the horizon. A low, fleecy flocking of clouds in the distance catches that vivid tint, but higher in the sky, almost above the truck, scattered wisps of cirrus are tinged, faintly, in a baby-skin pink. Behind these are darkness. Then the pink fades, the azure sky darkens and the line between night and light dissolves. White lights break out, pinpricks and dots and splotches, in the homes beside the road. That is when Lenny feels alone, when they fly past these acres of homes full of people who neither know nor care about what is happening on that broad concrete strip that cuts through their community.

"Pickett," he says, when they are alone in the darkness, "is this really going to be your last run?"

"I said so, and I ain't changin' my mind. I don't know if Mercury's goin' to hassle me or not, but I don't care. They can't make me drive. They'd have to put a gun to my head first."

"I feel strange," Lenny says, "knowing that this is it for the two of us. I was lucky with you. You respected me and we fit in pretty good together. I don't know if I'm going to find another arrangement like this one soon."

"You thinkin' of quittin' the business?"

"I haven't thought about it at all. My mind has been on Mynette back there, but it just came to me a few minutes ago. I was thinking of you, wondering how you must feel about giving it up. Then I realized that I was going to have to hunt up another situation. I don't know if I could adjust to another driver. He might not think of me the way you do. Maybe it would be better if I looked into another line of work. Maybe it's time for me to go back and get my master's."

"That's a laugh. I can't see it, Lenny. Not that you ain't got the smarts. I just can't imagine you sittin' in a classroom, takin' notes, writin' papers, readin' the same damn books day after day. Not you, buddy-boy. Maybe before, but not now. You've got too much of the wanderer in you."

"Maybe you're right. I do enjoy it. I really do."

"Damn right you do. I can see it myself. I loved it myself, once. I know."

"How do you feel, Pickett? I mean, knowing that when you get to California you're going to park the rig and climb down and maybe never drive a diesel truck again? Doesn't that bother you?"

"It scares the piss out of me. I don't know nothin' else. I've never done nothin' else. Hell, I'm even worried about what kind of a father I'll be when I'm home every night of the week. I've never been more than a part-time husband and a part-time father. Maybe Doris won't be able to stand me seven days a week. I don't know. I don't know much at all, except that I've got to get out of this business.

"It used to be different. I appreciated the business. I knew what I was, just a dumb Okie without a future. I was proud as hell when I became a truck driver. I figured this was about the finest, noblest profession that I could ever have hoped to spend my life at. It wouldn't be right to say that I wish I'd never done it. That would be denyin' too many good times and good people. And, anyways, I can't even begin to say what else I would've done if I hadn't bought that truck. I'd probably still be workin' on a derrick crew. It was good to me for a long while, but now it's gone sour. Maybe I should say that I knew all along that it was goin' to turn on me, but I stayed with it anyway and tried to hold it off as long as I could.

"It's like bein' a young man and fallin' in love with a real sharp-lookin' girl. You're blind to everythin' but her good points. She's a beautiful broad and she's a load of laughs and she's great in the sack. That's all you want to know. You're in love. Maybe you hear stories about her, stuff that ain't so appealin'. Maybe, somewhere in the corner of your mind, you know that she's no good, that she's peddlin' her ass on the side when she ain't with you. But you don't pay any attention to that because you think you're happy about the way things are and you don't want to upset the bed of roses. But one day, you can't ignore it any more. You face up to it and you tell yourself that the girl is a whore, no two ways about it. And not only that, but it's been a few years now and the sharp young tomato has wilted a little bit. In fact, she's dumpy and ugly and she drinks too much.

"There's two things you can do then. You can swallow your pride and go on living with the old whore because, after all, you're still in love with her. Or you can be a man and kick the old whore out of bed and start all over again. It ain't easy, but you do it. That's what I'm doin' now. It hurts like hell, some ways. I'm puttin' a lot on the line, buddy-boy. 'Cause there's one thing I know. Even old whores got pride. You kick her out of bed, chances are she ain't comin' back."

"You've got something, though, that nobody can take away from you," Lenny says. "You've been everywhere, you've done everything there is to do in trucking. Nobody can cheat you out of that kind of experience. You've earned it, Pickett. You've lived it."

"Just about," Pickett says. "Not that it matters any more. Two days from now, when I get rid of this load, I'll be just normal people. Saturday afternoons, I'll put the wife and the kids in the car and go for a drive, just like the rest of the workin' stiffs in their four-wheelers.

"And you know what? I'll probably shake my fist on the hills and yell at those dirty, slow trucks that take up all the road. Could be. I wouldn't put it past me."

They both laugh over that, but Lenny knows Pickett faces difficult days as he tries to adjust to life outside the truck. Then they are quiet again, and Pickett drives on, methodically rolling back the miles, pensive and subdued. They are nearing Cleveland when Pickett dips into the bottle of pills. Then Lenny knows who is going to be driving all night. He decides he will sleep. He is in the bunk, his eyes closed, when Pickett talks back to him.

"Lenny," he says, "what do you think's in that chest back there?"

167

"Hard to say. Can't be pills or grass. It wouldn't be worth the trouble and the money they're paying us. Could be heroin, I guess. But I hear that stuff is mob all the way. For a free-lancer like Billy-Frank, my guess would be cocaine. It's a big deal on the Coast. If you got a decent amount of that stuff together, it would definitely be worth paying somebody ten thousand bucks to haul it across the country."

"How much would you say, then? How much is a lot of it?"

"It's expensive, expensive as hell. Down in L.A., they might get seventy, seventy-five dollars for a gram, and that's not pure coke. There's about four hundred and fifty grams to the pound and by the time they get finished cutting it, they probably sell seven hundred grams on the street for every pound of pure coke. They can do that if it's good stuff, and you'd never notice the difference. So, add it up. That's forty or fifty thousand dollars per pound once you get it out on the street. We don't have to be haulin' too many pounds to make our ten thousand bucks worth the job."

"But what I'm tryin' to get at, Lenny, is how much a stiff like Billy-Frank is likely to have together in one place."

"Him? He strikes me as a small-time operator. Two pounds, I'd say. Three. That's quite a bit of coke. One thing bothers me, though. I can't figure why he'd be shipping it wholesale across the country. It seems to me that he'd make a lot more money just putting it on the street in Boston. Coke is hot stuff there, too. Unless, I don't know, he had more than he could handle, more than he wanted sitting around."

"Hard to believe, Lenny. Hard to believe that with what I'm carrying back there, some package stuck in the corner of my van, I could walk in and buy a small fleet of trucks, cash.

168

I could buy three new Petes and the trailers to go with 'em with what I've got in my van right now."

"That's right," Lenny says. "But don't get any ideas. You need six or eight dealers that you could trust to get rid of just a pound of that stuff in any reasonable time. It's like anything else, you need the contacts and the expertise. Besides, I've got a feeling that whoever that shipment is headed to, he's probably very serious about his business. I'm sure he'd be terribly disturbed to see you hijack his shipment right out of your own truck."

"Yeah. Wouldn't that be something, to see some big dope dealer, maybe Mafia, call up the Interstate Commerce Commission to complain about the lousy service he got from Mercury Movers? Can you imagine the number of rules and regulations we're breakin' with this load? I mean, besides the ones we always bend a little bit. If the ICC only knew."

"That's right," Lenny says. "Let's see, we never weighed Billy-Frank's shipment, right? That's a violation right there. We never gave him a copy of the manifest, either. That's another violation. Hell, we never even made up a manifest. That's another violation."

Pickett laughs over the sound of the engine. Picking apart the morass of regulations imposed by sundry bureaucrats has always been one of their favorite amusements.

"Hand me up that copy of the code book beside the seat there, Pickett. Switch on the light, so I can see."

Lenny leans out from behind the curtains, thumbs through the thick book and begins shouting, gesticulating, shaking his index finger, Bible-thumping style. Pickett looks in the mirror and, despite himself, begins to giggle.

"Here it is," Lenny says. "Right here in black and white. Part Ten-fifty-two. 'Handling of C.O.D. Shipments.' That's what we're talking about now, right, half C.O.D.? 'Every common carrier . . . shall maintain a record of all C.O.D. shipments received for delivery in such a manner and form as will plainly and readily show . . .' Shit, that's a violation. I don't have to read any more. *Clear* violation. There's more. Part One-fifty-three-point-one. 'Filing of contracts for transportation of property.' *Violation!* Part Ten-fifty-six-point-two. 'Establishment of rates stated in amounts per hundred pounds and not upon any other basis . . .' Violation! Ten-fifty-six-point-ten. 'Receipt or bill of lading.' Violation! Ten-fifty-six-point-fourteen. 'Signed receipt for shipment.' Violation! Jesus, we are in a shit load of trouble. We couldn't have broken more rules and regulations if we'd tried. We're going to leave a trail of busted rules from Boston to San Francisco."

"That's not all," Pickett says. "I'll bet cocaine isn't covered by a general commodities permit, either."

"You're right, Pickett. Violation! We don't have to worry about the cops if they catch us with this load. The fuckin' ICC will hang us before we ever get to trial for possession."

Pickett's laughter is solid and unaffected. He coughs, clears his throat, blinks his lashes to clear his vision.

"You keep it up and you're goin' to run us both off the road," Pickett says. "That's funny. That's rich, Lenny. Thanks. This cab was gettin' a little dreary.

"Listen, though, kid, I'd still like to know how much stuff we're carryin' back there. Ain't you got any better ideas?"

"Two, three pounds is the best I can guess," Lenny says. "I don't even know for sure that it's cocaine."

"Only one way to find out," Pickett says, and he begins kicking down through the gears, slowing the truck, pulling it into the gravel shoulder of the highway.

"Pickett, you're nuts. What purpose will it serve, knowing what you've got back there? Just take the money and run."

170

"Got to know," Pickett says. "You comin'? You're goin' to be awful curious if you don't."

"Okay. But don't open any of the packages, okay? They'll have our ass if they see that. We'll open the chest and see how much is in there, how big the package is."

"Good enough," Pickett says. "Put your damn boots on. I'm bringin' the flashlight and the screwdriver. Did you notice how the drawers of that chest were screwed shut?"

"I noticed. That's why I figured they didn't want us poking around in there." Pickett will not hear it. He has gone around to the side door of the van and Lenny can hear the door swinging open with a squeal.

Lenny steps down into the ground and walks around the van. A big tractor flies by, and its sound booms through the chamberlike emptiness of the trailer.

"Hold the light," Pickett says. "There's four screws in each drawer, two to a side. Might as well start at the top."

Pickett backs the screws out of the wood and lays them carefully atop the chest. When he has removed four of them, he pulls open the top drawer. It is empty.

"Bullshit," says Pickett.

More swiftly and less surely, he turns the screws out of the second drawer. His screwdriver slips twice and gouges the wood of the chest. He tosses the screws atop the chest with the others and he yanks open the second drawer.

Empty.

"God *damn*," Pickett says.

He squats deeper to work on the left-hand side of the lowest drawer. Lenny's hand quivers.

"Don't move the light, Lenny. Keep the fucker still."

One screw dropped on the top of the chest with the others. Two screws. Pickett leans over to work on the right side of the drawer. A third screw. The fourth, and this one

171

Pickett does not drop atop the chest. He holds it in his hand as he grasps the drawer by its two knobs and slowly pulls. It is heavier than the others. It offers resistance. Pickett yanks harder and it slides on its grooved track, slides slowly into view.

"Mother of pearl," Lenny says.

The drawer is crammed, back to front, side to side, top to bottom, with plastic-wrapped packages. Beneath their heavy translucent wrappings, Lenny can see brown butcher paper, wound with masking tape.

"Can't be coke," Lenny says. "No way it can be coke."

Pickett lifts one of the packages from the drawer. It is the size of a small box of sugar on a grocery store shelf.

"Feels close to a pound," Pickett says. He begins counting the packages.

"Fifteen, eighteen, twenty," he says. "What the hell can it be?"

"I have no idea. Meth crystals, maybe. I hadn't thought of that. I don't dare open one."

"You don't have to," Pickett says. "This one's got a leak."

Lenny moves the light to the package Pickett holds. There is a fine, granular coating between the thick plastic wrapping and the brown paper.

"Some of the small stuff sifted out," Lenny says. "Here, Pickett, give me your keys."

Pickett holds them out and Lenny takes Pickett's house key between his fingers. He passes the flashlight to Pickett and he holds the package in the thin beam of light. Gently, he pricks the plastic with the point of the key, and he works it carefully, tearing a tiny hole in the plastic without puncturing the brown paper. The hole is large enough for the tip of his smallest finger. He wipes the tip of his finger around the inside of the plastic, picking up a thin white coating of the dust. He wipes the tip of his finger against his tongue. He rubs his tongue against the roof of his mouth.

"What is it?" Pickett says.

"It's cocaine, twenty pounds of it. We're haulin' a million dollars' worth of cocaine."

Chapter 26

From the deck of his pool, Frank Rivera looks out on the San Francisco Bay. He sees white-shooted sailboats struggling through the Raccoon Straits near Angel Island. Across the water, he sees the San Francisco skyline, the city's monoliths clearly defined on this exquisite Sunday afternoon as they rise out of the downtown section. Frank Rivera sees the spindly Bay Bridge arching delicately from Oakland, onto Treasure Island and across into San Francisco. He watches a freighter with a vermilion-stained hull slice slowly under the bridge. He sees all this in silent panorama from the deck of his pool beside his split-level, oriental-style home near the top of the hill in Tiburon. It is a warm, seductive afternoon, as October afternoons tend to be on the hill in Tiburon. Rivera stretches on a chaise, closes his eyes, and feels the sun cascading over his body in liquid, buttery waves.

He tries to ignore the muffled ring of the telephone inside the house. He will hate to get up.

"Frank," says his wife. "It's your office."

173

Rivera nods, sits up in the deck chair, and drops his feet over the side, where he left his sandals. He shuffles off toward the house.

He walks through the tiled kitchen, down the shag-carpeted hall, and into his study. He closes the door and walks to the telephone.

"Rivera," he says.

"Mr. Rivera, this is Collins. I talked to the Freeman kid in Boston just now. He says the shipment's on its way. You won't believe who the asshole hired."

"I'm not in the mood for guessing games. Who the hell did he find?"

"Truck drivers. Two truckers who've never been near a load of dope in their lives. Freeman says one of them is a hard-nosed old S.O.B. who didn't want any part of it at first. The other one's a long-hair, if you can believe a hippie truck driver. Maybe he knows his way around. Still, I told the kid it was a dumb fucking idea. I bawled him out and told him we'd have his ass if things didn't go right."

"He already knows that. What makes you think it's such a bad idea? I give the kid credit. He's got some hot coke and he picks an off-the-wall way of getting it across the country. That might not be bad. Who's going to figure a couple of truck drivers for couriers? Did you know that a lot of weed that came in from T.J. used to get hustled across the country by hillbilly truckers looking to pick up a few extra bucks? This was back in the early sixties. It worked beautiful for a while. When do they make contact?"

"Freeman said they left this morning. They're supposed to call here Tuesday morning. You want me to set something up?"

"Yes," says Rivera. "But nothing direct. I don't want them driving right up to one of my warehouses. Just in case, because I hear this coke is hot as hell. I want you to find some secluded place, out of the way. That way, anything doesn't look right, you can spot it and get the hell out. You understand? It'll have to be right beside some road somewhere, but remember that those big tractors can't go everywhere. And one more thing. I want you to pick some road that's slow and hard to drive, just in case we have to chase that tractor. I don't want the truck to be able to run away on an open highway. You understand everything I'm talking about? You got any ideas?"

"I haven't had a lot of time to think about it, Mr. Rivera, but there's one spot that comes to mind. I was in Mendocino about six weeks ago, up along the coast. When you get north of here, the traffic thins out pretty good and the road is tough as hell to drive. There ought to be some spot up Highway One, up near Fort Bragg. There's this, too. Are you still thinking of shipping half the load down to L.A.?"

"So far," says Rivera.

"Then this is perfect. That banker from Woodside, doesn't he owe us a favor or two? Isn't he the guy with the big spread near Leggett, the one with a landing strip? I'll bet we could get the Comanche into there without any trouble. We could drive up the coast, pick up the load, then head straight for Leggett and split the stuff right there. Bring ten pounds back here and fly the rest down south. You're taking care of two jobs practically at the same time. How does it sound?"

"Don't rush me," Rivera says. He is irritated that someone else has thought so quickly and efficiently about this, but he must admit that the plan has merits. Still, to show that his is the final word on such decisions, he lets five, ten, fifteen seconds pass before he answers. He imagines Collins waiting tensely on the other end of the line.

"Okay," he says finally. "The plan has some bugs but we can work those out. I want you to take care of this per-

175

sonally, because this is important to me. Get in the car, drive up the Coast Highway this afternoon. Find a place to stay. First thing in the morning, you get out on the road and drive that highway until you find the right place. Make notes so that you can give those truckers directions, right to the spot. No fuck-ups. After they call, you and a couple of the men will take an Econoline and go back up there to wait for them. This is your baby, Collins. It's all yours. Any fuck-ups and you know who's going to catch hell for it."

Rivera does not wait for an answer. He drops the receiver and walks back to the pool. The sun is still bright and warm. Rivera reclines in the deck chair and looks out over the city and the glistening stretch of water. Somewhere out there, he thinks, are a lot of hypes who would get awfully excited if they heard what is headed for them now. All that coke, tracking toward them courtesy of a couple of crazy truckers. In his sun-numbed mind, Rivera dimly recalls an advertisement in a magazine. America, it said, moves by truck.

Rivera shrugs. Why not?

Chapter 27

"Not my Chippendale," yells Billy-Frank.

"Shut up," says Detective Sergeant Salvatore Zanalotti. "This fuckin' place is coming apart until we find what we're looking for. You can make it easy for yourself and for us if you tell us where you hid the stuff. Otherwise, we keep pulling things apart."

Special Agent Wheeler bends over the settee, his knife poised over the upholstery, waiting for Billy-Frank's answer.

"I don't know what you're talking about," spits Billy-Frank.

Special Agent Wheeler's knife rips into the fabric, slashing a wide diagonal gash.

"You bastards are paying for this," Billy-Frank says, "with your goddamn blood. Don't say I didn't tell you so before you started."

Detective Sergeant Zanalotti snarls back at Billy-Frank, but without real enthusiasm. He was charged up, all right, when they strode through the store, past the black clerk, and trampled back into the back room. But there his zest for the project faded. With twenty-two years on the force, Detective Sergeant Zanalotti has acquired an almost unerring instinct for these things, and what he saw when they burst into that back room told him that they had missed the boat on this one.

It looked promising enough a half-hour before. Even after the store had closed, the long-haired owner of the place, his black clerk, and two other freaks—"unidentified young male Caucasians in hippie attire," Wheeler had termed them as he spoke on the hot line—stayed behind. That was enough to set legal wheels moving in creaky process and to alert squads in the nearest precinct and in the Drug Enforcement Administration headquarters.

Twenty minutes later, a miniskirted girl with straight black hair down to her waist and a big shoulder bag knocked on the door, waited, then walked in when one of the four men came to the door. Wheeler yelped in pleasure at that.

"The big one's going down right now," he said to Zanalotti. "We've got 'em by the balls."

Zanalotti, for the first time, had his doubts. He tabbed the girl as a hooker; the big shoulder-strap bag was an absolute giveaway for a man who had spent seven years busting working girls. Hookers did not figure in a deal of this size. But he said nothing as he and Wheeler joined the group that was to make the raid.

Wheeler took the warrant in hand and rapped smartly on the door of the shop. The black clerk came from the back room and walked through the darkened store.

He opened the door two inches.

"Closed, baby," he said.

Special Agent Wheeler, who ten years earlier had been a second-string fullback on the University of Texas freshman football team, smashed the door with a forearm shiver that sent the clerk flying into a table covered with stacks of Rosenthal china. The door flew open. Special Agent Wheeler, Detective Sergeant Zanalotti and the rest marched briskly down an aisle, opened the door to the back room, and stopped in their tracks.

Billy-Frank Freeman, wearing only his shorts, sat on the floor, against the wall, a tepid bottle of Cold Duck lifted to his lips.

The second man lay naked and snoring in the middle of the floor. The third had his back to them. He was standing up against a table. His back was to the door and his pants were pulled down to his knees. His bare, hairy ass was gyrating, pumping. There was no girl visible, but, wait a minute, the bare-assed freak at the table seemed to have a shapely second pair of legs sprouting around his waist.

To Detective Sergeant Zanalotti, it did not look like your standard, everyday, million-dollar dope transaction.

Detective Sergeant Zanalotti at that moment would have wagered a month of free Sundays that Billy-Frank Freeman had somehow gotten rid of his cocaine and decided to have a cozy orgy to celebrate. Of course, he did not say this.

"Up against the wall, creeps," he said.

"You've got nothing on me," the girl yelled. "No money changed hands. You've got no witnesses. This was strictly a freebie."

So they poked and they ripped and they searched. They rapped on walls and, hands on knees, they looked for loose tiles and recently replaced floor boards.

And even as he rips open the guts of the Chippendale settee, Special Agent Wheeler, too, is beginning to catch on.

Last time we work with the local bozos, he thinks.

Typical federal screw-up, Detective Sergeant Zanalotti thinks.

Keep on trashing, Billy-Frank thinks. I was having trouble moving this junk anyway.

Chapter 28

Pickett is rumbling down I-80 outside Gary, his mind fixed on the road in his high-beams, when he notices the billboard beside the highway. There is a terse, four-word message in big white letters set against a black background, followed by a toll-free long distance telephone number. Pickett memorizes the series of numerals, and his lips move in recitation until he pulls a pencil from his pocket and commits it to paper on the margin of a weight ticket. The billboard flies past, but Pickett can still see it clearly.

TURN IN A PUSHER, it read.

179

Chapter 29

It grows in Pickett's mind.

It sprouts in the dark and lonely hours between midnight and dawn. Nourished by guilt, by frustration and, yes, Pickett will admit that there is some greed involved, this brassy and bizarre scheme flourishes and blossoms in his imagination.

Why not, damn it, he says to himself. He holds the cards; he will deal his own game and everybody else will play along with him. They have no choice. He knows he must compensate his battered conscience. And is it fair that he should have been duped into taking such chances, doing such a job, for such a pitifully small portion of the treasure they are smuggling across the continent?

Of course it isn't, he tells himself.

Can it be done? Yes, he assures himself. Yes, it can be done. With a little bluff, a little daring, a little of the old Pickett brashness. They will play along with him. The stakes are too high not to stay in this hand, even if Pickett does raise the ante.

Lenny will not like this, he thinks. Still, the kid has nerve. He has a habit of doing things just for the hell of it. And if all goes well, there will be money for him, too. There will be money for both of them if this goes well.

They are nearing Davenport when the sun sneaks up behind them. Driving into the sunset one night and being at the wheel when the sun rises in the mirrors the next morning can be an unnerving experience. It can also be gratifying, a cause for some pride, to have stayed on the road, driving on, covering the distance between these astronomical benchmarks. Pickett has done it too many times to be impressed, but sunrise does brighten his mind this morning. Now, with the sun lighting up the countryside, with the Mack roaring straight into its own massive shadow, Pickett can wake Lenny.

"Lenny," he shouts. "Time to be up, boy. The old man wants some company. How about it, kid?"

"I hear you, Pickett. Be right down. Slept too damn long anyway. I can feel it without looking outside. Arms and legs feel like wood."

He stretches, slips out of the bunk and into the seat. He pulls on his boots.

"You must be wired tighter than a color TV, Pickett. You're not even blinking. How many pills did you pop last night?"

"Who's countin'? It takes my mind off food. Anyway, I had some thinkin' to do. I want you to tell me what you think of this idea of mine."

"No. I refuse. I refuse to move until you pull over and let us get some breakfast. I've had two packages of cheese-and-peanut-butter crackers and one vending machine orange soda since we left Boston. You give me food for my body and then you can give me food for thought. You can consider this a mutiny if you want."

"Okay. But you got to hear this. I been cookin' it all night. It's a honey. We need fuel anyway. We'll stop at the next place and you can run in and get something to take out."

"That's the best you can do? All right, all right, I understand. You want to get back and see John William. There's a place about a mile ahead, I think. I'm chowing down good. Ham, eggs, toast, the works. At the rate you're going, I think

I'd better order a bag of burgers and some sandwiches, because you won't be wanting to stop for lunch, either."

"You know how I feel, Lenny."

"Sure. No harm in hustling, just so long as nobody wants to check our logs. We'll be okay until midnight, then we're taking our chances. Here's the place. You want anything? You sure? I'm bringing you something anyway. You'll get hungry. You've got to eat something, Pickett. You must have been popping those pills like they were after-dinner mints."

Pickett gracefully arches the truck beside a service island. Business is steady on this Monday morning. He has barely finished with the fill-up when Lenny jogs toward the truck, one white bag under each arm. The smells are inviting when Lenny climbs into the cab, but Pickett does not eat. The amphetamines have robbed him of his appetite.

"That will do us until tonight," Pickett says. "You want to piss, you can just hang 'er out the window. This crate ain't stoppin' till the gauges read dry."

Lenny sits the bags on the floor of the cab. He reaches into one sack, finds two slices of toast, then opens a styrofoam container and gingerly picks out a rubbery fried egg. He covers that with the two slices of toast and attacks the sandwich.

"I'm listening," he says when he has swallowed his second mouthful. "What's this you've been hatching overnight?"

Pickett clears his throat.

"Goes sort of like this," he says. "I started thinkin' about how much money that cocaine is worth and how much we're bein' paid. When we took the job we agreed on the price. It seemed right, I'll admit. It seemed like a lot of money, presumin' we really weren't takin' that many chances. And I guess we weren't, judgin' from the way things have been goin' so far.

182

"Well, that's just fine. But then we find out how much cocaine we're carryin' back there. Hell, I never figured that stuff was worth so much, so little bein' so valuable. I mean, you hear about these arrests with the cops confiscatin' a suitcase full of heroin worth a half-million bucks. But when you see the facts of it, right before your eyes, it's hard to accept. I can still hardly believe how much that chest of drawers is worth.

"But you tell me so and I believe you. And that sets me thinkin' some more. Man, they're playin' us for first-rate chumps. Payin' us a lousy ten thousand for haulin' a million-dollar shipment. That sucks. It's like an artist, say, some poor fellow who lives in an attic. Can't even afford to buy bread because nobody wants his paintin's. Then, one day, somebody comes along and buys every last one of his paintin's, pays the guy enough that he can afford bread and even beans to go along with it. He's happy. He knows nothin'. He doesn't know that the sharper who bought his paintin's is sellin' 'em for thousands of dollars, makin' a fortune. That ain't right, is it? Billy-Frank and his pals are playin' us the same way. They're playin' us the way Earl Scruggs plays his five-string."

Lenny nearly chokes. This is too much at eight in the morning, the pent-up speed rapping of a pill-popping truck driver.

"Pickett," he says, "where the hell did you come up with that story? The one about the painter?"

"That," Pickett says, waving his hand, "is out of a movie I saw once. But that ain't important. Thing is, we're bein' taken for chumps, and I don't like bein' taken. And I'm doin' something about it."

Lenny looks up from his second fried-egg sandwich.

"What did you have in mind?"

"We've got their dope, don't we? They want to see it

again, they can come up with some more cash. Otherwise, forget it. What do we care? I'm headed home. I've got five thousand already. They don't like my new deal, I'll dump the fuckin' chest into Flamin' Gorge and they'll never see it or me again. They don't know who we are. They got no way of ever findin' us again. When I call those fuckers this afternoon, I'm goin' to tell them that they ought to bring along a little more cash when we get together. Say, a hundred thou'. That sounds like a nice, even amount. They're still makin' a hell of a profit. They'll go along with me. I know it."

"Me too," Lenny says. "I'm sure they'll go along with it over the phone. But it'll be different when we get there. They'll tear us to pieces.

"Pickett, you don't cross people like these. They don't like being fucked over. They like it even less than you. You don't bargain with them and you don't break your deals. Or they'll break you. They play rough."

"I know, I know all that. I've thought about it. But there's got to be a way. I'm not exactly sure how to go about it. Hide it, maybe, tell them we want the money before we let on where it is. They kill us, the dope is gone for good. Something like that. I've got time to think about it. I don't have to call until tomorrow morning. I'll think of something before then."

"Pickett, if I never meant it before, I mean it now. You are one crazy mother. They don't come any crazier than you."

Pickett looks over at him.

"You're turnin' normal on me now? You? You're tellin' *me* what's crazy and what ain't? Man, you changed quick. Okay. Fine with me. Can't offer you a thing once I park this Mack, anyway. You want no part of it, I'll understand."

"I didn't say that, and you know it. Maybe you're crazy,

184

but so am I. You're not pushing me into anything I don't want to do. Anyway, they'll squash you like a mosquito if you try it alone."

"Could be," says Pickett. "I guess I could use the help."

"Better believe it," Lenny says. "What are you trying to do? You trying to cut me out of your big deal?"

They are near Council Bluffs when Pickett marks his twenty-fourth hour at the wheel.

"All day and all night," Lenny says. "Time for relief, Pickett. You overdid those joy pills. Come on. I can handle the rig just as well as you can through this country. If you're not sleepy, at least try and relax over here."

"I'll do it to please you," he says, "but I'm hangin' in okay."

He slows to the side of the road and the engine rattles beneath them as they switch seats. Pickett slaps his own skull as if to jolt himself out of his driving consciousness.

"After a while," he tells Lenny, "a guy gets riveted to the seat. You can't take your eyes off the road. Somethin' in your mind keeps sayin', oh, you can pull over in another mile or two. The miles keep pilin' up and pretty soon you've driven halfway across the country and you don't know how. Maybe it's those dividin' stripes between the lanes. Scary."

For the first time in more than eighteen hours, Pickett feels his body again. His back is hunched, as if he were still at the wheel. He straightens, but the muscles and the vertebrae resist. Slowly, painfully, he presses his back against the seat. His shoulders, his arms and legs, they are all the same. They seem to be atrophying in the driving position. And food. Pickett thinks about eating for the first time since Boston. The sandwiches seem unappealing to him now, but he will let the idea of eating simmer for a while. Then, so quickly and so stealthily that he is barely conscious of it, sleep overtakes him. Lenny knows then that Pickett was

185

reaching his limits for his last couple of hours. Road fatigue in its advanced forms is a terrifying experience. The hypnotic effect of the road combined with the body's absolute sodden weariness and the haphazard effect of a stimulant can cause a man to drive off the road without ever knowing it. Hallucinations are not uncommon, especially at night. Drivers swap stories of nodding off at the wheel and waking forty or fifty miles down the road.

"Road crazy," the truckers call it. They discuss it the way young mothers talk about diaper rash.

Seven hours of driving brings them across Nebraska. This is drudgery for Lenny, nothing but work. He fights to keep his concentration as they cut across the even, unchanging landscape made more drab by the chill of the approaching winter. Pickett sleeps through, until they bull past North Platte.

"We out of Nebraska yet? Good. I plain forgot to tell you. We're turnin' off of 80 when we get to the state line. Take the junction for 80-South toward Denver. We're takin' I-70 west from there. Got business in Utah. Moab, Utah."

"What are we doing there?"

"You got a gun?" Pickett says. "You have a pistol that can't be traced back to you? You know any place we can get one?"

Lenny shakes his head.

"I do," Pickett says. "This guy ain't never let me down, no matter what I needed. If I need a gun now he'll fix me up."

"I don't understand, Pickett. You've already got the Ruger."

"Sure. And that Ruger ain't goin' to mean tiddly-shit when I try to collect that extra money on Wednesday. You said it yourself. These guys play rough. We need a little firepower just to show we can bite back."

"I don't know," Lenny says. "I don't like the idea."

186

"The idea is if we have guns to show, we won't need 'em."

"I never shot a gun in my life."

"Don't worry," Pickett says. "You'll get a chance. This guy has plenty of room for target practice."

"Anyway, Pickett, I'm not sure we want to drive 70 tonight. The radio said there was a storm moving into the Rockies. That road is going to be hell in the snow. It'll be a lot easier on 80."

"That'll take us three hours out of our way if we do it like that," Pickett says. "I'll take my chances with the snow. Pull in for fuel when we get outside Denver. Then we can go till mornin'."

The thought of wielding a gun against dope peddlers does not cheer Lenny. His gloom deepens as they drive toward Denver and the cloud cover overhead turns thicker, darker, lower. When they ease into a truck station after dark near Denver, the attendant checks the dipstick, adds a quart, and fills the twin hundred-gallon tanks.

"Headed east?" he says. "The storm must have been on your tail all the way through."

"We're going into the mountains," Lenny says. "Bound west, toward Utah."

The attendant whistles.

"Don't know if I'd do that," he says. "They say it's the first real big one of the season. This one's going to stick. Hope you got your chains."

"We've got 'em," Pickett says, as he walks around the tractor to climb into the driver's seat. They cast off down the highway.

Colorado rises steadily, imperceptibly, from the Kansas line to Denver. In twelve hours of driving, the westbound traveler finds that he has climbed from less than a thousand feet above sea level to Denver's mile-high altitude. Outside

187

Denver, though, the Rockies rise abruptly. They burst straight out of the high plateau so that, seen from the east, Denver is framed against the rugged, thick folds of the mountains. West of Denver, within twenty miles of the city limits, Interstate 70 climbs into the heart of the Rockies, toward Loveland Pass with an elevation of nearly 12,000 feet.

Soon, Pickett and Lenny drive into the storm. Snowstorms on the road are not unlike rattlesnakes, deadly but usually offering fair warning. Light flecks of snow begin fluttering from the sky; perhaps bits of sleet will drop against the windshield. These first flakes will not stick. They are pulverized by the wheels and they only wet the road surface. Then the flakes will become large, whiter. They may begin to build on the road's surface and the traffic will cut slushy troughs. Then the wind may increase and the flakes will fall faster than the wheels can crush them. The road will be covered with snow. Snow tires and chains will churn up packed chunks of snow and the driver is in another realm.

Usually, this is a benign, processional series of events. This time, though, the pattern is nasty and accelerated. The storm hits them suddenly, as Pickett urges the Mack up into the mountains, down-shifting, playing with the engine's narrow power range so that it is willing and eager in the lower gears, running with a torquey growl. The rush of the snow is immediate. Dime-sized flakes swirl in their headlights and the wet pavement turns to glare ice quickly. Pickett runs with his low-beams but switches on the highs every seven or eight seconds to check for curves and road signs. He is intense, his concentration total, because this weather demands responses and actions that are positive, yet delicate. Every move is critical. All of the truck's driving eccentricities are amplified. Normally, they are annoying, but in these conditions they are insidious. Stops, climbs, and turns must be anticipated. There is no margin for jerkiness. Pickett does not ordinarily use his clutch in shifting. He glances at the tachometer, listens to the engine, matches the engine RPM with the speed of the driving wheels and meshes the gears carefully. But on ice and snow, he can take none of these chances. He clutches with every shift and he releases the pressure slowly, carefully, so that the gears engage smoothly and the wheels do not lock. When he brakes, he pumps the pedal rapidly, slowing the rig but still keeping the wheels rolling.

When he nurses the Mack around a corner and still feels the tractor sliding toward the outside of the turn, he knows they need the chains. He stops as close as he can to the edge of the road, because by now the shoulder has been obliterated. They pull on their winter jackets and Pickett zips up his Mercury coveralls, too.

They open the locker on one side of the tractor and Lenny pulls out the big electric torch. From a rack above a fuel tank comes a set of chains for the driving wheels. Lenny spreads the chains behind the wheels, then Pickett climbs back into the cab and Lenny motions him backward. Then they kneel in the snow, blowing on their hands, to fasten the hooks that will pull the links snug against the rubber. The cold steel is unfamiliar to their fingers after the summer months, so the job takes longer than it should. Their toes are numb by the time they have finished and climbed back into the cab.

Now it is a matter of loafing along, concentrating on the road ahead, coaxing the rig patiently around curves and nursing it up grades without spinning the wheels and losing traction. They drive deeper into the mountains and the storm thickens. Here, the snow already has blown and drifted three and four feet high against the sides of the road, some of it from this storm, some tossed aside by road graders earlier in the night, some of it remnants of an earlier snow-fall.

Lenny cannot sleep. He will watch this one through with Pickett as they crawl along the road. Over Vail Pass, the wind gusts heavier and the snow drives across the wind-shield in sheets so thick and so fast that they cannot dis-tinguish individual flakes, only thousands of blurred white streaks that blend into a pristine mask which bounces their headlights' beam back into the cab.

Outside of Dillon, the road narrows, for the Interstate highway is still not yet completed here. As Pickett eases the rig over the pass and haltingly points it downhill, he can feel the wind bucking, trying to shove the empty van across the road. Then the gust doubles and redoubles. The snow is a solid wall and their headlights cannot pierce it. Pickett and Lenny cannot see five feet ahead.

White-out.

Lenny has seen it only once before, driving on the east side of Nevada's Mount Rose on a skiing trip. He was terri-fied, helpless. He sat in the car, emergency lights blinking, unable to see the hood on his Volkswagen. In less than thirty seconds, the wind stilled and it was over.

Now, in the night, in a mechanical behemoth that can burst through guardrails as if they were cardboard, it has happened again. Pickett does not panic. He brakes the truck gradually, keeping tractor and trailer straight. When they have stopped, he reaches for three flares he had brought from the locker and hands them to Lenny.

"Walk to the back of the truck," he says. "Walk right be-side the van so you know where you are and you won't get lost. Light one of these and drop it right behind the van. Then light the other one and heave it as far back down the road as you can. But don't go wanderin' off. If anybody's comin' up behind us, this is the only thing they'll ever see.

Otherwise, they'll rear-end us for sure. Then toss the third one out in front of us. I really don't know what side of the highway we're parked on. Hell, I don't even know if there is a highway, anymore."

Lenny takes the flares, holds them in his left hand and grasps the grab-bar on the side of the tractor as he dismounts. The van shields the top of his body from the wind but his legs are still caught in the gale that nearly upends him as it whips under the van. Lenny feels his way to the back of the truck, then pulls the plastic sheath from one end of the flare. He uses his thumb to open the top of the cover, exposing the red scratch box. This he touches to the naked tip of the flare. He scrapes them roughly, abruptly, and on the third try the friction does its job and the flare catches, red and hot. He tosses this two or three paces away and he works in its red glow as he lights the second flare and throws it overhand, end over end, the burning red tip cartwheeling into the blizzard until it is swallowed up by the snow and the darkness.

Now he steps back through the snow to the front of the tractor. He lights the third flare and throws it out past the smeared beams of the headlights. Then, abruptly, it disappears, as if it snuffed out. That, Lenny knows, is not supposed to happen. He clambers back into the cab to ask Pickett for another.

"Forget it," Pickett says. "It didn't go out."

"Come on, Pickett, it had to. It must've stuck in the snow."

"You'll see," Pickett says.

Abruptly, no more than four minutes later, the insistent, howling wind becomes only a breeze. The flakes waft gently to the ground. The Mack's headlights thrust out and Lenny sees why the third flare disappeared so swiftly.

Ahead of them, no more than ten feet ahead, is a guard rail with snow banked against it in a gentle drift. Beyond that is only blackness, the blackness of an abyss. They have stopped less than four steps from the apex of one of the most acute turns on the highway.

There is nothing to say. Pickett releases the brakes and the compressed air hisses beneath them. He notches the truck into gear and he yanks the wheel hard left to make the turn. As they drop down toward Glenwood Springs, they pull in behind a snowblower that scrapes the roads and shoots the snow in a heavy cascade above the treetops. It is slow going, strictly first-gear driving, but they do not complain.

They are out of the mountains before daybreak, making time for Moab.

Chapter 30

Moab, Utah, is a smattering of hamburger stands, motels, and an erstwhile shopping center on the edge of Utah's canyon country, where the earth runs rich in the red oxides that have been simulated but never captured in so many square miles of Kodachrome film.

Northeast of the town is Arches National Park, where the rust-shaded sandstone twists and stretches in surreal configurations. East are the La Sal Mountains. Just north of town, the Colorado River gushes toward Dead Horse Point and its confluence with the Green River beneath steep cliffs in Canyonland Park's remote reaches. South of town, a few miles beyond the last neon sign, a rough dirt road pokes into a bare and isolated region the locals call Spanish Valley. It is

down this road that Pickett steers the Mack just after daybreak on Tuesday, five, six miles down this road until they
reach a narrow wooden bridge.

"We'll walk from here," Pickett tells Lenny, awake now
after their bouncing ride. "Truck's too heavy for the bridge.
Not far to go now. Just around the bend."

Around the bend is a shack, its corrugated steel roof
stained the color of the grainy brown wood with which it is
shingled.

Pickett walks to the screen door, opens that, slaps his open
palm against the side of the house.

"Jack! Pack Rat Jack! Wake up, you sleepy old fool, you
got visitors out here! Put the coffee on, you tired old bastard!"

Lenny looks around. There is a shed, the same color and
condition as the ramshackle building where Pickett is raising
such hell. There are no other signs of habitation in this arid,
lonely valley.

A voice from inside:

"Let an old man sleep, God damn you. Go away and don't
come back until the sun's so high your only shadow is in the
soles of your feet."

"I don't have that kind of time, Jack," Pickett shouts.
"This is Pickett. J. W. Pickett. I'm comin' through on the fly
and I need some service. You're the man, far as I'm concerned."

Silence inside. The door opens. The man must have
stepped out of an 1880 mining camp tableau, Lenny thinks.
He wears full-length red woolen long johns. The fuzzy
growth around his cheeks and under his chin suggests not
that he is cultivating a beard, but simply that he has not
shaved in two weeks or more.

"J. W. Pickett," he says. "You put a few miles on the road

since the last time I saw you, I bet. Nineteen sixty-five, I think. Maybe sixty-six. You were driving a White then. Picked up a brand-new washer-dryer for your wife, as I recall. Come in, Pickett, come in."

"This is my relief man," Pickett says. "Lenny Lewis. Just about my partner in most ways, I guess."

"Good," says the man. "Come on in. Got plenty of coffee. I been up awhile. Coffee ought to be just about ready by now. I had no idea it was you, Pickett. It's not that I'm antisocial. I just hate doing business with strangers before breakfast. How're they working out, that washer and dryer?"

"Still going strong," Pickett says.

"Good, good. I don't like to think I ever sold a piece of defective merchandise."

"Jack," says Pickett to Lenny, "is what you might call an outlet for certain goods that get misplaced from shipments."

"Right you are," says the man. "Established since thirty-six, same location, steady clientele. All the old-timers like J.W. know about me. You want something, I've either got it or I can get my hands on it. What'll it be? Set of power tools? Stereo set? How about a bottle of booze? Special this week, twelve-year-old scotch for twenty-two bucks a case. This is the good stuff. Tax time comes, you might want one of those pocket computers. Got a crate of those little beauties. Winter's here. Got some nice goose-down jackets, very best.

"You see," he says to Lenny, "I don't deal a lot in cash. Mostly, it's with truckers who trade me something in their load for something I got and they want. Simple bartering, oldest way man has ever done business. They lose a carton here or there, they blame it on thieves and the insurance covers it. They're happy and I keep building my stock. I've got stuff in that shed you wouldn't believe. Electric pencil sharpeners, golf clubs, scuba gear, auto batteries, hiking boots,

194

record albums. I've got eight dozen Nehru jackets that somebody stuck me with a few years ago. Are you in the market for a few nice Nehru jackets?"

"What we're lookin' for," Pickett says, "is a gun."

"A gun. Rifle, shotgun or handgun?"

"I was thinkin' of a handgun," Pickett says.

"Stay here," the man says. "Pour yourself some coffee. I'll go back and see what I've got. Guns I keep in the basement, not out in the shed."

He returns with his arms full of boxes, looking like a shoe salesman taking on a finicky buyer.

He opens the first box.

"This one," he says, "is a nickel-plated .45 automatic. Here, heft it. It's a real fancy model. Argonne Forest Commemorative model, it says. Damn pretty gun. You could hang that one in your living room."

"I don't need anything that fancy," Pickett says.

"Okay. This one's a Beretta .25. Look, small enough you could palm it like a magician, hide it right in your hand. The only problem is, you couldn't stop a good-sized rabbit with it. This one's a lady's gun, mostly."

"Something heavier," Pickett says.

"Okay. Maybe this is the one you want. Mr. Smith and Mr. Wesson are real proud of this one. Police Special. It's a .357 Magnum. Lot of the big-city cops are using these instead of their standard issue .38s. It's got a wallop. I got this one in snub nose and four-inch barrel lengths. Snub nose isn't real accurate for long distances, but it looks better. More businesslike, if you know what I mean."

"I'll be enough of a scattershot without any help," Lenny says. "I'll go for the big barrel."

"Big one it is. You need ammo? I'll throw in a box of fifty cartridges."

"How much?" Pickett says.

"Depends," says Jack. "You haulin' anything I might be interested in?"

"Not this time," says Pickett.

"No, I didn't think so. You bug-haulers never do. Okay, let's say eighty-five for the gun and the shells."

"Sold," says Pickett. "How about some target practice?"

"Right behind here," says Jack. "There's a bunch of tin cans out in the garbage. Take a few out back, sit 'em up against that hill and blast away."

They do that. Lenny holds the gun uneasily, and he loads the chambers as Pickett tells him. The gun is heavy, but somehow it balances nicely as he holds it, arm extended. He sights down the barrel, through the notch, and tries to remember what Pickett has told him. Hold your breath. Squeeze the trigger. Don't blink. He squeezes.

The report and the kick are as though a firecracker had exploded in his fingers.

"Again," Pickett says. "You were close. Just so long as you're in the ballpark."

They feed forty rounds through the gun. Lenny snaps off single shots and then he booms two, three in succession, learning to recover from the recoil and straighten his arm to fire again.

"That's forty," Pickett says. "We'll save these last few. Jack, I hate to run, but we have to be movin' along. I feel like I got a bargain."

"No bargain," Jack says. "I got a half dozen of those two years ago from some trucker who wanted a color TV for his wife. I gave him a real nice console. Now this eighty-five will keep me in groceries for a couple of weeks."

"Fair enough," Pickett says. "Now we've got to go. I've got a couple of phone calls to make."

Chapter 31

"Mr. Rivera, I think you ought to listen on the extension. I've got one of the truckers on the line and something's come up. You ought to hear this."

Come up? Rivera thinks. This is no good. Things are not supposed to come up in a deal such as this. He presses the lighted button on his phone in the executive bathroom of a certain large chemical plant near San Jose. He hears Collins' voice.

"Out of the question," Collins is saying. "You made a deal. I suggest that for your own sake, you live up to the terms of it. We think you're being paid a rather generous amount."

"Generous, my ass," says another voice. "I ain't dumb. I know how much this load is worth when you retail it. I know. A million dollars. I may be a dumb Okie truck driver, but I know a few things.

"You ever traveled through Utah or Wyoming? Let me tell you about this pretty spot in the southeast corner of Wyoming. No, listen to me for a minute. See, there's this dam in eastern Utah across the Green River. The water's been backin' up for years into this deep, wide gorge that must be thirty-five, forty miles long and two or three miles wide in some spots. Called Flamin' Gorge. Hell of a pretty sight. But the thing that's most impressive about this place is how far out of the way it is. There's two or three roads that go around it and most times of the year, say this afternoon, you could drive right up and be all alone. And you know some-

197

thing else? If I was to stuff a certain chest of drawers full of rocks and toss it into the gorge, I'll bet nobody would ever see me. And I guarantee that nobody would ever find that chest again. Am I comin' through okay?

"See, since I know how much you're goin' to make off this load, I'm sure you won't really mind givin' up just a little bit of your profit margin in order to pay some out-of-the-ordinary expenses. It's a shame the way transportation costs have gone up these days. Maybe you'll just have to pass the extra costs on to your consumers. I'd say that one hundred thousand dollars seems like a reasonable figure. Otherwise, you ain't never hearin' from me again. And I'll tell you beforehand, you don't even want to waste your time lookin' for this chest. 'Cause Flamin' Gorge is an awful big place."

"It's impossible," says Collins.

"Put the man on hold," says Rivera. He waits until he sees the light flashing under the button. Then he speaks again.

"Collins," he says, "how much can you get together now if I give you twenty-four hours? I don't want you dealing with any shys, but money from our cash resources?"

"In an emergency, I'd say sixty-five, seventy thousand dollars. I'd have to work at it but I could do it. Sixty-five, seventy thousand that we could remove from our assets without having the whole mess fall down around our ears."

"Good," says Rivera. "Let me talk to the man."

"Listen," he says when he hears the connection. "You don't have to know who I am, except that I'm the guy who signs the pay checks around here. That still means something. At least it did the last time I looked. I don't ordinarily involve myself so closely in the day-to-day workings of my company, so you can see that you have created quite a stir around here. Yes, you have raised a hell of a commotion. I think I can say that. You say you know the value of that shipment to me. My friend, you don't have the whole story. It's true that in small quantities this substance fetches a very enviable sum, but it would be a big mistake to project those figures over such a great amount as you are bringing across the country. I must consider employees, storage costs, and working overhead, all of which increases drastically when one handles large amounts of this product.

"Then, there is simple supply and demand. When such a large quantity of this commodity enters the market and becomes widely available, the price goes down. I would not ordinarily be this frank with a stranger, my friend, but this is an extraordinary request you make and, therefore, I am taking extraordinary measures. I will tell you now that I do not intend to retail all of the cargo you are carrying. I have associates in Los Angeles who are willing to buy half the shipment wholesale from me. Although this decreases my potential profit, it also cuts down on my overhead. And, of course, the less time I have this product on my hands, the less risk I happen to be taking. So, as you can see, my profit on this shipment is not as great as you might imagine. But I won't deceive you. That shipment is worth a great deal to me, a great deal, indeed. I want it. I'll handle this like the businessman that I am and that I presume you are. Your offer is unacceptable. My counteroffer to you is sixty thousand dollars, payable in cash upon receipt. That is my final offer. Any more and the transaction will not be profitable enough for me to pursue. What do you say?"

"I'll take the sixty."

"I hoped that you would. Tomorrow afternoon is not too early, I hope. Stay on the line. Give my employee your telephone number, so that he can get back to you from a pay telephone to give you the details. Thank you, sir. It was a pleasure."

Frank Rivera, hunkering over the toilet, feels a surge of satisfaction. There are still some things that require his personal touch in this operation, some things which only he can salvage. Collins! That cocaine would have ended up at the bottom of some gorge in Wyoming if Collins had handled it all the way; Rivera is positive of that.

Rivera flushes the toilet, hitches up his pants, washes his hands. He does this without haste, savoring the feeling of his masterly performance just now.

He walks from the washroom and into his outer office. There, Collins is waiting for him.

"You didn't mean that, did you, Mr. Rivera?" he says. "You're not really giving that man sixty thousand?"

"Start putting that money together, Collins. You're taking it with you when you meet the man tomorrow. As for giving it to him, I want you to play it as it goes down. If you must, give the man his money. If you think he's not really prepared to enforce his bluff, then all the better. Economize any way you can. But no unnecessary risks. And get me that cocaine.

"Oh, and Collins . . . if the Freeman kid in Boston starts wondering why he doesn't get paid for this shipment, you be sure and tell him. Better yet, let me talk to him. I don't want to lose him. He's not much of a judge of people but he must have some damn good contacts in Bogotá."

Chapter 32

"Wheeler," says The Boss, "how about stepping in here?"

Special Agent Wheeler does not waste time in doing that.

The Boss is sitting behind his wide walnut desk when Wheeler walks in. He swivels his black leather executive chair. He motions Wheeler to a chair.

"This is interesting," he says, shoving a yellow sheet of paper at Wheeler. "What do you think of it?"

Wheeler recognizes the paper. It is a standard form used to record information phoned in on the WATS "pusher line." Except for crank calls and scattered leads to some inconsequential dealers, the line has been a failure. Americans, apparently, have been reluctant to turn in pushers even when they know that someone else will be picking up the tab for the telephone call. Thus, Wheeler reads the form with some skepticism.

Phrases leap out toward his eyes as he scans the paper. "Billy-Frank Freeman," they say. "Silver Jaguar."

"Interesting," Wheeler says. "Like you put it sir, very interesting."

"Is it accurate?"

"It is, sir, up to a point. Freeman does drive a car of that description and he does reside at that address. But as for the rest, I can't believe that he could be dumb enough to carry twenty pounds of cocaine in his car. Certainly, he could not carry it all beneath his seat."

"That's not what it says, Wheeler," says The Boss. "It says, quote, 'You'll find what you're looking for under the driver's seat.' It doesn't mention twenty pounds. Isn't there a possibility that he's carrying a portion of the shipment there?"

"A possibility, yes. But I would say not. Up to now, he has done a scrupulous job of confining his illegal activities to that antique shop. He's quite a canny type."

"Just the same," The Boss says, "this seems too specific to ignore. You've got the basis here for a warrant. I want you to get that and search his car."

"Sir, don't you think a twenty-four-hour stakeout is advisable? That *is* the procedure."

"You had his store staked out for ten days, Wheeler, and the only thing it got us was a fifty-five-hundred-dollar bill for damages. Get that warrant and hold onto it until he gets into the car. I want this done right."

"Yes, sir," says Wheeler. "There's only one thing that doesn't jibe. Why in the world would a call like this have come from a pay telephone in Moab, Utah, of all places?"

"Wheeler," says The Boss, "be thankful for miracles. Don't scrutinize them too closely."

Chapter 33

Off the highway, through dark and empty town streets, up the lane where Pickett lives. The rattling idle of the diesel resounds off the house until Pickett turns the key and the engine gasps, shudders, dies.

"You can get in a good six or seven hours' sleep," Pickett says. "We'll leave about eleven. I want to get up early and visit John William in the hospital.

"You can use the spare room," Pickett whispers as he swings open the door to the house. "The bed ought to be made. Get your rest, Lenny. You'll need it."

Lenny knows his way. He leaves Pickett standing alone in the living room, acclimating himself to the feeling of being home again. Pickett sits and pulls his boots off, then stuffs his socks inside. He wants to see his wife, but he is reluctant, fearful. He is not sure how he can face her after all that has happened since the last time he sat in this house. Be a man, he thinks. She wants to see you. Go and be with her because, after all, she might never see you again if things go wrong tomorrow.

She has swaddled herself in the bedcovers, stretched out on her own side of the bed, not encroaching on his territory even though he has been gone for days. He undresses. The bed creaks when he puts his weight on it and bends over to find her mouth. He kisses her.

"Pickett," she says. "You're home. I didn't expect you until tomorrow. You must have hurried."

"I told you I was comin' straight through. Had to make a little detour or I'd have been here sooner. How's John William? Did you visit him last night?"

"I spent the evening there," she says. "He's doing okay. They're still keeping him foggy, but he's getting along good. I told him you're coming. He understands. He'll be awful happy to see you."

"I'll be happy to see him," he says. "It's good to be back. And, honey, I'm sorry I was ever gone."

"It's okay now," she says, and she kisses him. "How long can you stay?"

"I've got one little errand to run tomorrow," he says, "and then I'm home for good."

"Pickett. What do you mean by that?"

"I mean," he says, "that I ain't goin' back on the road. I've done my last truckin'. I'm goin' to be home for good, beginnin' tomorrow night."

"Don't say that, Pickett. Don't say it if you don't mean it. Don't do it or even think about it just 'cause you think it's what I want. I've made out okay up till now. Don't let what happened to John William force you into something you don't really want to do."

"I'm sayin' it," he says, "because I mean it. I'm doin' what I want to do. You know damn well how obstinate I am. Don't think you could force me into something like this. It's my decision, for better or worse."

"I'm happy," she says, and she knows that if she had not done more than her share of crying during the last week, she would be weeping with joy right now. "I don't know what we're going to do for money, but we'll manage. We'll make out."

"After tomorrow," he says, "I hope it won't be such a problem. I figure on pickin' up a good piece of change for this job I'm haulin' tomorrow. If everythin' comes out okay, we'll have plenty of time to figure out how we want to live for the rest of our lives."

"What are you talking about?" she says. "I thought you were coming back from Boston with an empty van. You said you would deadhead right back."

"I did," he says, "almost. Just one little item that I have to deliver up the coast tomorrow. Nothing to worry about. I'll be back for dinner, back in time to catch the evening visiting hours at the hospital."

"I don't understand," she says.

"Don't worry. When you see what I'm bringin' home tomorrow, you won't care that you don't understand. I'm settin' us up for life, baby. You'll see. You, me, John William, and the baby are goin' to be situated real nice."

"Okay," she says. "But the important thing is that I'll have you home with me. The rest of it, the money and all, doesn't matter. We'll work things out somehow. I'm just happy to have you here."

"Trust me. And tell me, honey," he says, his lips moving against the tender part of her neck, "did you miss me?"

"A little bit," she says. "I missed you a little."

204

Chapter 34

"Fm. ARCO station at n. end of Ft. Bragg, 13.6 mi. alng. hiway 1 to Bl. Glch. brdg."

That is the last line in the instructions which Pickett scrawled in pencil, on the back of a blank weight ticket, in the pay telephone booth at Moab, Utah. Lenny reads the instructions as they surge on toward the rendezvous. And so, Lenny looks doubtfully over at Pickett when they shoot past the Fort Bragg road at Willits and hurtle northward.

"Pickett," he says, "all the directions this guy gave you are north from Fort Bragg."

"Exactly. That means they'll be expectin' us to be comin' north up Highway One."

"Right."

"Which," Pickett says, "is precisely why we're goin' to loop up north and go south on One. I really don't know whether it makes any difference, but we might as well get everything we can in our favor. You know, the element of surprise and all that."

"You are a truly amazing man, Pickett."

"Yeah? Talk to me in a couple of hours and we'll see about that. If you're still throwin' bouquets at me then, I might catch a few."

Approached from either north or south, Blue Gulch is the second of three indentations within a two-mile stretch of the California coastline north of the town of Fort Bragg. Here, State Highway One, known otherwise as the Coast

Highway, is a gray ribbon between brooding bluffs and the edge of cliffs high above the Pacific surf. The two-lane asphalt highway bends slightly inland to follow the contours of each of the gullies which flank Blue Gulch. A narrow white bridge constructed in 1946 leaps across the Blue Gulch chasm. At the south end of the small bridge is an unmarked gravel turnout, perhaps one hundred feet long and varying from ten to thirty feet in width. At its edge is a cliff, and more than one hundred feet below is the Pacific. All of these features make the Blue Gulch bridge turnout uniquely suitable for Collins' purposes. From the edge of the turnout are visible the two bends in the highway as the two flanking gulches twist the highway inward. A car approaching from either direction can be spotted nearly a mile away before it ducks out of sight. Thus, Collins has both intimacy and a strategic lookout. Except during the tourist season, the road is nearly deserted on weekdays. The only town of consequence near Blue Gulch is Fort Bragg, nearly fourteen miles away. Several miles north of the spot is Westport, which consists of perhaps two dozen homes built around a gas station, a general store, and a gallery displaying the works of North Coast artists. North of Westport, Highway One is at its most scenic and tortuous as it follows the ragged coastline and then loops inward to Leggett, a small town on the edge of California's logging country. It is at Leggett that Pickett and Lenny turn onto One, where Pickett drops the Mack into its lower gears to climb a steep grade into the verdant and rugged hills which separate the coastline from the rest of the state.

Here Pickett and Lenny fall in behind a logging truck struggling to pull up the grade with three enormous redwood trunks pyramided on its rail trailer. They slow to a crawl, but they do not dare to pass on the twisting road.

Pickett works the gears, watches his brake temperature, tugs at the wheel with motions that are both deft and desperate. This is tough work. The Mack, built for open highways, is out of its element here, like a football lineman stepping into a girl's playhouse, fitting broad breadth through narrow passage, every move cautious and calculated. And, most worrisome of all, the pavement still is damp in patches from the thunderstorm which rolled through in the morning and which now seems to be regrouping over the ocean for another sally soon.

"No mistakes, no fuck-ups," Pickett says again, his eyes never leaving the road. "If we do what we say we're goin' to do, if we follow it right down the line, right to the letter, then we can do it. Give it to me again from the top."

"Okay," Lenny says. "When we spot the Econoline, parked by this turnout, you drive past about twenty yards, then back up slow. But you keep the driving wheels on the asphalt, not on the gravel, in case there's trouble and we've got to get out quick. 'Cause there's no traction on wet gravel, right?"

"Go on," Pickett says.

"So when they give us the wave and we know it's them, you angle the van onto the shoulder of the road and put on the brakes. You park, but you leave the engine running. Then you climb down and walk around the van to give yourself cover. I watch them, ready to give you a blast on the airhorn if there's any trouble. And I pull out the Magnum to give them a good look. You've got your Ruger in your holster, covered by your jacket."

"You forgot about the money, God damnit."

"Right. Before you get down from the cab, before you even set your brakes, I yell down and tell them we've got to get a look at the money before we do anything. I tell them to throw the bag, the briefcase, whatever it is, out where we can all see it. Then you come down and come around the side of the van. You give the money a good look to see that it's at least close to the sixty thou. Then you put the money at your feet, not grabbing it so they think you're going to split, but close enough that nobody's going to take it away from you. Then you tell them how to unlatch the van door and you watch the guys who walk to the trailer to make sure they don't try to screw us up. Meanwhile, I'm covering them with the Magnum.

"That's right so far, isn't it, Pickett? There's just one thing. I think you ought to draw your Ruger at one point, maybe after you look through the money. Just so they know you're no sitting duck."

"Good idea. I'll wear the Ruger outside my jacket. I'll keep it in the holster for a while because I need two hands to look through the money, but after I'm finished with that, I'll draw it. That way they won't try to fuck us over. They'll know we mean business. So where were we?"

"You were telling them how to unlatch the van door. You're standing right next to the money, watching them to make sure the guys who are unloading the chest don't screw around with the truck. When they get it out, you ask them if they want to check the merchandise. No, that's wrong. First you tell them to shut the door of the trailer and then you ask them if they want to take a look inside the chest. If they don't, you pick up the money, walk around behind the trailer again, climb up and we take off.

"But remember, Pickett, don't turn your back on them. You're just supposed to back away until you're beside the back of the trailer. Then, when you're out of their sight, you turn and hustle back up to the cab."

"Yeah, Lenny, I know. Believe me, when I get my ass out there in the open, there ain't no way anybody could make me turn my back on those fuckers."

"Just checking, Pickett. Then, if they do want to look inside the chest, you back off to the side of the van facing them. You give just a quick glance to make sure the door's closed right. But you don't get more than three or four steps away from that money. Then, when they're satisfied, you grab the money and come back to the cab, the way we just talked about it, and then we get away."

They are silent for a few moments as the road levels off. Pickett, whose eyes have not strayed from the road while they talk, uses the straight road to blast by the logging truck, the Mack's engine howling as Pickett pushes it to the limit.

"I don't know, Pickett."

"What do you mean, you don't know?"

"I mean, it all seems so easy. Something's got to go wrong."

It is their own plan, hatched somewhere between Moab and Winnemucca, Nevada, based on Collins' directions, some fragile assumptions about the road, and Lenny's hazy recollections of Blue Gulch from a drive up the coast years earlier.

"Kid, I keep tellin' you that nothin's goin' to go wrong if we keep our heads and follow the plan right down the line. We might have to make some off-the-cuff changes here and there, but the basic plan is good. It's a business deal, right? These guys don't want any trouble. Oh, they're prob'ly pissed as hell about getting snookered out of all this money by a couple of dumb-ass truck drivers, but that doesn't mean they're goin' to gun us down. There wouldn't be any percentage in it. All we have to do is make sure they don't get greedy and try to keep the money when they get the dope. They do that, there's goin' to be trouble. But if we act like we know what we're doin', there won't be any problems.

"Hell, Lenny, we've pulled crazier stunts than this for a whole lot less money. Remember that day in February, two winters ago, when we hauled across Echo Summit just 'cause we had a delivery in Placerville and we were anxious to get home?"

"I remember."

"Fuck, yes. There was trucks all over the side of the road, some of 'em wheels-up, but we went right on through. When we hit that patch of glare ice up near Kyburz, I thought we'd had it. Wasn't that somethin'?"

"Shitfire, boy, that was just plain fuckin' dumb. We didn't make a penny extra for takin' that chance, but we did it anyway. Maybe we are takin' a chance here. Maybe we are, but it's worth it. Anyway, it's too late now to change our minds. We can't turn around on this road till we get to Fort Bragg. Besides, I've been nervous about haulin' that dope ever since we left Boston. I'll be glad to get rid of it."

"Okay, kid, here's Westport. That bridge can't be more than three, four miles from here. Get that cardboard and the masking tape."

Pickett brakes the truck and guides it to the side of the road. He climbs down with the cardboard in one hand and the masking tape between his teeth.

He tears off an oblong of cardboard, places it over his name and serial number on the driver's door and then tapes it in place. He does the same to the door on the other side. He lays strips of tape across the identification numbers on the van and he tapes cardboard over the truck's plates, front and rear, and over the small interstate tabs fastened in neat rows to a plate at the rear of the van.

An old woman watches them closely as she sits on the porch of a home that has nearly succumbed to the rigors of the ocean elements. She wonders where these fools are

210

headed, because she knows, as Collins does, that anyone passing through Westport is going far out of his way.

Collins moves his head nervously, side to side, standing on his toes to watch the two bends in the highway. Collins has a lookout to do this, but he is edgy. He wants this job done right for Rivera. He would like to bring back both the money and the cocaine, but he will not try too hard. Collins has heard that truckers can be rough and unpredictable. After all, Rivera has seemed happy enough to let the sixty grand go, and Rivera would be furious to the point of killing someone if Collins somehow botched this job.

All this Collins tosses in his mind as he waits on the turnout at the south edge of Blue Gulch bridge, dressed in red flannel pants and the red-and-black check woolen shirt so popular with hunters in this area. Collins and the man who waits in the van and his lookout all would pass scrutiny as hunters who have stopped for a moment to admire the view of the ocean below them. Of course, they would be tabbed immediately as first-time hunters, because their clothes are still pressed, still fresh from the department store, but the ruse is good enough; it would certainly explain the two shotguns and the Winchester semi-automatic in the gun rack behind the back seat of their white Econoline van.

Pickett and Lenny spot the Econoline as they round the bend north of the turnout. Collins and the third man—short, squat, homely, and wearing on his reptilian face a dull stare of impassive malevolence—are holding shotguns, barrels angled toward the ground, when the Mack crosses the bridge, gears down, brakes to a halt. Pickett is looking, surveying the terrain, measuring their impromptu plan against the realities of the spot Collins has chosen.

Nothing wrong, he thinks. Nothing much different than he imagined it would be. No special problems.

Lenny, meanwhile, has been scanning the green hills, looking for a hidden man within the clumps of scrub brush beside the road. He sees none.

"Looks okay, Pickett. This is it."

Pickett jams the transmission into reverse and the truck rolls backward down the highway until it is even with the Econoline.

Once more, Pickett sweeps his eyes across the scene. He notes: no fence, no barrier, no guard rail. Nothing but a long drop-off at the edge of the turnout. He notices, for the first time, a patch of pavement, a triangle of asphalt, extending from the south end of the turnout into the sand and gravel. Ah, he thinks, that will be useful, because the rest of the spot is still moist from the morning rainfall. That splotch of pavement, he knows, will provide welcome traction when they pull away. No wheel-spinning there.

When they back to a stop, Lenny rolls down his window. This is wild, he thinks. What do you say to a dope dealer, maybe a mobster, who knows you're trying to squeeze $60,000 out of him even while he totes his shotgun?

"I think you gentlemen are interested in obtaining a certain chest of drawers," he says.

"Back it up to the Econoline," Collins says, waving his shotgun.

"Time to get rough," Pickett says. "Show the fucker your gun."

Lenny pulls the Smith & Wesson into view and tries to waggle it casually.

He says: "I'm having a little trouble hearing you. Why don't you throw the money out on the ground? Then my hearing might improve."

Collins nods to the frogfaced man beside him. The man

212

reaches through an open window of the Econoline. There is a black canvas bag hanging from his fist when he pulls the arm out again. It is a gym bag. It says "University of California" on the side. Collins nods again. The man tosses the bag onto the ground near a small puddle.

Pickett is watching. When he sees the bag, he eases the truck forward and then backs it again, this time aiming the trailer into the turnout, about a dozen feet from the Econoline, the cab still on the road and nearly blocking the highway.

He sets the brake. He pulls the holster around his waist, he cinches it and dismounts. He nearly stumbles off the second step and he lands clumsily.

Straighten it up, Pickett, he thinks. Don't choke now. Lenny levels the gun, watches the three, and calls out an okay. Pickett squares his shoulders and walks to the bag.

He squats and pulls the zipper open. There are packets of money inside, but Pickett cannot bring himself to lower his eyes for longer than a blink. He watches the two men and their shotguns warily.

Lenny sees him and sees his problem.

"I'm watching," he yells down at Pickett. "I've got 'em. Just check the money." He speaks boldly but his voice is on the edge of quivering and his palms are wet against the cross-scored walnut on the butt of the gun.

But it is convincing enough for Pickett, who lowers his head and rummages through the bag. There are packets of twenties, fifties, and hundreds bound with paper strips. Pickett cannot shake the feeling of being exposed. He knows only that there is more money here than he has ever had in his hands. He will be happy with this. He zips the bag, rises to his feet, and automatically, he brings the bag up with him, in his hands.

"Put it down," shouts the frogfaced man beside Collins. "We haven't seen the coke yet."

Frogface levels his shotgun at Pickett.

Pickett does not realize what is happening, does not understand how he has provoked the man. Then he hears Lenny's voice, calmer and more certain this time.

"Lower the gun or I'll kill you. You hear me?" Lenny says. "Pickett, it's the bag. Just drop the bag."

Oh, you dumb fucker, Pickett thinks. All this planning and you have nearly bobbled it all. He drops the bag to his feet. Frogface lowers the shotgun reluctantly.

Pickett feels the sweat on his back and he feels a breeze blow in from the ocean. It chills that perspiration on his spine. He shivers.

"The chest is the only thing in the van," he says.

"Carry it out," Collins says. He speaks straight ahead, toward the two drivers, not at Frogface.

"No way," Pickett says. "Go in and get it yourself. It's a two-man job and my man ain't leavin' the cab."

He pulls the Ruger carefully from the holster and cocks the hammer. For a long moment there is silence, and for the first time Pickett is aware of the waves washing against the shore at the foot of the cliff.

"Okay," Collins says. "Woody, over here."

This is the lookout. He walks away from the edge of the precipice and takes the shotgun that Collins holds out to him.

"How about opening it up for us?" Collins says to Pickett. "I don't want to spend all day fumbling with that latch."

"Okay," Lenny yells at Pickett. "It's okay. I'm watching."

So Pickett does, but he hooks his foot around the handle of the black bag and he drags it with him to the van. He thinks: Damn, the kid is cool. He sits up there like a movie

214

director, movin' people around. I love that kid, he thinks. I love him like my son.

Pickett also trusts him, because he replaces the gun in the holster, turns his back on the shotguns to open the door, and swings it wide. He kicks the bag over to the end of the van, kicks it a few feet at a time. He draws his gun as Collins and Frogface walk into the trailer and the lookout stands, momentarily outgunned, beside the Econoline.

Collins and his helper do not bother with the ramp. They carry the chest to the edge of the opening and lower it to the floor of the van. They jump to the ground and grunting and cursing quietly, they heft the chest off the floor. They carry it clumsily to a spot several feet away from the Econoline and they drop it there. One carved leg splashes squarely into a puddle, but no one seems to notice.

"Crowbar," Collins says, breathing heavily with the exertion. Frogface walks again to the Econoline, reaches again through the open window, and comes up this time with the tapered shaft of steel.

"Bottom drawer, if you're interested," Lenny says, but they ignore him. They rip the top drawer apart, with Frogface yanking viciously on the crowbar. They pry the second apart and the wood splinters loudly. Frogface puts his full force on the third drawer and it gives way without protest.

Collins reaches inside and picks up one of the plastic-wrapped packages. He has come prepared. He pulls a thin stainless steel spoon from the pocket of his woolen shirt. He takes a cigarette lighter from the same pocket and he hands these to Frogface while he opens a jackknife and slits the package less than an inch. He works his fingers through the opening and comes up with a pinch of white powder, looking not unlike a certain popular laundry detergent.

"Flake," he says. "That's good."

He rubs the pinch of cocaine onto the spoon and flicks the lighter. He holds the flame beneath the spoon and he watches the powder dissolve in the heat to a clear liquid.

"Not a trace," he says. "This is one hundred per cent stuff."

Pickett and Lenny feel forgotten. Even the lookout seems more interested in the coke melting in the spoon than in what the two truckers are doing.

Pickett turns and latches the door. He is bending to pick up the bag when he hears Lenny's voice, suddenly on the edge of panic.

"Pickett," he says. "Smokies."

Then, louder, to the three men who have opened a second package: "Cops, you assholes."

Pickett runs around the trailer, climbs into the cab and throws the bag onto the floor.

"Highway Patrol," Lenny says. "Right around that bend. Looks like just one cruiser. You want to pull out?"

Pickett looks past Lenny, to where the three men have shoved their guns inside the Econoline. They are stuffing the plastic packages back into the chest, hoping to look, Pickett supposes, like three touring hunters who have decided to give their chest of drawers a good airing. They stand around the chest to block it from view.

"No," Pickett says. "We'll stay till he's past us."

"Back up," Lenny says. "Back off the road or the guy will stop for sure."

Yes. Pickett remembers the paved spit that extends into the gravel turnout. He shifts to low reverse and clears the white stripe that borders the highway when the patrolman cruises past, the engine on his black-and-white Plymouth murmuring as he rounds the corner. He passes them by without a second glance and disappears around the next bend.

Lucked out again, Pickett thinks. He jabs the accelerator, releases pressure on the clutch, and the Mack, still in low reverse, lurches backward. The van smacks solidly into the Econoline. Pickett hears the tinkling of glass from the headlights and the groan of twisting sheet metal.

The three men standing beside the chest in the gravel yell in unison. Pickett looks over at them. He pulls his foot from the accelerator. Then he looks over at the men again and he sees that they are as scared and as stunned as he. They seemed paralyzed, not quite grasping what is happening. Neither does Pickett, for a long moment. Then he sees what he has done. The three men are outside the Econoline. Their guns are inside. And Pickett has his Mack in low reverse gear, backed right up against the Ford, which is itself less than five feet from the edge of the precipice.

Now Pickett knows. He has them. He has the bastards.

The Mack's transmission has two reverse gears. In low reverse, the lowest ratio of all, the Mack has enough torque to shove a house off its foundation. So the Econoline, sliding on wet gravel while the Mack's driving wheels find traction on the splotch of pavement, is no problem. Pickett feathers the clutch with his left foot and toes the accelerator with his right. The Econoline offers only token resistance. It slides a foot, two feet, three. Pickett, watching through his mirrors, sees the Econoline teeter on the lip of the cliff and then disappear over the edge. They hear it slam against an overhang. Then it bounces straight down to the gray-sand beach.

Now Pickett dumps the transmission to a forward speed and the truck grunts toward the bend, headed for Fort Bragg. Before they make the turn, he glances back into his mirrors. He sees:

Three stunned and angry men in new hunting clothes, still standing in the gravel.

One badly mistreated chest of drawers.

One black thunderhead, moving up fast.

And then the rains come.

Three miles away, Pickett stops the truck beside the road. Until now, they have been speechless, not quite ready to accept what has just happened.

Pickett unstraps his holster and lays it beneath his seat.

"We did it," he says. "We fuckin' did it, Lenny."

They roll into Fort Bragg. Pickett stops at a filling station and he walks into a phone booth. One more call to tie this all together, he thinks. He flips through the phone book to the number of the local Highway Patrol barracks.

"Just a citizen," he says to the man who answers. "I thought you ought to know that three guys ditched a white van off the cliffs north of Fort Bragg."

"Can you tell me where?" the man asks.

"I sure can," he says. He remembers the scribbling on the back of the blank weight ticket.

"Thirteen-point-six miles north of the ARCO station in Fort Bragg," he says. "Blue Gulch bridge."

Chapter 35

The next day, the afternoon newspaper in San Francisco runs a second-page story about the three men who were arrested by the California Highway Patrol near Fort Bragg as they tried to hitchhike down Highway One with twenty pounds of cocaine stuffed beneath their shirts and jackets. There is a photograph of them being led to the courthouse. They are trying to hide their faces with their checked woolen hunting shirts. The shirts and the men look very wet.

Chapter 36

The Mack is parked in the street, looking out of place among the subdivision homes. It looks big to Lenny as he wheels his motorcycle into Pickett's driveway, bigger and scruffier than he remembers it from a week ago. The front of the tractor is spattered with bugs and road grime. Trailing from the stack, along the right side of the trailer, is a diminishing streak of black soot. No, Lenny thinks, it is definitely out of its element here. This truck belongs on a highway, hauling a load of freight.

Pickett appears from around the side of the house.

He seems happy, Lenny thinks, happier than he has been in months.

"Hey, kid, I was startin' to think you'd forgotten about me. Where the hell you been?"

"I've been around, unwinding, trying to settle back into the real world. Did a little hiking, drove down to Santa Cruz for a day. Relaxing. Wondering what I'm going to do for a job."

"Funny you should mention that. Come on, let's go inside. Doris is gone to the doctor. She's getting check-ups

219

every two weeks from now on. I want that baby to be healthy. My family's gettin' only the best."

"I got a call three days ago from Mynette," Lenny says.

"No surprise. She likes you. Likes you a lot, that's easy to see. She find a job?"

"She's got a job as a sales clerk, but I don't think she'll last long at it. She's not the type. I doubt if she'll stick around Boston forever. She'll be moving on, hitting the road in a few months. Maybe less. Most people wouldn't understand that, but I think you do."

"I understand it," Pickett says. "I just never expect to find it in a woman. What did she have to say?"

"A funny thing happened, Pickett. Just three days after we left, two narcotics agents arrested Billy-Frank right outside his house. Searched his Jag and they went straight for the driver's seat. Isn't that strange? They came right up with three joints. It wasn't exactly what they were looking for, but I think they were satisfied."

"See, Lenny? You can't cheat the law forever."

"No? How often did anybody catch you screwin' around with your logs? They were always phonier than a businessman's expense account.

"Anyway, his girl friend saw the whole thing. When Mynette found out about it, she told Annie that old Billy-Frank was lucky they only found a few joints of grass, all things considered. Annie flipped when she found out. Went back to Kansas a day later."

Pickett laughs.

"Some people," he says, "belong in Eureka, Kansas. Others belong in Boston. And there are a few that don't belong anywhere and have to keep travelin' back and forth."

"I'll buy that," Lenny says. "How about you?"

"I had a place all the time," Pickett says, "but I wasn't ready for it. I never thought I'd be able to enjoy spendin' a whole mornin', just paintin', but that's what I've been doin' out back. I finished with the fences and I went to work on the trim around the windows. I'm havin' a hell of a time."

"How's John William?"

"Comin' along. He'll be in the hospital for a while, but he'll be all right. It was a damn good doctor who worked on him. I'll be thankful for that the rest of my life."

"Did you count the money when you got back?"

"Fuckin'-aye right I did. Sixty even."

"How did you explain the money to Doris?"

"At first, I told her not to worry, just to hold onto the money and forget how I ever brought it home. But I couldn't keep my mouth shut. I was ashamed of carryin' that shipment but I was too proud about the way we ripped off those guys. When I saw the story in the paper the next day, I had to tell her about it. Jesus, that was somethin' I'll never forget. Did you see the story? I was ready to call up the papers and tell them it was me, that I was the one who screwed those creeps. When I took the job from Billy-Frank, I promised myself that I would do anything I could to screw these people. I did it to Billy-Frank with his grass but even when I got the sixty grand out of these others, I felt like they were gettin' away with something, like they had won and they were still usin' me. But when I backed into the van, with them holdin' the dope outside and with their guns inside, I saw it all. The first time I hit the Econoline was an accident. Pushin' it off the cliff, that was my idea."

"Some idea," Lenny says.

"I liked it," Pickett says. "What were you sayin' about that job? 'Cause I've got one for you, if you want it."

"You going back on the road?"

"No. I told you. I'm finished with that. I don't want it

any more. But I've been nosin' around. I've got the money for a good down payment on a couple of earth-haulers. Been talkin' to a lawyer. He says he thinks I can spring one earth-movin' permit from the public utilities people. And I know of a guy in Concord that's got another one up for sale. That's the start of a company, me and one other good man. There's good money to be made with all the freeways that are bein' laid around here. You could do the work, Lenny. You handle that Mack like a pro. You could learn to work a big off-the-road machine real easy. Pay's good. And you'd be home every night for dinner."

"Thanks, Pickett. I'm flattered. Right now, though, I'd rather drive the roads than build 'em. I miss being on the move."

Pickett nods and smiles. He expected that.

"Okay," he says. "Before you go, I want you to take a decent cut of this money. I've still got it in the black bag; the tax man will step on me for sure if I put it in an account. Part of that money's yours. You were nervier than I was that afternoon. We did it together and you deserve part of it."

"No money," Lenny says. "I don't need it. I live simple. It's yours and you deserve it. Any man who spends thirty years of his life bulling semis across the country ought to get a pension like that. But I would like to have one thing."

"Anything you want," Pickett says. "Just tell me."

"What were you planning to do with that Mack?"

"Trade it in," Pickett says. "It'll go as part of my down payment on one of the off-the-road machines."

"I'd like to have it," Lenny says. "That's why I came. I've been doing some scouting around during this last week. I found a broker who says he can find me two or three loads a month with canned fruit from Salinas to New England.

222

Sounds like a good deal. I go to work in two days if I can come up with a tractor."

"It's yours," Pickett says. "But only if you'll take another five thousand for repairs and maintenance. That tractor's got a lot of miles on it. If something major goes wrong, it could put you out of business. So let me throw in another five thousand. If you don't spend it, you can put it together with the Mack for a good down payment on a real rig."

"Sounds good," Lenny says. "Matter of fact, I stopped by that Peterbilt lot on my way over. They're back-ordered seven months, but that new cab-over of theirs looks like it's worth waitin' for."

Pickett whistles.

"Peterbilt! Kid, you're startin' out on the right track. You've got a helluva future if you keep movin' in that kind of style. Stay right here. I paid off the Mack last week. I've got the pink slip in the bedroom. I'll sign it over to you right now."

Pickett returns. Carefully, he puts his signature on the front of the ownership papers and hands the slip to Lenny.

"Here are the keys," Pickett says. "You can load your bike, but you'll have to bring the van back to the Mercury terminal in a couple of days. They weren't exactly overjoyed about me duckin' out of the lease, but they know there was nothin' they could do. I told 'em I'd bring the van back in a week or so."

"I'll take care of it."

"Okay. It's all yours. Don't forget to watch your revs when you're shiftin', 'cause the power band's just a couple of hundred RPM wide, around twenty-one hundred. Check your dipstick every mornin' and watch your tire pressure, especially on them drivin' wheels."

"I know, Pickett."

"Yeah, you do. You do, all right."

223

"Good-by, Pickett."

"Keep the rubber underneath you, kid."

Pickett watches Lenny walk the motorcycle into the van. He watches the kid step up into the cab without hesitation. The engine catches quickly and he toes the accelerator, the Mack coming alive once more. Lenny leans out of the window and flashes Pickett a thumbs-up. Same to you, Lenny. Then the kid clutches, notches into gear, and sets the truck into motion smoothly and without strain.

Pickett hears the burbling of the diesel after it turns the corner. It is not a cacophony but a familiar song that is urgent and strong and vital even as a gust of wind comes up from the east and snatches the sound from his ears.

". . . And that new storm that just moved in yesterday from the Pacific is raisin' all kinds of hell in northern California, Oregon, and Washington, higher elevations in Idaho and Nevada. Chains required on Interstate 5 for a stretch fifty-five miles north of Redding. Highway 101 north of Leggett, snow and ice on the pavement, carry chains. Interstate 80, Baxter to Truckee, snow and ice on the pavement, storm's heavy and the California Highway Patrol says traffic is slowed to fifteen miles an hour over Donner Summit. Carry chains. Interstate 80 North, Interstate 90, Interstate 15, all report hazardous conditions. Traveler's advisories out for U.S. 10, high winds and patches of glare ice just out of Missoula. High winds on the Yolo Causeway, just out of Sacramento. Hell, you get the picture, you gear-jammers. Gonna be some tough drivin' the next few hours. But you'll get 'em through. Hell, yes. You always do. We know who makes the country run, you mother-truckers. You bet! Keep 'em rollin' . . ."*